THE LAST OF THE WINTER ROSES

THE LAST OF THE WINTER ROSES

Jeanne Savery

Walker and Company
New York

All the characters and events portrayed in this work are fictitious.

First published in the United States of America in 1991
by Walker Publishing Company, Inc.
Published simultaneously in Canada by Thomas Allen & Son
Canada, Limited, Markham, Ontario

Library of Congress Cataloging-in-Publication Data
Savery, Jeanne.
The last of the winter roses / Jeanne Savery.
p. cm.
ISBN 0-8027-1162-6
I. Title.
PS3569.A8384L37 1991
813′.54—dc20 91-6569
CIP

Printed in the United States of America
2 4 6 8 10 9 7 5 3 1

For the two to whom I owe so much:

My mother and, in memory, my father.
No one has been envied so often, by so many
as, having my parents, I've been envied.

Hey, come on, Mama. No blushing.
You can't help being just a trifle wonderful.

— 1 —

"IT'S A *WHAT*?!"

Several voices attempted to shush Arthur, Lord Winters, but none had much hope of succeeding. Only Lady Ardith, his youngest child, refrained from attempting the impossible. Besides, it was too late: the earl's booming intonation had rung through the hushed house.

"Another granddaughter, you say?" He raised his fists and shook them.

The maid, Mary, bearer of the bad news, winced.

"Always girls," bellowed the earl. "Girls, girls, and more girls."

Silence followed—except for a giggle which escaped the poor maid. Everyone's gaze—save that of Lady Ardith—followed Lord Winters as he tramped across the Axminster carpet, stamped back. He raised his arms again. Again he shook his fists. All but one of those gathered in the room held his or her breath. Once again Lady Ardith ignored her sire.

"Another demmed girl." He glared around the room. "Ten thousand pounds to the man who gives me a grandson, then."

The silence this time might have been described as stunned. Even Ardith turned away from the bowed front window out of which she had been staring. A glance at the others revealed much what she expected: Bertie eyed his wife, Ellie, in a speculative way; Ellie looked everywhere but at her husband. Terrance grinned at Maud; Maud—the hussy—winked at Terrance. Married not quite three years,

Maud had yet to present her father with a grandchild of either sex. Clarence's gaze was tipped upward towards where his wife lay, recovering from the delivery of their third daughter in four years.

"Ten thousand pounds, I say."

"It is hardly fair, Papa." At Ardith's clear alto, Lord Winters rounded on his heel and glared. His choleric temper did not faze Ardith, however. "Ellie was told to have no more children," she said. "Another might be fatal for her, but look at Bertie." Everyone looked at him. "You can know what he's thinking as if he were saying it."

Bertram had the grace to blush.

"Then there is Cecilia. She desperately needs a rest from bearing brats, but Clarence desires a son as badly as you wish a grandson."

Clarence turned red, too, but from anger rather than chagrin. His glare was very nearly as intimidating as his father-in-law's.

"Maud has, up to now, been too selfish to allow herself to get *fat*. The money *may* change her mind, but don't count on it. She likes better-than-even odds when she gambles."

At that comment Maud did indeed look thoughtful.

"There is also, of course, the minor point that *one* of your daughters is unwed and disqualified from your grand offer," added Ardith lightly when, in truth, she felt like railing at the lot of them.

Lord Winters looked a trifle shamefaced, but there was that much-to-be desired grandson—a boy of his blood he could adopt and to whom, after an appropriate change of name, he could leave his fortune if not his title. He didn't dislike the cousin who would inherit the title, but his fortune . . . He huffed. Twice. "Just whose fault is it, Ardith, that ye remain unwed?"

"Probably Aunt Sibley's and the inheritance she left me. *You* did your best, of course." Oh, yes. He'd done his best. But her Season had been one huge jest, ending in the biggest jest of all. Ardith felt a long-hidden bitterness surge up once again. She met her father's eyes. "I am what you made me, Papa."

"Yes, and you're a grand lass, Ardy." He smiled fondly at his favourite, though most irritating, daughter. "Well, well, you say 'tis unfair, but *I* think not. I don't withdraw my offer."

Ardith read fear in Ellie's eyes. She noted Terrance looked pleased—although Maud's lovely features were marred by a pout. Aware the pair were always up to their necks in debt, she didn't wonder at it. Not one to pursue lost causes, she turned towards the door.

Lud! The maid waited there, eyes demurely cast down and hands properly folded—her ears obviously on the prick. She'd heard all the details of the ridiculous offer; the whole world would know before the cat could lick its whiskers. "Mary," Ardith asked severely, "how is my sister?"

"Doctor said mother and baby be right as a trivet, Lady Ardith."

"Good." Ardith picked up the short spencer she'd discarded earlier and walked out into the hall. "I will have a word with her before I leave."

Another flurry of conversation followed Ardith out of the drawing-room. The words "storm" and "snow" and "cold" caught her ear, but Ardith thought she'd rather be trapped in the carriage in a blizzard than stay another night in her sister's house surrounded by the men of her family. Most assuredly Great-Aunt Sibley was to blame for Ardith's lack—or so they considered it—of proper respect towards those same men. If she stayed, there would surely be another battle, and she was tired. She'd return to her small estate and her work and regain the contentment she'd somehow lost over the long winter.

Ardith entered her sister's bedroom where the Winters girls' old nurse was adding coals to the already hot fire. "Hello, Nanny. Is she sleeping?"

"Ardith?" The voice came from the high bed, a weak, sleepy voice.

"I'm here, love. I wanted to congratulate you and peek at the newest little Hawke child before I go."

Lady Cecilia Hawke's hands moved restlessly. "Must you go, Ardith?"

"I must. There is another storm brewing and I'd prefer to be home in case I'm needed there. Oh, isn't she sweet."

"It's another girl, Ardith." Her voice sounded weary.

"Yes. A lovely little girl." Ardith cooed at the bundle laid in the cradle, which had been handed down in the Hawke family for four generations.

"But . . ."

"Don't think of it, only rest and enjoy the child. You know you love your children, Ceci."

"Yes, but . . ."

"Shush. You're tired and you wanted a son. Don't let the disappointment make you love your daughter less."

"Oh, I *wouldn't*, but . . ."

"Sleep, now, love. Nanny will take good care of you and the child. I must go, or I'll end up in a snowdrift."

Ardith kissed her sister's cheek and moved briskly from the room. A heavy woollen, dark grey travel skirt dragged around her limbs with the force of her stride.

As she opened the door to her room she asked, "Fremby, dear, are we ready?"

Miss Fremby's official position was that of the female companion propriety demanded Ardith have since she was too young to live without proper chaperonage, but the thin grey-haired lady had become so much more. She was a true friend and confidante.

"You mean to hold to your decision?" asked Miss Fremby.

"I mean to take us away from here as quickly as possible." Ardith bit her lip. "If I don't go I'll have words with Clarence. He's set to make Ceci the invalid my mother became. It is outside of enough, Fremby!"

"Some women are delicate. Childbearing is hard on them. Once you've calmed down, perhaps you can write him and explain to him. I believe he cares for Cecilia but doesn't understand," soothed Miss Fremby. She motioned to the footmen to carry down the trunk and boxes. To lighten things, she asked Ardith, "Have you seen the latest from your admirer?"

Spread on her pillow was a knot of cheap ribbons. "Poor creature. Wasting his bit of money. This must be the third gift he's given me. I don't like it, Fremby." She shook her head.

Ardith slipped into her spencer and a plain, almost mannish bodice disappeared except for a chin-high collar which, with its rows of fine tucks circling her throat, hinted at a man's creased cravat. She picked up a sable-lined cloak and followed the old woman. Downstairs her family awaited her in the hall.

"Ardith," sputtered Clarence, "it is insanity to set off now. Our old coachman is never wrong. He predicts heavy snow before the day is out."

"With a modicum of luck I'll be home before it breaks. It's a mere two stages, after all." Ardith's family lived in one another's pockets, as the saying went, the most distant less than a day's travel from others. "Papa?" Ardith leaned forward for his kiss. She nodded to the rest, adding a special, encouraging smile for her oldest sister, Ellie, who still looked very like a frightened rabbit.

When she and Miss Fremby were underway, Ardith sighed, an ambiguous sound which she followed with a chuckle when Miss Fremby patted her arm. "I'm a sad trial to you, aren't I, my long-suffering friend?" she asked as the team leaned into the harness and the journey began.

"Cold weather won't hurt us, Ardith. I, too, will be glad to return home. I miss Summersend whenever we leave it."

Summersend was some ten miles from her father's estate, Winter Hall, and about thirty from Clarence and Cecilia's house. The small but pleasant manor had been built by a long-dead ancestor to house a less-than-noble ladyfriend. Later it had sheltered indigent relatives who were not wanted permanently at Winters Hall. Eventually the property had been ceded to the spinster daughter of the then earl. That eccentric lady, her great-aunt, had willed it to Ardith.

Ardith's most urgent reason for wishing to be home was the imminent foaling of her favourite mare. Ardith's concern for the mare would not have been an excuse acceptable to her family, however, so she had not mentioned it. Cecilia, especially, would be insulted—and rightly so—if she knew her sister's relative concerns. Ardith sighed again.

"What's troubling you so deeply, Ardith?"
"I'm not certain. I'm so restless and unsettled and bored I suppose. It's this long winter, I think. It's gone on and on and on."
"Spring is very late this year." Miss Fremby cleared her throat before her next encouraging words: "It will come."
"When I can begin schooling my young stock, I'll come out of the megrims. You'll have to be patient with me until then."
They were silent then, suffering the jolting and swaying stoically. Ardith judged they were all of seven miles from home when their luck failed. Snow, pouring suddenly from laden clouds, was lashed by gusting winds. Their pace slowed, slowed still more, and Ardith pushed aside the storm covers from the window. Could her coachman manage?
Again the wind increased in strength, rocking the unstable carriage. Snow blew through the gap around the door. They slowed to a crawl as conditions went from uncomfortable to intolerable. It became clear, however much the idea appalled her, that she must order them to the nearest shelter. If she were correct in her estimate, it would be Rohampton Park. Or perhaps they were farther than she thought? Maybe it would not be necessary to take shelter at the Park? Ardith opened the trap behind the driver. The groom bent over to her: John, her coachman, was preoccupied with maintaining the road.
"Where are we, Owen?" she yelled.
"We just be coming to the crossroads, milady."
"Drat. There is nothing for it, Owen." She gritted her teeth and gave the order she knew necessary—such a nasty turn of fate! "Turn and head for Rohampton's. And hope Saint John is *not* in residence," she added under her breath.
Their luck held bad. True, they turned into the long winding drive through Rohampton Park land, but not far up it a windblown drift, a freak of the lay of the land, brought them to a halt. "Blast and bedamned!"
Fremby chuckled, an unusually husky sound. "Ardith! Such language!"
"You've heard me use worse. Are you up to it, Fremby?"

"Have I a choice?" laughed the wiry woman.

The voice sounded hoarse, and Ardith peered through the gloom. She berated herself for putting the older woman into danger. "You wait here while we unharness the horses. I'll have Owen strap what we'll need to the harness. John and I will lead the team and Owen will help you. It's not half a mile to the house. We'll be there before you know it.

John led the way. The horses broke a path for her feet, but Ardith ducked her head against the blustery gusts of windblown snow. She'd told the coachman they'd not need the trunk, but she was certain he'd try to get it for her. John was twenty years her senior. Yet he'd suffer in her service, because it was the role for which he'd been born. Ardith felt there was something sad about that, then decided blowing, blustery weather must call forth a philosophic bent she'd not known she possessed.

"The Hall is just ahead, milady," called John. "You'll be warm in no time now."

"And you?" she shouted back.

"I'll see to the horses, milady."

She couldn't fault that pronouncement, and he didn't expect her to. "John, truly, we'll need nothing from the carriage. Please do not go back into this storm for such a fribblish reason."

"We'll see, milady."

While Owen helped Miss Fremby into the house, Ardith waited to see the portmanteau and the large hatbox unstrapped. She took the latter and moved to the door. Miss Fremby had already disappeared, led up to a room by the Rohampton housekeeper.

"Good evening, Ransome. Is your master, perchance, in London?" she asked hopefully.

The butler looked down his long nose, but Ardith noted a twinkle in his old eyes. "Nay, milady, he is in residence. As there are no other guests he'll be glad of the chance that landed your ladyship on our doorstep."

"Dear me. I wonder how Rohampton allowed himself to be trapped with no way to amuse himself." There was almost as much ice on her tongue as coated her garments.

She felt guilty and ducked a rueful look at Ransome. He appeared impassive, except for those expressive eyes. Maybe her old friend was amused by the fact she had no choice but to enter a house into which she'd sworn she'd never again step foot, but Ardith felt quite differently about the ill luck stalking her. Why had that storm not held off for another hour? "Bored is he?" She received a nod. "Well, I fear I'm coming down with a chill and had best keep to my room. Ah, Mrs. Lander."

Ardith held out her hands to the housekeeper who had known her forever. They were ignored. Mrs. Lander had strict notions of proper behaviour, and once Ardith put up her hair her friendship with the housekeeper had waned. Now the woman dipped a curtsey and turned to lead the way to a bedroom on the second floor.

"I've put Miss Fremby in the room across the passage, Lady Ardith. Hot water will be up directly, milady. *And*," she added, a touch of disapproval not totally concealed, "a maid to see to your needs."

Ardith had been made aware long ago how scandalised the local people were that she kept no lady's maid, so she ignored the reprimand. "Thank you. I am tired and would like my dinner on a tray. Something light and hot, if you will. And please send the same up for Miss Fremby."

"Yes, milady."

Ardith warmed cold fingers before the fire. Her nose twitched in irritation as a wet wool smell rose with the steam from her skirts. When certain her fingers wouldn't tremble, she slipped off her spencer and started on the tiny buttons at the back of the blouse, turning as the door opened. She expected a maid with a can of hot water. Instead her eyes met the deep-set ones of her nemesis, St. John Worth, Marquis of Rohampton. They stared at each other.

Ardith had never understood why the man was so idiotishly attractive to her. She'd met many more handsome: the marquis's face was a study in harsh planes and hard angles, high cheek bones and strong jaw. His hair was never quite tamed, silver dusting each temple in contrast to the much darker hair rising from his forehead in, as usual, something of a tangle. Slim waisted and broad shouldered, and much taller than average—perhaps *that* was it: Rohampton was one of the few men tall enough to make her feel small and feminine. Not that she wanted to feel small and feminine, but still . . .

"Tired, Ardith?" A London dandy would have drawled that question with bored languor. Rohampton's tone indicated only a characteristic interest. "Could you not come up with a better excuse?"

"If you had the sensibility of a goat, you'd pretend to believe me, St. John."

"Goat?" He shook his head. "Bad metaphor, Ardith, my love."

She felt warmth in her cheeks and turned back to the fire, hoping its heat would cover the blush. Then, remembering the buttons undone at her neck, felt further embarrassment that she'd allowed him to see she was in disarray. Ardith did up the buttons. At least he wasn't twitting her about finding her *en deshabille*. "I'd appreciate it if you'd go away."

"When I have your promise you'll come down to dinner in a proper manner."

For a moment she balked, then, unwilling to argue, drawled, "As you will." Lost causes had ceased to appeal to Lady Ardith. They hadn't since her Season five years previously. That had been a lost cause indeed. Silence followed her comment. She turned. The door was closed, the room empty. Drat the man. He moved like the red Indians about whom she'd read, the ones who stalked deer never making a sound. It was unnerving.

An hour later she knocked on her companion's door. "Fremby?"

"Just a-a-a—*achoo*—moment."

Ardith opened the door. "You are ill." Hearing the accusation in her tone, Ardith was put to the blush for the second time that evening. "Oh dear. I shouldn't have said that." She apologised, "I'm sorry."

Fremby chuckled. "There was a draft, the windows rattling the whole of last night. I wonder if I've taken a chill."

"You should have told me. . . ."

"With all to-do last night with your sister? Don't be foolish. Let me look at you." Fremby watched as her charge made a defiant turn. It ended with a glare which dared her friend to say one word. Fremby, ignoring the show of incipient temper, nodded. "If you mean to put Lord Rohampton off," she said, "you've managed about as well as may be."

Understanding was in the warm look in her friend's eyes. Ardith grinned. Fremby's mouth spread in an answering smile. Ardith had had little choice as to a gown, but of the two in the portmanteau, the old green merino with high round neck and long straight sleeves was the least attractive. She'd bound her long hair tightly around her head in braids, leaving the strong bones of her face exposed and, she hoped, intimidating.

"Well, I suppose we must go down," said Lady Ardith.

"A-a-a-choooo."

"Oh my."

"Don't worry, my dear. I'll be fine as a fivepence after a night's sleep. This room is much warmer than the one I had last night."

"I could have had a word with Cecilia's housekeeper. If only you'd *told* me, Fremby."

"It seemed to me the house was unsettled enough without my making a fuss. But that corner room had too many windows."

"Corner room? You weren't in your usual room?" Fremby shook her head on another sneeze. "Whyever not, I wonder?"

Ardith frowned. She'd been unprotected if Fremby hadn't been in the room which connected to her own. *Had someone tried her door?* She'd thought it someone coming for her to help her sister, but when she lit her candle and unlocked the door, a maid was just then approaching down the corridor. No, she must have dreamed it.

Fremby sneezed through the four courses of the dinner. She continued to sneeze when Rohampton, instead of staying at table with the port, moved with them to his library for coffee. Ardith wasn't certain she approved. She'd never liked coffee.

"A-a-a-chooo."

"This is absurd." Rohampton strode to the bellpull and yanked it. When Ransome entered, St. John ordered a tisane prepared and then helped Miss Fremby to her feet. "You are to go to bed at once. You needn't worry I'll ravish your ewe lamb. I'll not even try."

Ardith's head turned sharply. All right. She knew she wasn't particularly attractive. That had been made clear to her as she watched her three lovely sisters grow up. The Winter Roses, they'd been called as they were presented to the ton at intervals of two or three years. Soft and small and nicely rounded, with identical heads of glowing golden hair and lovely heart-shaped faces, they'd been, each and every one, a beauty.

Until Ardith. The youngest. When Lady Ardith's turn in London came, the wits called her the Long-Stemmed Rose, in reference to her height. It had *not* been a compliment. She'd grown taller than her sisters at an early age and never quite learned what to do with the long legs and arms with which she'd been blessed. Or cursed. Only when she was riding did she feel as if she were correctly proportioned.

Worse, instead of blond hair, hers was long and dark, nearly straight, and too thick and heavy to be easily handled. Not for her the flyaway curls her sisters achieved with so little effort. While they enjoyed fine features set in soft milky complexions, she had strong bones under skin that was naturally darker than fashionable, a nose just a little too long for perfection, a mouth much too large for beauty, and a chin far too firm for a woman. If there weren't a portrait of a long-dead ancestress hanging in the picture gallery at Winters Hall, a lady Ardith resembled down to the small mole beside the corner of her mouth, she'd have believed her mother, poor thing, had wronged her father, herself the result.

"I wish you would unbend, Ardith," said St. John as he prowled closer. "We used to be friends."

Oh yes. Once. In a period of her young life when she'd badly needed a friend. But then she'd grown up. And gone to London for her Season. And he'd turned from friend to foe and she still didn't understand it, still felt the pain of disillusionment.

"Ardith?"

"Once upon a time, long ago, we were friends. Then you showed me even friends are not to be trusted."

"Those idiots' behaviour was explained to you. The fools thought their trick hilarious. They didn't plot against you that night, Ardith, but against *me*. A silly bet which should never have been made."

"What a coup for the ugliest maid on the Marriage Mart," said Ardith softly. "Three proposals in as many minutes."

"*Mine* was serious."

"Was it? I don't believe you, of course."

"I might have convinced you, but, coward that you are, you ran away. I came to see you the next day, but you'd disappeared."

"So my father told me. But you're an honourable man." She went on just as thoughtfully: "I assume you sobered up, saw what you'd done, and came to make amends. Well, I refused, saving you from folly, St. John." She forced herself to chuckle. "Aren't you glad I ran? You'd not abide a coward for a wife."

Ardith could see the renowned Rohampton temper simmering in the tension behind his tanned face. Something, some energy, seemed to crackle around him like summer lightning. It was an effect she'd sensed before, but until the fiasco in London never directed towards herself.

"I wish I could knock your father into flinders. I told him not to present you. You weren't ready for a Season."

"The Winters girls were presented when they reached eighteen. I turned eighteen." She shrugged.

"You weren't ready, dammit."

"St. John," she said mildly, "that's no language to use before a lady."

He grinned. "But then, you've sworn you're no lady, haven't you?"

"That joke is too old to deserve comment. I was twelve at the time. And I hadn't learned to be a lady."

"I think it was then I discovered exactly who you are," he

said, opening a snuffbox with practiced ease. He closed the lid and put it back in his pocket when Ardith's nose wrinkled involuntarily, a smile softening his harsh features. "I forgot that you think it a dreadful habit."

"Well, it is."

"So it is." He came to the sofa and settled himself beside her. Ardith had to force herself to remain unmoved. But, out of the corner of her eye, she let herself note his relaxed rangy body and knew her pulse was racing. "That day. What a temper tantrum you threw, Ardith." He chuckled at the memory.

She grimaced. "I do not care to be reminded of all the follies of my life, St. John."

"Folly? It was no folly. Your father richly deserved that blistering tirade. I admired your vocabulary, little one."

Little one? St. John was the only person she knew who could call her little and make her believe it wasn't a deadly insult. But then he was so tall, so . . . She turned her thoughts sharply. "If I'd realised you'd followed me into the stable yard, I'd never have allowed myself to lose my temper, but it is the only way to cope with Papa. He despises people who will not stand up to him."

"It wasn't the first time you'd lectured him?"

"Lud, no. I was five when I first looked him in the eye and told him what I thought of him. I was standing on a mounting block that time. He'd caught me trying to get on the back of one of his nastier hunters and objected, you see.

"At which point he realised he had a fire-eater on his hands . . . and began your course to ruin."

"Neither fish nor flesh nor good red herring." She nodded, wondering a trifle wistfully if she'd have been better off if she'd not brought herself to her father's attention. Perhaps if her mother had remained at home, had not taken herself off to Bath after Ardith's birth and remained there, a recluse until her death a little more than a year previously . . . But if she'd been raised as her sisters were, would she be better off? She thought of those sisters, their ham-handed husbands, and decided she much preferred her independence, the life she'd made for herself, thanks to Great-Aunt Sibley, to whom she'd run after that never-to-be-forgotten scene when she'd been the butt of St. John's monstrous joke. Blast St. John.

"Where," asked St. John, drawing her attention back to him, "did you find a copy of John Heywood's sixteenth-century collection of aphorisms? I know it isn't in the library at Winters Hall."

She had to think to remember the quotation she had just tossed off. "Aunt Sibley, of course." Ardith snatched at the opportunity to turn the conversation from personal subjects. "Have you read his comic interludes? I enjoyed them very much. In winter when there was little else to do, Aunt Sibley and I would take parts and . . ."

The discussion ranged widely after that, Ardith surprised by St. John's breadth of interest. She'd known him to be intelligent. Anyone would know that after only the briefest of conversations. But she had not known he was something of a scholar.

"Ardith?"

She turned her head, realised he'd lifted her hand from her lap and was playing with her fingers. She jerked herself free and stood, shocked by her first instantaneous desire to ignore what he was doing. She *didn't* like the feelings his touch aroused. It was *impossible* that she could like anything about this man after what he'd done to her.

"Ardith, don't glare." He eyed her, a lazy look from under heavy lids. "You'll get lines, you know, if you go on that way."

"Oh, you are . . ." Words failed her.

St. John rose to face her, and she forced herself to stand steady, although he was much too close. Then his sober look disarmed her.

"Ardith, we've enjoyed a pleasant evening. I'm sorry I spoiled it for you." When she would have spoken, he shook his head. She closed her lips, waiting for him to continue. "If the weather-wise are correct, we are in for the worst storm of a very bad winter. We may be snowed in for days. Truce, Ardith? Until you leave? I'd rather not spend the next week wondering when and where you'll stab me."

Her eyes widened. Did he truly think her capable of such violence?

"With that sharp tongue, Ardith," he explained, his eyes narrowing with amusement. "It can cut more deeply than you know."

Days. She and Fremby might be forced to remain under St. John's roof for *days*. Her heart beat faster and she decided it must be irritation. But days?

"Truce, little one?"

"With conditions," she decided.

"I'm listening."

"No references to . . . my Season." She knew he'd understand she meant the cruel jest which had hurt her so badly. "I've listened to enough lies concerning that." His mouth tightened. "St. John?"

"We'll see."

She shook her head, forcing herself to walk away. "Then no truce."

"I did not lie to you, Ardith."

She threw him a scornful look. "That is lie one thousand and one."

"I haven't spoken to you enough in the past five years to have offered you a *hundred* and one lies." A muscle jerked in his cheek. "All right. No references to your last evening in London, although we might talk about your stay there other than that."

Compromise. Ardith believed in compromise. Besides, the feud was years old and every day of it she'd missed their friendship. She tried to read his mind behind his dark eyes. Serious eyes. Drat the man. She'd never been able to read him. Oh, she'd thought she could. Once. Back before that awful night when he'd raised her hopes only to—No. She wouldn't think of her humiliation and shame.

"I'm tired, St. John. I spent the night hours sitting up with Cecilia. I'll say good-night now."

"Ceci? Oh Lord." Ardith heard a rueful note in St. John's voice. "I forgot. Are she and the baby all right? Did Hawke get a boy this time?"

"My sister is fine. Another healthy girl. Father made a cake of himself, however." She moved towards the door, wanting, *needing*, to get away.

"Your *father* did? *Not* Hawke?"

For a moment she dithered, a yawn escaping as she did so. She met his eyes and read understanding. "Truly, St. John, I'm very tired. I'll explain another time. Good-night." She opened the door.

"Truce or not?" he asked, a sharp note in his tone.

"Oh, truce, I think. I'm a guest here, whether I will it or no, and I did learn a few manners from our governess, despite being truant from the schoolroom more often than not."

"Ignore your hours with the vicar as tutor when you learned Latin and mathematics. More important, your father taught you something men are taught, Ardith. Unintentionally, I'm sure! You have a sense of honour and more pride than is good for you. And courage. As much courage as any man I've ever known. That has made life difficult for you, hasn't it, m'love?"

Her cheeks warmed at what she knew were compliments, and, unable to answer, Ardith hurried from the library before St. John could say more. She'd never learned how to deal with compliments, believing they were undeserved when directed at her person and distrusting them otherwise.

But blushing! At her age it was ridiculous. She'd blushed *three times* since entering the Rohampton front door. Oh, if only the storm had held off and she'd managed to reach Summersend!

— 2 —

Ardith awakened far more abruptly than she liked. The rings rattling along the curtain rod made a horrendous noise. Worse, a bright, if odd, light flooded the room and caused her to blink. She made a mental note to remind Amy not to do that. Ardith much preferred adjusting to a new day slowly and in stages. She blinked again, wondering when the bed curtains had been changed from pale yellow to heavily embroidered blue. Blue?

Ardith sat up, eyes wide, and stared around the room. Rohampton. She fell back against her pillows. A truce. Could she hold truce with St. John and not betray all those odd yearnings she couldn't quite eradicate? Days passed when, busy with her beloved horses or working long hours in the still-room on medicinal brews or potted salves, she'd not think of him at all. But this winter—this long, long winter—there'd been little to occupy her. All too often her thoughts had drifted towards Rohampton—and its owner.

"Coffee, tea, or hot chocolate, milady?" The young maid spoke each word carefully.

Ardith turned towards the thin child who looked barely old enough to be in service and wished for nice comfortable, plump, and cheerful Amy. But hot chocolate sounded good. She ordered it and stretched as the maid went through the doorway.

Rohampton Park. For five years she'd avoided it despite gossip about her behaviour. St. John's behaviour, actually. A smile of sorts twisted Ardith's mouth. Everyone wondered just what St. John had done to insult her so. So, let them wonder. Her family had given up arguing with *her* and fawned all over *him*, so no one could think *too* badly of him.

She'd been twelve when she met St. John. Furious with her father, Ardith had saddled her mare and ridden as if all the devils of Hades were following. Under pressure from a well-respected dowager who'd gotten wind of Ardith's activities—which were generously set down to her mother's abdication of her duties—Lord Winters informed Ardith she was too old to spend all day every day in the stables. When he'd caught her there again, he'd lost his temper. The result? If she wished to act like a boy, he'd roared, she'd be reared like a boy. She would join the class the vicar taught for local youths. Angry, Ardith had ridden too far and become lost. St. John, twenty-three at the time and riding the most magnificent bit of horseflesh she'd ever seen, came across her as she was debating with herself what to do next. He'd overcome her proud denial that anything was wrong and escorted her home.

Once home she'd said all the things she'd planned to say to her father—with St. John, the head stableman, a coachman, and three stable boys for audience. Finishing the tirade directed at her blustering father, she'd turned too quickly and caught her heel in the hem of the despised habit, which was another recent innovation, the same dowager having convinced her father she must no longer be seen rampaging around the countryside in breeches. She'd almost fallen, but had been caught by large well-shaped hands. Embarrassed, she'd stared up at the knight-errant she'd all but forgotten. He'd winked at her. Instant hero worship filled her young breast.

"Your chocolate, milady."

Ardith shook away the memories and pushed pillows behind her back. She accepted the cup and saucer and forced herself to really look at the maid. "Thank you, child." The girl twisted her hands in her apron, her gaze sliding towards the fireplace where a new fire burned but a hod of ashes awaited removal. She looked nervous. "What's your name, girl?"

"Betty, milady." The maid sidled a pace towards the fireplace.

"You're new to your work?" A jerky nod answered her. "And worried you'll make mistakes?"

Red flowed up thin cheeks. "I'm alwuz makin' mistakes, milady."

"How long have you been in service, child?"

"Near two months, milady." Another step took her closer to the latest proof of her incompetence and a disordered mind.

"You worry too much, Betty, and that makes you forget exactly what you should do. Do one thing at a time. Take the ashes away carefully so you don't strew dust. Then go to your next duty. Remember now. Take each task one at a time."

Good advice, thought Ardith as Betty again disappeared out the door. Only, in her own case, it was one day at a time. The wind had dropped, she noted, her gaze drifting to the uncovered windows, but snow still fell in huge, wet, white clumps. How long? How long before she could get back to the peace and security of Summersend?

A few minutes later Ardith debated the merits of beating John around the ears. She'd told him she'd no need of her trunk, but when she opened the huge armoire, she found her things put away neatly, the drawers to the side containing chemises and petticoats. Ardith sighed. One reason she'd not wanted her trunk was that without it she had an excuse to dress drably with no touch of fashion. Not that her normal style of dress was exactly *fashionable*. But now she had no excuse to look as unattractive as possible.

Not that it was possible to look too attractive in any case. She was no soft blonde with curls and blue eyes and pouty mouth. She was as she'd always been, a great gawk of a girl, too tall, too thin some places and too big others—such embarrassing "others"—and much too dark. She chose a morning gown in deep rose, devoid of frills and lace, and dressed, avoiding as much as possible the large oval mirror which showed all her faults too clearly. At Summersend there were few mirrors and the only one in her room was small, suitable for checking her hair each morning.

As happened too often, Ardith had forgotten to braid her hair before retiring. Now, as she struggled with snarls, words better kept to the stables escaped her. A muffled sneeze interrupted her, and, holding the brush in one hand, she went to her door. "Fremby?"

"Good morning, love. I was just—*a-a-a-choooo*"—Fremby sniffed, wiped her watery eyes, and drew in a deep breath—"about to go down to breakfast. I see you aren't quite ready. *A-a-a-choo*!"

"What *are* you doing out of bed? That cold is worse, is it not?"

"My dear." Fremby sneezed again. "You know I don't pamper myself, but I'm not stubborn about caring for myself either. So don't go ripping up at me."

Ardith tipped her head. Truly, Fremby was a sensible woman. She'd taken to her bed with no arguments when she'd come down with a quinsy nearly a year ago now. The putrid sore throat and fever had frightened Ardith, who had come to depend on her companion's friendship and support. And love. There was more love between herself and Fremby than between her and any of her sisters. Even Cecilia, the closest to her in age. "You aren't coming down because I need a chaperone, are you?"

"I have no concerns leaving you with Lord Rohampton. He has an odd kick in his gallop, as the saying is, but he's an honourable man. I thought I might take a look at his still-room after breakfast and make up a draught. It would help a great deal, I'm sure." She sneezed again and followed Ardith back into her charge's bedroom.

At home, Ardith thought, I could simply tie this mess of hair back with a ribbon. She hated fighting the length and weight and more than once had come close to cutting it, but something always stopped her. Now she wrestled it into a bun at the back of her neck and stuck pin after pin in to hold it. It is such a nuisance, she thought. "Now I'm ready," she said with a last fleeting look in the mirror.

"Someday you will allow me to teach you ways of dealing with that magnificent hair, Ardith, dear." Fremby's tone held a wistful note.

Ardith frowned. "Give it up, my friend. I learned long ago there was *nothing* to be done. Even Henri threw up his hands in disgust." Well, in a way. The fashionable London hairdresser had wanted to crop it and curl it, and when Ardith refused he'd gone off in a huff.

Fremby had offered help a number of times, but Ardith had laughed off the suggestion. Maybe she *should* let Fremby show her a trick or two? Maybe there was a way, but for what purpose? Running from that question, Ardith moved with unstudied grace—and more speed than proper—into the hall and down two flights of stairs to the breakfast room. Fremby, trailing behind, stopped often to sneeze and blow her obviously painful and very red nose.

"Good morning, Ardith. Miss Fremby."

Oh blast, she thought. She'd hoped St. John had broken his fast earlier and was occupied with estate problems. "Good morning, St. John." Ransome seated her, then Miss Fremby and discreetly served them breakfast. "I assumed you'd be long gone."

"I *live* here, Ardith."

She felt heat in her cheeks. "I meant I thought the storm would have had you out overseeing repairs."

"I did that hours ago." He looked at her chaperone, who was picking at a boiled egg and ignoring the toast and sausage on her plate. "You are worse this morning, are you not, Miss Fremby?"

"I'm afraid there is little one can do but wait out a cold, my lord. If you have no objections, there's an infusion I'd like to make if I may use your still-room. Ardith and I have found it efficacious for the symptoms."

"Anything you like," he said doubtfully, his eyes going to meet Ransome's. The butler's eyes widened in chagrin. "I'm not quite certain of the state of the still-room. After my mother died . . ."

"I'm sure I'll find all I need. The ingredients are common enough."

He nodded and turned back to Ardith. She ignored him, eating with her usual appetite despite her nervous concern at being under his roof. He was, as Fremby had pointed out, an honourable man. Or was he? He *had* taken part in that jest which had sent her fleeing London . . . hadn't he?

"What are you thinking that makes you look much like the stormy weather we're having, Ardith?" asked St. John, his voice devoid of expression.

Startled, she looked up at him. His features were emotionless, but quite obviously he would insist she answer. She searched for one.

"Are you worrying about Summersend?" he asked, finding it for her.

Ardith very nearly sighed in relief. "Yes. I've a mare about to foal. It's her first and I wanted very much to be there."

"Ah. Which mare?"

"Lightly." She flinched when he straightened and stared at her, a scowl more intense than hers—on which he'd just commented—twisting his dark brows. "Now," she asked, "why are *you* so stormy browed?"

"Would that be Ever-so-Lightly out of High Water by Hell's Last Hope?" he asked, his voice a dangerous-sounding growl.

Ardith grinned. Oh what fun! "Wanted her yourself, did you?" She felt a certain unworthy glee at having bested him. "Where *does* Tarkington come up with the names for his stock? I've often wondered."

"How did you talk him out of Lightly?"

"I'll never tell."

He eyed her, a speculative look which faded as he shook his head.

"No. Definitely not. I didn't get him to sell her with the bribe of my magnificent body," Ardith said tartly, quite without thinking. She blushed a livid red when Ransome, shocked by her words, stifled an embarrassed laugh.

"He'd have *given* you Lightly, if you had," said St. John. Her host was apparently oblivious of the fact she'd said something completely unacceptable.

St. John neither smirked nor twitted her, and Ardith sent him a shy look of thanks. His teeth flashed in a quick grin, but that was all, and she turned back to her breakfast, the flush receding slowly. How *could* she have said such a thing! But old habits never completely die, and St. John had let her say whatever she pleased to him during her growing-up years, had *encouraged* her to say whatever came into her head.

"I'd still like to know how you did it, Ardith."

She debated the notion of letting him wonder before giving in to his coaxing tone. "He wanted to breed High Water to my Black Lightning." She shrugged. The trade was obvious once one knew that.

He nodded. "I've a new stallion of my own you might like to see. Ajax is rather special."

"Oh?"

The conversation continued with stable talk long after Miss Fremby excused herself. Ransome was dismissed and assuming she'd ever been out of it, Ardith fell in love with St. John all over again as he allowed her the sort of discussion she loved. Horses, well-known breeders and their stables, equine illnesses and medication, and the training up of young stock all figured in their swiftly paced dialogue. The time passed quickly, and too soon Ransome came in to remove the last of the now tepid coffee and the empty teapot from the table.

"When the weather clears I'll take you to see Ajax. You'll be green with envy, my girl."

Ardith ignored the improper appellation as she ignored all such he'd tossed her way. She also tried to ignore the feel of his hand against her back as he directed her to the library, but that was much more difficult. They entered the huge but comfortable room, the wood polished to the sort of gleam only centuries of rubbing achieved. She loved the smell of books, the faint scent from the applewood fire, the ambience that made one relax whether one willed it or no. "You don't have to entertain me," she said.

"No. I don't, do I? But since I've nothing else to do," he teased, "I might as well. Chess, perhaps?"

Was that hope she heard? Ardith glanced at him, turned to really look when she noted the anticipation in the gaze fixed on her face. "Chess?"

"I haven't had a decent game in weeks," he admitted.

"Weeks?"

St. John glanced around the room, his hand behind his

ear. "Do I hear an echo in here?" He dropped the pose and moved towards the game table where he lifted a case of chessmen from the drawer. "I've been here for months now," he said as he set out the black king. "I had visitors earlier, but they are long gone. The Season, as you'd know if you kept track of such things, started early this year since hunting has been impossible, and London is already frantic with entertainments. So, as I said, weeks. Will you humour me? I'd like to see if you've improved. Do you still use that crazy intuitive system that often comes very close to defeating me—despite your lack of discipline?"

Ardith strolled nearer to watch as he set out the last pieces. Finished, he picked up the two queens and held them behind his back, moving them from palm to palm.

"Choose."

She chose, winning the white queen and the privilege of beginning the game. Quiet reigned. Two minds, one brilliantly logical and one intuitively brilliant, fought and challenged, feinted and defended, neither really achieving a solid advantage over the other.

Finally Ardith sat back, staring at the board. The last flurry of moves had seen a good number of pieces taken. Her king was, she noted, once again in danger. She looked up and faced the man smiling at her. "I think I'm in trouble."

"Yes," he said, his tone judicious, "I do believe you are."

There was a look in his eyes she didn't understand. And his words, that tone—just what did he *mean*, what *could* he mean? He couldn't be suggesting . . .

He smiled warmly and she turned her eyes and with difficulty her thoughts, to saving her king. She managed it. Once. But a few minutes later she was trapped. Flipping her king with her finger, she tipped him over and settled back in her chair.

"I thought I had you half a dozen times, my love. You are always a delight and a surprise."

"Don't."

He didn't pretend to misunderstand her. "Don't call you my love? But you are, have been for years. Don't compliment you when you deserve compliments? Whyever not?"

Ardith shoved back her chair and moved towards the heavy drapes shutting out the cold and the view. Not, she conceded, once she'd lifted one aside, that there *was* a view. Would the snow never stop?

"Ardith?"

"Our truce won't last if you don't stop treating me to such fustian, St. John."

He lolled in his chair. "I've never understood why you have such a low opinion of yourself."

"We'll discuss something other than my inadequacies or we'll discuss nothing at all." She turned, worked up for battle. "Thanks to Aunt Sibley I can look forward to an agreeable life, St. John. If it weren't for her I'd have remained at home, fighting with Father, playing aunt to all my nieces, and eventually disintegrating into a bitter spinster." She shrugged. "Spinster I am, but I'm not bitter." She tipped her head at the expression turning his features into something fiercesome. Taking a deep breath, she went on. "Since I'm satisfied with the life I have, I don't wish to discuss the past. One word, St. John, and I'll go to my room."

He stood, towering over her. "Word one: you are not inadequate. In any way." She stalked from the table. St. John caught her and turned her around, his fingers biting into her shoulder. She stared straight through him. "Your family is much to blame," he said. "Your mother, for instance, had no business forgetting her responsibilities after you were born and running off to Bath."

"My mother ailed until the day she died," objected Ardith. "Some women—"

He interrupted her. "Then there were those idiots who ruined my premature proposal, which didn't help. Lady Sibley was the last straw. We'd have wed long ago if you'd not had her protection—protection only a recluse such as she could have made so impenetrable. Worse, she willed you a home in which you still bury yourself." He shook her lightly. "Don't deny you were buried! I tried often to see you after you took refuge with your aunt. I still do off and on, but I'm never let past that closed gate."

And I'm never informed, she thought ruefully, because keeping St. John out is a standing order of long duration. How could I have known . . .

He shook her gently. "And don't ask why. I want you for my wife, Ardith. I have, I think, since you threw that tantrum at age twelve." A muscle twitched in his cheek. "I could hardly ask you *then*, could I?"

Then? "I don't understand you." Ardith fought the fluttery feeling his now-gentle hands on her shoulders induced. "You could have any woman. You are titled and wealthy; you are not in any way repulsive. Drop the handkerchief and any of the well-trained beauties cluttering the Season will pick it up." She shook her head again. "Why do you persist in teasing me?"

"I am not teasing you. When you believe that, you'll understand me perfectly."

"Let go of me, St. John." It took all her control not to tremble. "Now."

He dropped his hands from her shoulders where his thumbs had rubbed softly and, she believed, without conscious direction, against the skin bared above the modest neckline of her dress. His touch drove her mad and only the strictest of self-discipline had allowed her to demand her release. His features firmed and she wished she'd not objected. They stared at each other until Ardith dropped her gaze.

"A luncheon will be laid shortly, Ardith," he said, obviously attempting to return to something approaching normality.

"I never indulge in lunch," she lied without a qualm. She turned to the shelves beside her, chose a book—not quite at random—and reaching for the door, ducked a quick look at Rohampton. "Thank you for the game, St. John." She, too, knew the rules of a truce. "I'll see you at dinner."

Once the door shut behind her, Ardith drew in a long shuddering breath. One of these days he'd make her truly angry. He'd jest once too often about marriage and she'd say yes—simply to watch him squirm out of the trap he'd laid for himself. In her room, Ardith threw the biography of Sir Walter Raleigh onto her bed and paced between her door and the windows. Why *did* he persist? Why did he insist he was innocent of that plot which had sent her running from London? Could he be? Was he?

Her mind, will it or no, conjured up scenes from her Season. About a month into it, she'd been very nearly nineteen. She was rather looking forward to her birthday since her father had told her to choose the form of entertainment and allowed her to draw up the guest list. Lord Winters had been amused. Only twenty people when he'd expected something like two to three hundred. Not a ball, as each of her sisters had demanded, but a dinner. The *names* on the guest list had had him roaring with laughter.

It hadn't mattered to her he had nothing in common with half the list or that that half had nothing in common with the other. The women she'd invited were, one and all, certified blue-stockings. The men were horse-mad, either breeders such as Ardith had since become or sportsmen who liked talking to a silly girl who was surprisingly well informed about the only subject to interest them. She didn't have to pretend as did most young ladies thrown into the Marriage Mart who would become glassy-eyed before the end of some interminable anecdote.

In age, the guests had ranged from those just older than Ardith herself to a couple from her grandparents' generation. She wondered what sort of fiasco the dinner would have been. She'd never know since she'd run away a week before it was set.

She'd attended that last ball. Neither of the two young men coerced by the hostess into asking her for the "privilege" of being her partner had been quite so tall as Ardith was. The pimply one had fled her side as soon as the music ended; the other, a trifle older, returned her to her chaperone before escaping by offering to fetch her some lemonade. He hadn't returned, of course.

She'd spent half an hour with a new friend, another wallflower who scorned the social scene on principle and had a burning determination to *do something* about the poor who were all around them. It was clear to Ardith that the young woman had no notion what she might do, but even to *want* to do something seemed a better ambition than the common one of finding a husband—any husband. Ardith had been bored and unhappy, as she'd been all too often since her arrival in London.

The Marquis of Rohampton arrived long after Ardith had given up on him. The hostess was saying good-bye to other guests and greeted him a trifle coolly, scolding him for not coming earlier. He'd met Ardith's gaze across the room until she'd blushed and turned from him. When she'd looked back, he'd moved from the lady of the house to Lord Toby, her son, where whatever was said brought a faint flush to the Marquis's cheeks. Ardith had wondered about it, but not for long. She was preoccupied with hoping St. John would ask her to dance. A dance with St. John would go a long way towards making the evening worthwhile and, at the least, would be a break from the nearly intolerable boredom she felt—which he'd undoubtedly recognised, knowing her as he did.

Rohampton moved away from Lord Toby, occasionally pausing to converse with an acquaintance, but apparently with a goal in mind. Ardith's heart was painfully full, fearing he was courting one of the young ladies also watching him, their eyes either avid or bashful or even one or two hoping his eye did *not* fall on them, since they'd given their hearts elsewhere and had parents who would not care about their feelings if a wealthy marquis could be brought up to scratch.

So she had been pleased when eventually, just as the small orchestra struck up a particular favourite of hers, he stopped by her chair and almost summarily gestured towards the dance floor. Under other circumstances she might have objected to his manner, but not when she could take the floor with one of the biggest prizes in the marriage stakes! She wasn't for him, of course, but she knew his request roused jealousy in other maidenly breasts and she couldn't help the glow that gave her. Besides, it was fun dancing with St. John. He was tall and coordinated and made her feel as if she, too, were graceful and *almost* as if she were beautiful. Those feelings blocked from her mind the fact he seemed different—unsure or nervous?

That particular country dance was one which started slowly, with a deliberate pacing of steps. As the music continued the tempo increased until many couples, laughing and heated, dropped out. At the end only a few pairs, including Ardith and St. John held the floor. The music reached its climax and St. John bowed. Ardith curtsied and felt a heavy lock of hair slip down over her shoulder. She reached for it, but St. John shook his head, offering her his arm and guiding her towards the door.

"We'll find a place where you can fix it," he soothed. He raised his free hand and touched her face gently, a silent comment on the flush of mortification burning her cheeks. She glanced up, blushing more when she noted the soft look in his eyes.

"The lady's withdrawing room is that way," she said.

"You don't want to go where all the tabbies will ogle you and then gossip about what a hoyden you are, your hair falling down, so." His eyes widened in pretended shock. "Why, they might even label you *fast*."

Ardith shuddered, not at all amused. "You are correct. Find me your room, kind sir." He seemed to know where he was going, but when he turned down a barely lit hall towards the back of the house, she stopped. "St. John," she said, doubtfully.

"I want to talk to you." When she didn't respond, he added, "Ten minutes, Ardith, that's all I ask."

Again there was that look in his eyes as he reached for her hand. When he put it on his arm and continued walking, she didn't balk, her mind in turmoil. What could he possibly have to say to her that required privacy? It could *not* be what she secretly wished, of course, because a man so marvellous as St. John would never offer for a woman so totally unsuitable as herself. So what? Oh no. Her hand tightened around his sleeve. Something had to have happened. To her father? To one of her sisters, perhaps?

"St. John . . ."

"No," he interrupted, reading her concern, "there's nothing wrong. Shhh. It's just down the hall now. Come."

He opened a door and she found herself entering a small room, a sewing room, she decided as she noticed the screen in one corner, a sewing basket and a sturdy stool on which a lady might stand to have her hem pinned.

St. John, too, looked around the room and frowned. "This isn't quite what I had in mind, but it will do." He picked her up and set her on the edge of the good-sized table which would be used for the cutting of material. He didn't remove his hands from her waist. "Ardith, we've known each other for nearly seven years and I believe we have become friends." She nodded, a choked-up feeling and a faint but growing hope, making it impossible to speak. "I have wanted to say something to you for some time now, but felt it proper to wait."

"Yes?" she croaked when he seemed at a loss.

"I suppose the best way is to just ask. Ardith, will you marry me?"

"No, me," said a laughing voice and Lord Toby stumbled around the edge of the screen. "Me, Lady Ardith, choosh me."

"No, no, he'sh an idiot, Lady Ardith," said Mr. Freemantle. "I'm the one to choose. Marry me and make me the, er, the happiesht of men."

Since the latter was known to have debts all over town, Ardith didn't doubt her marriage portion, at least, would make him happy. She felt confused, embarrassed, and after one glance at St. John who seemed less angry than she thought proper, she tugged, trying to loosen his too-tight grip around her waist. The young men fell to their knees, one after the other, each trying to outdo his rival in flowery speeches and reasons why she should not agree to marry the other.

Ardith ignored them, stared at St. John. In the iciest tone she could manage, she asked him to release her. For a moment he didn't move. Then, nodding, he lifted her down. "I'll talk to you tomorrow, Ardith. This was a fool notion."

"Yes," she agreed. "I believe it was." A fool's notion to make such game of her. How *could* St. John have been a party to it? She knew, even while realising they'd played a joke on her, the others had a modicum of excuse in the fact they were well-to-go, half-sprung if not quite disguised. Their state of inebriation was disgusting, but that bothered her less than that St. John would agree to take part in such a tasteless jest.

Ardith gave him one last darkling look before passing into the hall. Before giving way to tears, which she held back with effort, she found another room farther on. There was just enough dim light from outside to allow her to make out a settle and, closing the door, she felt her way to it, collapsing into one corner and crying long and hard.

It was too bad of St. John, raising her hopes that way only to dash them brutally. Was that it? Had he guessed the dreadful secret she thought she'd kept from everyone? Had he guessed how she felt about him and decided to teach her a lesson? Oh, it was laughable that she, the weed amongst the Winters bevy of roses, should aspire to wed a man far above the rank of, and much wealthier than, the men her lovely sisters had captured!

Well, he'd shown her what he thought of her. And that was that. She couldn't face him. Nor anyone. Not after this. So, what to do?

Ardith stared blankly out the window in her bedroom at Rohampton Park. She clearly remembered what she'd done. She'd washed her face in a bedroom on the floor above and fixed her hair to the best of her limited ability. She'd gone down to the front door where a solicitous footman called her carriage and took word she was unwell to her sister Ellie, her chaperone that evening, that she was returning home but that the carriage would return.

Back at her father's townhouse, Ardith gathered a few random items of clothing into a band-box, searched her various reticules for every bit of her remaining pocket money, and, sneaking out the side door had the luck to find a hackney-carriage just dropping a fare at a neighbouring house. The driver, thinking the plainly dressed female a servant dismissed from her place, took her to the proper stage-coach inn. She'd bought a place on the waybill and waited for nearly three tense hours, before dawn and the coach arrived simultaneously; she escaped to Summersend and her Aunt Sibley.

It had been years since she'd allowed herself to remember the details of that last evening in London. A surprising number of details, actually: the look on St. John's face when the first of his friends had appeared, for instance. Had he briefly been as horrified as she now thought? Surely not. That was merely her memory playing tricks on her. She *wanted* to believe he was telling the truth, that he hadn't been a party to the plot to mortify her, but what she clearly remembered was his silence.

She'd better keep to the facts. St. John had been talking to the son of the house. They'd talked for some time, obviously plotting. Then he'd danced with her. He'd had the responsibility to get her away from the chaperones since he was the only one of the three culprits she'd trust, the only one she'd go with.

Oh, stop thinking about it. It was past history. Ardith flopped in a most unladylike manner into the comfy chair before the fire and scowled. It was over. Over. *Long* over.

And now? Now she was enjoying the enforced companionship with St. John—except when he made her angry. If he'd forget the past, she'd *like* to be friends again. He was her nearest neighbour, and it wasn't pleasant being on the outs with him. Well, she'd see. The snow had stopped but the wind had risen again. She'd have to spend the rest of today and tomorrow and perhaps the next day as well under his roof before the roads would be clear enough for her to go on.

So much time. Anything might happen. So, she'd keep in mind the possibility of their returning to their old easy relationship. It wouldn't hurt to think about it, at least. Assuming he behaved in a reasonable fashion, who knew what might come of it? Oh, to be *friends* again.

— 3 —

THE SECOND MORNING of her stay at Rohampton Park, Lady Ardith stopped on her way to the breakfast room at the landing overlooking the hall where Mrs. Lander and Ransome argued with a poorly dressed lad. The youth's teeth chattered in his head, but he held his ground against their combined force.

"What the devil is all this racket?" St. John approached, a napkin clutched in one hand. St. John, thought Ardith, would resolve the problem. She waited quietly, not wishing to put herself forward into what was obviously a matter of estate business.

"Well, lad? You're Matt Martin's boy, are you not?" The shivering youth nodded. "Speak up. Why are you here?"

A muddle of voices answered. St. John looked from one to the other before raising his hand and turning to stare at Ransome. All other sound disappeared.

" 'Tis his mother, milord," said the butler. "I don't know what the boy thinks *we* can do."

"Do," asked St. John forcibly, "about *what*?" He was, thought Ardith, fast losing patience.

"She needs the midwife, m'lord," said the boy carefully forming his words between teeth clenched against the clatter he couldn't otherwise control.

"Midwife. She isn't here."

The boy went red in the face. "No m'lord. She be drunk as a sow."

"The devil," said St. John ruefully and raised his eyes to the stairs, as Ardith now feeling she had a place in the discussion tripped quickly down the remaining flight. "Good morning, Lady Ardith," he said formally. "Breakfast is served if you'll be so good as to go along to the breakfast parlour. Ransome, escort Lady Ardith—I've a problem here," he went on. "But I'll join you once I've dealt with it."

"Just *how* will you deal with it, St. John?" said Ardith, making no concessions to propriety. "Young man, how far is it to your home?"

"Just on four miles, m'lady," he said shyly.

She took his arm and led him towards the fireplace at the right of the door, one of two flanking the wide entrance. "Now, you sit down and pull off those boots and get out of that wet jacket. Mrs. Lander, bring the boy something hot to drink. He's chilled to the bone. You've been," she went on, directing her question to the boy, "to find a midwife, is that correct?"

"Yes'um. Babe's early, see," he explained earnestly, "but midwife's deep in the bottle."

"Yes. That would be Mother Tandy. She's a disgrace and it is obviously too far to get Mrs. Clark under present conditions." Ardith didn't need to think about what to do. "If you will wait while I change into something warmer, I will go with you."

Ardith started for the stairs, ignoring St. John's abrupt order to the contrary. She halted on the first step as Mrs. Lander appeared with a steaming mug, which was handed to the boy. Ardith ordered supplies from the housekeeper who looked towards St. John for corroboration. It wasn't given.

"Ardith, you will *not* leave this house."

"Will I not? You, perhaps, will go to the woman's relief?"

"But *you* can't be of any use," stormed her harassed host.

Ardith smiled a trifle grimly. "Oh yes I can." She lifted her skirts and ran up the stairs. At the landing she turned and told St. John, "It would help if you were to order out some strong beasts so the lad and I might ride back to his home." She turned and disappeared, not waiting to see if he complied. It made no difference. She would go with the boy even if they had to slog through the drifts.

Behind her, St. John stared at Mrs. Lander. "What is one to do with such a wrong-headed and stubborn piece of work?"

"Help her," suggested Mrs. Lander. "I thought of her when Timmy here first arrived but then thought you'd not approve. She has the reputation of having good light hands. She's said to be a great comfort at a lying-in, milord."

"Lady Ardith?"

Very little shocked St. John, but the thought of Ardith involved in the awful business of aiding in the birth of children, achieved it. On the other hand, the boy looked to be terribly anxious, and his mother, a sensible country woman, had brought several children into the world already. If the family felt there was need of a midwife, then most likely there would be need.

"Very well," he said. Although still disturbed by the information Ardith was a midwife, St. John suppressed his natural feelings. "Find the things she wanted, the clothes and what have you. I'll have horses brought around." Once having decided to cooperate, his mind worked in its usual competent fashion. "Perhaps the sleigh with the farm team could get through with the least difficulty. Take Timmy to the kitchen and find him dry clothing and warm him up. He may return later when the weather is better."

"No, sir."

"No?" St. John stared down his nose at the boy who stood firm, although obviously inwardly quaking. "Well?"

"No, m'lord, sir. I be needed. M'father broke his leg yisterday or he'd have come hisself for help. As it is, I be needing to see to the beasts and keep up the fire and take care of my family while he's tied to a chair. M'lord," he added, belatedly tugging at the hair at his forehead.

St. John repressed a smile at the youthful dignity of the boy's explanation. "So be it. Go with Mrs. Lander and warm up. She'll find you dry clothing."

As Ardith returned to the ground floor, Mrs. Lander, followed by two footmen carrying large baskets, entered from behind the green baize door to the kitchens. The butler was organizing warm carriage robes. Another man placed heated and wrapped bricks close to the fire to maintain their warmth.

"Bricks? Carriage robes? I'll be riding, Ransome."

"No milady. They are turning out the home-farm pair and the old sleigh. His lordship will be here directly."

"I've put in food for the family, milady," added Mrs. Lander, respectfully. "Bread and a hearty stew and some cakes for the children. I also put in a jar of pig's foot jelly, which Mrs. Martin may need. It'll make a good sustaining broth for the poor dear. When the weather clears, which I'm sure it soon will, I'll send over more."

"Very thoughtful of you, Mrs. Lander. I'm so worried about the mother I hadn't thought of the rest of the family." The door opened, letting in a cold draft and some spitting, wind-blown snow. Ardith asked, "Are we ready? You shouldn't have turned out a man to drive me. I'd have ridden."

"I will not send a man out into this. I will drive you myself."

She blinked. Why was he so angry? Well, this was no time to worry about it. The footmen carried out blankets, bricks, and baskets as Ransome led her to the door. "Explain to Miss Fremby and tell her that I have no idea when I'll return. She'll understand," she said over her shoulder.

"Yes, milady," said Ransome and this time there was nothing but respect in his bland features. The twinkling look she'd come to expect from him was absent.

Many hours later Ardith stared down at the infant she worked on frantically. A deep fatigue filled her. The poor thing wouldn't live, of course. Even if she could get it breathing. She let her eyes rest on the woman lying straight and still on the bed. It was touch and go if the mother survived. Oh Aunt Sibley, what more can I do? asked Ardith of the empty room. If only . . .

"What now, Ardith?" St. John stood in the low doorway, his head bent. There was no expression on his usually expressive features.

"I can't get the babe to breathe. I've tried everythi—" She glanced up, her eyes wide.

"You've thought of something?"
"Cold water, St. John. Bring me a big bucket of very cold water."
His booted feet clattered down the steep stairs even before she finished speaking, and very soon he was back with the water. She plunged the child into it, pulled it out, and put it back into the heated water she'd had ready for its first bath. She tried again and shook the infant. "Hell and damnation, *why*? Why won't you breathe?" she hissed softly. Even in her anger at her helplessness she remembered her other patient.
St. John watched, equally helplessly, as tears ran down her face, glistening streaks in the firelight. He thought she'd never looked more beautiful. Then, watching her rub the baby's legs, he reached for a tiny arm, rubbed it, imitating her motions. It was no use. He knew it. She knew it. Soon they'd have to give up. When she did would she allow him to comfort her?
He looked at the large, obviously ancient hand-carved cradle which lay near the hearth. He watched as, finally, gently, Ardith cleaned the baby, dressed it in the waiting robe, and lay the dead child into it. The tears hadn't stopped.
"My man?" Mrs. Martin's voice was breathy, weak, but if she wanted her husband then husband she'd have. Ardith looked up at St. John. He nodded, knowing the difficulties of getting a man with a rough splint on his leg up the narrow stairs to the bedroom!
Once again he went down the stairs. The chunky farmer sat sideways in a chair, the broken leg propped across another and his body half fallen onto the table where one fist clung to a nearly empty mug. Drunk. Well, under the circumstances, perhaps it was understandable.
A few low curses, encouraging noises from St. John, and soon the farmer stood awkwardly by the bed. "Mary?"
"I'm so tired, Matt."
" 'Twas bad, luv. 'Twas a bad'n."
A weak smile greeted these words. " 'Twas bad."
"Now you rest." His huge paw gently patted the small

work-worn hand. "You rest and get strong again." He glanced towards the cradle, then away.

The woman went to sleep, falling deep into it the way the ill so easily do. Ardith nodded to St. John, who helped the man back downstairs accompanied by more curses as the broken leg was bumped once or twice. Then the stairs creaked under returning weight. Ardith picked up the candle and hurried out onto the landing. St. John stopped a step from the top, and for once their eyes were on a level.

"Is there anything more we can do?" he asked.

"She needs care. Losing a child is always bad. Then, too, she's worried about her family, and that won't do."

"Poor Tim left hours ago to get his aunt. The woman is a widow and will help." He raised his head, listening. "In fact, I think that must be them now. Hear the bells on the harness, Ardith?"

Ardith looked at the woman on the bed, looked around the room. She was so tired her head spun. But, when the rosy-cheeked aunt climbed the stairs a few minutes later, she pulled herself together to give instructions. "I fear fever." She ended her explanation of what must be done and how.

"I do be hearing about you, m'lady. The women you help rarely have the fever. Don't know why that should be, but I'm not stupid," she said cheerfully. "I'll do for m'sister just as you say. She'll be right as a trivet in no time."

They turned to the bed as the patient stirred. "Belle?"

"I'm here, m'very dear."

"I lost my baby, Belle!"

"You be still now. You aren't the first to do so and you won't be the last. You do be thinking of Timmy and the little ones and get well. And of Matt. He's a good man, Matt. There'll be other babes."

Ardith quailed at the rough sympathy, but it seemed to do her patient good. She realised there was nothing more she could do for the family, that the sister could and would do what was needed, but, worried, she reiterated her instructions anyway.

When she finished, the aunt shook her head in mock

despair. "It'll take a mort o' water to be washing everything that way," chuckled the buxom country woman, shaking her head, "but like I said before, I'll do just as you say, m'lady."

Ardith looked at the cradle. Again tears pushed at the back of her eyes. If only . . . but, as Aunt Sibley had once told her, she must put such things into the Other Hands. At some point one had done all one could and could do no more, but it was so sad, so wrong. Why couldn't she have thought of something more? Something which would have helped?

"Babe's early, m'lady," said Belle, seemingly reading her mind. "They almost never live. M'sister knows that."

"But . . ."

"Come, Lady Ardith," said St. John from the doorway. "The team is still in harness and it is too cold to leave them standing."

"But . . ."

"Is there more you can do here?" he asked gently.

"No."

She turned away, knowing the sister would be far more comfort to the bereaved family than she could ever be, but she couldn't help her feeling of failure. There must have been something she could do. Suddenly St. John reached for her, pulled her into his arms, and carried her down the steep stairs. Ardith thought she must be more tired than she knew. It felt *good* to lie against his chest, to let him care for her. She allowed her head to fall against his shoulder. His hand moved to her hair and played with a strand which had escaped her braids.

But it was wrong, his carrying her this way. "I am able to walk on my own two feet, my lord."

He smiled down at her. "No. You might fall and then where would we be?" He shook his head and she felt the brush of his bristly chin moving the tangled hair along the side of her head. "No," he said again. "Much better safe than sorry, my lady."

Safe? Held this way with his chest rising and falling, his arms, strong but gentle around her? He called this *safe*.

"You are teasing me, my lord. It is very bad of you."

His arms tightened. "I assure you, Ardith, you are fair and far off if you think I'm teasing." He entered the kitchen and glanced around. The children slept on one pallet, their father on another. The son of the house rose from where he lay on the settle. He tiptoed towards them.

"Is she worse?"

Ardith, her cheeks heated, soothed his fears from her position in St. John's arms. It was really too bad of him to embarrass her this way. He knew what he was doing, too. Oh, she'd get him for this somehow.

"Your aunt knows what to do, Timmy," said St. John. "Lady Ardith gave her strict instructions. I'll send over a man to help you until your father is able to get around again. But now I'm taking Lady Ardith home. She's very tired."

Ardith knew it wasn't so much that she was tired. She was, of course, but it was the loss of the child. Never before when she worked alone had either of her patients died. And her aunt had accepted tragedy with more fortitude. Was there something she'd forgotten? Was there anything?

"What is it, Ardith?" St. John slowed the team.

She sat rigidly beside him. "There must have been something . . ."

He transferred the reins to one hand and put the freed arm around her shoulders. "Ardith, you did all you could." She resisted him when his arm tightened.

She replied in a harsh voice. "I've heard crying helps. I suppose I could do that."

St. John nodded to himself. It was as he'd thought. She didn't know she'd cried when she'd given up on the babe. "Tears are a help sometimes."

"As a man you'd not know, of course."

He pulled her closer. "Actually I do know."

The admission made her relax slightly into his embrace. What could he mean? "St. John?"

"When my father died." Again he was silent for a long moment. "I took the news with appropriate stoicism, but as soon as I could I ran away to my secret place. You remember."

Yes. She remembered. Once, when a mare she loved had had to be destroyed, he'd taken her there. It was a perfect little dell where high banks hid a wide place along the stream. Wildflowers had nodded along the edge of the water and sunlight had sparkled down through the young spring leaves of dripping willow fronds. So still. So private. How many years had it been since she'd thought of that? "A little cold today for your secret place."

"So it is. Perhaps you could pretend right here is a secret place?" He hugged her closer. "I won't tell."

"You never did, did you? When I'd get weepy over some silly girl thing."

"You *were* a girl, Ardith."

She chuckled a rather watery chuckle. "I'd often forget that. I was so different from my sisters, you see."

"Yes. Very different."

She stiffened.

He hugged her. "Did I say that was a bad thing?"

"You didn't have to."

"Ardith, has it occurred to you that if the doll-like sort of woman appealed to me, I might have offered for any one of your sisters as they grew up? Even Ellie would have been much of an age to be my wife. I'd have been a trifle young then to marry, but since none of them interested me, it doesn't make any difference, does it?"

"But they are so lovely," said Ardith wistfully.

"There is more than one kind of beauty, m'dear. I happen to prefer your style." Again he pulled her close when she tried to pull away. "Stay, now. You are very tired, are you not? I have you safe. Sleep if you can and I'll have you home as soon as I can."

Home? Sleep? thought Ardith. While you have me tucked under your arm this way, I'm to sleep? Oh no, St. John. I'm finding this far too nice, too comforting. . . . She yawned. No, I'll not sleep, not waste a moment of you treating me as if you cared, treating me the way I've longed to have you treat me. . . . Another yawn and another. Because it won't last. You'll change again. She snuggled close, gradually relaxing.

Then, in her mind, she saw the two of them working over

the newborn infant. The babe . . . the poor babe. Once again tears streaked her cheeks.

The tears had stopped and Ardith slept when St. John pulled the tired team to a halt before the doors of Rohampton. He lifted Ardith down from the high seat. A groom ran up and asked shyly for news of Mrs. Martin, who was his cousin, before taking the team and sleigh away. St. John entered the huge foyer, where he was again inundated with questions.

"Quiet." St. John's tone was such no one disputed the order. He glanced around, his eyes meeting various members of his staff, a faint expression of surprise on his face. He shifted his burden slightly and Ardith stirred in his arms. "Surely you have something with which to occupy yourselves elsewhere?"

There was the faintest touch of arrogance in his tone, and, depending on their natures, servants blushed or squirmed or sidled quickly out of sight. Soon only Ransome, Mrs. Lander, and Fremby remained.

"Lady Ardith is exhausted," he said quietly. "I will take her up to her room. Hot water, Mrs. Lander, and lots of it. Then a tray. *Not* an invalid's tray, but good hearty food."

Ardith woke as he spoke. Her cheeks reddened as she realised where she was. She met Fremby's eyes and, noting the quirk in one corner of her companion's mouth, knew it denoted suppressed humour. Well, it was funny, she supposed, St. John, her worst enemy, giving orders for her comfort. But he shouldn't be carrying her. She squirmed slightly and was held more tightly.

"St. John! Put me down at once."

He was halfway up the first flight of steps and ignored her.

"At once, St. John."

"Take a damper." When she objected to the cant phrase, he sighed. "Ardith, put that stiff-necked pride of yours in your pocket and let someone care for you. Whether you know it or not, you are exhausted."

"I can certainly climb a few steps."

"No."

That was that. She knew from long experience that when

St. John had that particular black expression on his face there was no moving him. She had no choice, and, realising that, all the starch went out of her. She collapsed against him. Her body was aware, contrary to her will, that he knew what he was doing. She relaxed despite herself.

"Better."

"Ohhhh. You wait until I'm rested!" She yawned, a jaw-cracking yawn.

"Willingly," he chuckled. "When you're back in form I'll spar with you as much as you wish."

He walked down the hall and opened her door without setting her down. As he entered he took one last look towards the stairs, noted no one was in sight, and, letting her feet slide down his body, held her close. For an instant he just held her, then putting his hand under her chin he tipped it up. "This is taking unfair advantage, Ardith."

She didn't know what he meant. Then she did as the hand holding her chin firmed against her throat and his mouth came down on hers.

Oh, she thought wildly, it is only because I'm so tired. It must be. Why else would one's knees give way, would one's hands clutch at the cold material of the caped driving coat he'd not yet removed. It was torture. Or at least it seemed a form of torture. Then it was over.

She was surprised to find herself sitting in the chair before the fire, too bemused to wonder how she'd gotten there. "Miss Fremby will help you, Lady Ardith," he said with cold formality, confusing her still more. "For once in your life, allow someone to aid you."

Ardith didn't argue. By the time the meal he'd ordered arrived, she'd finished her bath and been helped into a night-dress and robe. Fremby helped her to the small table. Ardith was almost too tired to eat but managed to get down most of the sliced beef with horseradish sauce, the thick soup, and a compote of mixed dried fruits, well soaked and floating in one of Mrs. Lander's deceptively innocent fruit brandies. Those fruit brandies had been known to lay out strong-headed men. Ardith was asleep before Fremby had her well tucked in.

* * *

St. John stood at the foot of the stairs and searched Ardith's face for signs of her ordeal, his hand clasping hers. Her chin rose a notch. He grinned and handed her down the last step into the foyer. For a moment he stood there, smiling warmly. Then, putting her hand on his arm and refusing to let her go, he led her towards the dining-room. There he seated her with due ceremony and motioned to Ransome to begin serving.

The rest of the night and a day had passed since she'd fallen asleep after her bath. She'd slept late, then dozed off and on the whole day. This was the first time she'd seen St. John since that fierce kiss just inside her bedroom door and she wasn't certain how to deal with him now.

Besides, there was another vague memory—or dream, perhaps?—of St. John leaning over her in the dim light shed by the smouldering coals of a fire badly in need of attention. She remembered—or had imagined?—his hands resting on either side of her relaxed body. Had she looked up into his stern face or had she not? Had he leaned over her? Had he kissed her gently? No. Surely not. It *must* have been a dream. Surely St. John would not invade a young unmarried woman's bedroom in the middle of the night! But it was so unsettling not to know.

She kept her eyes firmly on the soup ladled into her bowl. The silence stretched until Fremby cleared her throat, startling her into looking up, and into remembering her manners. "Oh dear," she said, chagrined. "I forgot. How is that cold, Fremby, love?"

"Much better, m'dear. I found the herbs I needed, although," Fremby turned to her host, "that still-room is a disaster, Lord Rohampton. Someone should take it in hand."

"Perhaps you and Lady Ardith would do so? I've been lax. An estate's still-room is much too important to be ignored. Will you help repair its deficiencies?" he asked politely, not looking at Ardith.

"I would be pleased to do so. It will take the whole of the summer to collect and replace the herbs. Most of what you have are old and have lost much of their efficacy."

"I thank you, Miss Fremby, for your offer of help." Finally, he looked across the table to Ardith. "Will *you* help, too?"

Ardith felt her cheeks warm. Why did he have to look at her that way? So thoughtful and with a curious sort of encouragement in his eyes? "Someone at Rohampton should be trained," she said. "Every estate needs a person knowledgeable in the use of herbal remedies. I'll train someone." Now what? Why that smug look? "Mrs. Lander may send her choice to Summersend once the weather warms." Now, drat it, why did he look so black? "Our still-room is, though I say it who shouldn't, the best equipped in the county." He still looked like a thundercloud!

"I'd prefer it," he said, "if you were to do the teaching here." He went on before she could speak. "That way you can include the collection and storage of herbs in your training."

Ardith glanced at Fremby, who raised her napkin to her lips, a strange sound smothered by the white linen. "Are you all right, Fremby?" Surely that hadn't been a laugh!

"I'm quite all right, Ardith."

But her voice sounded strained, and Ardith wondered at it before turning back to her host. "St. John, I do not believe that possible."

"Why? You no longer have the excuse that you'll never again enter my home. You've been here days now and what damage has been done you? None."

No damage? Didn't he *know* how he had harmed her? No, perhaps not. She *must* forget that kiss, forget the feel of his arms around her, his strength and gentle care of her—care he'd give anyone in need. "Well, until spring arrives nothing may be done. I'll think about it."

Another silence stretched her taut nerves. She waved away several of the dishes offered her for the next course, her appetite disappearing for reasons she didn't understand. Fremby again introduced a topic of conversation and Ardith, knowing it was required of her, forced herself to concentrate and add her mite to the discussion of the war in the Peninsula. The third siege of Badajoz had begun early in March. On the twenty-fifth, Fort Picurina was successfully stormed despite heavy fire and rockets. St. John was tight-lipped about the many dead and wounded, wondering if the partial victory had been worth it.

Ardith remembered that one of those listed as wounded was a friend of his, who was with the Fifth Division. "I'm sure," she said, "that Colonel Westman can't have been badly hurt or surely there would have been further word. We're into April. Word of his death must have arrived by now, so you *must* assume he's recovered."

"So I hope. His home is in Northumberland. I sent a groom with a note to his mother as soon as I read the report. Another is in Dover awaiting the hospital ships returning the wounded to England, and if Cameron *is* sent home he will be brought here—assuming he can travel further. It will be much better for him than a hospital where he will be one amongst many."

Ardith nodded. "Dr. Waingarden is a good man. He'll do as much for your friend as any well-known London practitioner could do."

"At this point we do not even know how badly he was wounded. Perhaps, as you suggested, he has healed and returned to his regiment."

St. John shrugged away the topic and asked whether Ardith felt up to a game of chess. She did. They finished their meal and adjourned to the library where Miss Fremby settled before the fire with work candles and some mending she'd coaxed out of Mrs. Lander's hands. Ardith, preferring the fight at the game table to verbally sparring with her host, was glad it was not necessary to talk to St. John. She feared he'd open a topic of conversation she wouldn't know how to handle. Ardith forced all thoughts of that kiss from her mind and settled down to the battle.

Hours later, having won one game and lost two, Ardith yawned. She stretched, her eyes closing—and then opening them to see St. John observing her, a flush reddening his high cheekbones. Ardith forced herself into a more ladylike posture and glanced around. The candles were guttering, the fire low. Fremby had disappeared at some point; she and her host were alone.

"It's later than I'd thought," she said. "We'd best be off to bed."

"Yes." There was a deliberate note in his voice. "That's an excellent notion."

She rose from her chair so quickly she almost tipped it over. She glanced at St. John—looked at him more closely and away, a flush rising up her neck and warming her flesh. There was a hot look in his eyes she found exceedingly disturbing. He couldn't mean . . . could he? "St. John . . . ?"

"Don't be a fool, Ardith. I meant exactly what you thought I meant, but it's impossible. I know that. And *you* know why you must leave me."

"I don't." She turned to face him.

"You *are* a fool then. Leave or be ravished, my beauty." He leered with the histrionic words but immediately sobered. "Ardith, you tempt me far too much for any man's control."

"Me?" All fear fled at the extravagance of his words and she laughed. "Oh, St. John, you are such a tease."

"You're playing with fire, Ardith."

She frowned. "You sound serious."

"Damn you, woman, I warned you!"

He grasped her arms and pulled her close. She barely managed to raise her hands to his chest, to hold some little distance between them. A frown creased her brow; her eyes searched his face; a gasp slipped between her lips as his lowered to hers.

His mouth was hot; his tongue traced her teeth, retreated, touched her lips. His arms tightened and she heard him moan. "I must let you go," he whispered against her ear, and she found the moist heat of his breath nearly as unsettling as the kiss had been. Despite his words he didn't release her; one of his hands went to her hair, pulling out one pin after another, allowing the heavy locks freedom. His hand slid into it, grasping handfuls which he pulled around and over her shoulder as she leaned back against the hard muscle of the arm around her waist. "Beautiful," he whispered. "I knew it would be beautiful. So lovely."

His words were a mesmerising murmur and Ardith found

she couldn't move except for the tips of her fingers which clenched into his shirt, relaxed, bent again against his chest.

"Stop me, Ardith. This is wrong. But for so long have I desired to hold you, make love to you, teach you . . ."

She jerked away, panting, his words echoing vague undefined yearnings she recognised briefly before she pushed them from consciousness. His hand slid down her arm and grasped her wrist tightly.

"You must let me go!" she said.

"You don't want me to."

"You must."

"Ardith . . ."

"I must go."

His fingers tightened painfully before tense muscles relaxed slightly, and gradually he released her. He turned to place his hands on the game table, leaning onto stiffened arms. "Go. Ardith, go now while I can let you."

She hesitated, then turned and almost ran for the door.

"Ardith?"

She paused again, her hand on the handle.

"Tomorrow I will get you home. Somehow. I no longer trust myself with you here where you tempt me with every move of that graceful body, with every look from those magnificent eyes. The mouth that draws me, the form that haunts my dreams, the hair, that beautiful hair."

Ardith slammed the door behind her. She didn't dare listen to more of his lovemaking. It was as dangerous—perhaps *more* dangerous—than his touch, because the things he said were untrue, but were words she'd always longed to hear. If only she weren't such an ugly duckling!

Back in her room she giggled almost hysterically: if she had stayed, if she had allowed herself to be seduced, would she have conceived the grandson her father wanted so desperately? What a fine joke that would have been!

Berating herself for such unsuitable thoughts, Ardith forced herself to prepare for bed, but it was a long time before she managed to fall asleep. And when she did, she dreamed, then woke from those dreams to find her skin damp and flushed and the sheets a wrinkled uncomfortable mass entrapping her . . . as St. John's body and arms had trapped her in her dreams.

Tomorrow. Tomorrow she would go home. Home to Summersend and with any luck the end of winter. This *must* be the last storm of the season. She couldn't take any more. She had to be outside, out among her horses, active with their training, busy and, *under no circumstances* could she let her mind dwell on the unbelievable sensations St. John had brought to birth within a body she'd formerly believed she'd known and understood.

— 4 —

NEARLY A MONTH after their return to Summersend, Ardith and Fremby prepared to travel back to Cecilia's. The christening of her newest niece was a family occasion she could not avoid.

To Ardith's surprise, St. John's curricle followed them as they turned into the posthouse where they made their only change of horses. He pulled to a stop beside them and jumped down to open their carriage door.

"Will you join me for refreshment, ladies? I'll order a private parlour for us and we can rest before going on to the Hawkes' house."

"You are invited to the christening, my lord?"

"Yes. I've been asked to stand god-father."

St. John seemed complacent about the honour and Ardith wondered about it, thinking it an odd request to make of such a man-about-town. Then she recalled seeing him hold one of the Martin children, cuddle her and play with her curls, and decided it wasn't so strange. But god-father? When *she* had been asked to be god-mother? Ardith gritted her teeth. Her family had gone too far in their efforts to push her and his lordship together!

"What should I order for refreshment, Miss Fremby?"

"I'll admit, Lord Rohampton, I'd enjoy a dish of good strong bohea. This journey is nothing like our last, but I think the damp chill is almost worse than the biting winds of the blizzard."

Ardith had intended telling Rohampton they must get on but had, she realised, been lost too long in her thoughts.

She could not now contradict her friend; Miss Fremby's pleasure in the proffered treat was too obvious. She followed Fremby out of the carriage and, hesitating only a moment, placed her fingers on St. John's offered arm.

"I'll have," she said curtly, once established in the parlour, "a few words to say to my delightful family when I see them."

"So I should hope!"

"I refer to this embarrassingly obvious ploy to bring us within speaking distance."

"Hmmm. Ardith, you are adopting just the attitude they will expect. Treat the whole as quite commonplace and confound them completely. They'll have no notion at all what you are about."

Ardith thought about his suggestion, met his eyes, and noted the unholy laughter lighting them. She chuckled. "I see. If I treat you as a total stranger, am polite to you but otherwise ignore you, they will be quite at a loss, will they not?"

"No, no, you still do not understand! Treat me as you did before—as a *friend*."

Ardith sobered, turned, and walked towards the window. "I can see where it would make them very happy if I were to do so, my lord."

"You fear it will give them ideas?"

"They have those ideas. How I treat with you will not change that one iota. But their hopes!" She swung around, her spine rigid and her head high. "I would not like to raise false hopes, my lord."

St. John turned to Miss Fremby. "I have set up her back somehow. I am always reduced to 'my lord' when she wishes me to know I have offended."

"I see." Fremby nodded, her wide-eyed expression that of a student receiving enlightenment. "Perhaps, my lord, if *you* were to treat *her* with a certain coldness, she could be as polite and friendly as she pleases and still confound her family," she suggested with equally false innocence.

"Hmmm. It is a likely notion. What say you, Ardith?"

"I might like the idea better if I thought I could trust you to carry out your end of the bargain."

"A wager!" Her brow quirked at his suggestion. "A wager to liven our visit. You will, for the period we visit the Hawkes, treat me with the easy ways you once used as a matter of course. I, on the other hand, will treat you with all the cool indifference of a total stranger. The first of us to break from the mold will owe the other." He paused, stroking his chin. "What would be, do you think, an appropriate wager? Miss Fremby? This was after all your suggestion."

"I was brought up to abhor the habit of wagering, Lord Rohampton," said Fremby primly. He started to apologise but was stopped in midsentence when she raised her hand and shook her head. "However, my lady, my lord, perhaps if you lose, sir, you will agree that the maid you wish to be trained in the stocking and use of the Rohampton still-room will come to Summersend, and you, Ardith, will agree if you lose to go to Rohampton and train the woman there."

"I like it," said St. John, grinning.

"I don't." Ardith scowled.

St. John stared at her. "You think you will lose."

"I think nothing of the sort! I merely have an alternate wager to offer. If you lose you will allow Lightly, when she is ready, to be bred to your new stallion. I will in turn give you the right to breed any mare in your stable to my Black Lightning."

"Tempting." St. John rubbed his chin thoughtfully. "I've a mare I'd like to show to that stud of yours. But you haven't seen my new stallion, Ardith. What makes you think it an even trade?"

Ardith's eyes widened. "You chose the animal, did you not? It isn't one you won on a wager and have not yet rid yourself of his contaminating presence, is it? I mean Ajax, who—"

"Be easy, Ardith. I paid a long price for the brute. I've great hopes of him."

"Then that's all right. I trust your judgement of horseflesh, St. John."

"My God, Ardith, do you realise you've just given me a compliment?"

"A very limited one, you'll agree. It is *only* your judgement of bloodlines and conformation I trust."

"Well, it is something, at least."

Ardith frowned. Had he actually sighed before muttering that last? Drat the man. The more she saw of him, watched him, listened to him, the more she was inclined to the notion she'd misjudged him, that those fools really *had* played a tasteless joke on him when they'd interrupted his proposal. That it had been a real proposal! And if that were so . . .

But no. It was irrelevant because it was too late. Her life was no longer that of a young lady whose only hope in life was to get married. She'd been her own mistress far too long to put herself under a man's authority. The thoughts went round and round as the light refreshment of fairy cakes and cut sandwiches were laid out, the innkeeper bustling around his servants like a sheepdog herding his sheep.

"Well?" asked St. John as the door closed and the three were again alone. "Is it a wager?"

"Hmm? Oh, the stud. Yes. I suppose so."

St. John studied her for a moment before turning to Miss Fremby, who was also looking closely at her charge. They exchanged a bemused look and St. John shrugged. Miss Fremby shook her head. She began an innocuous conversation which, eventually, Ardith interrupted. "I believe, my lord, it would be best if you let us get a head start. I do not wish to arrive at my sister's in tandem with your curricle."

"I understand, of course. However, I will go first. My team hitched to a sporting rig will pull far ahead of you, riding in a closed carriage as you are. If you tell your coachman to dawdle a bit, there will be no question of our arriving at the same time. So, if we must break up this delightful *tête-à-tête*, I will settle with the landlord and be on my way. I will greet you later, ladies, as if we were meeting for the first time." He headed for the door, where he turned, his hand on the latch. "Ardith, you might warn your servants that we have not talked. Also that they aren't to mention you were snowed in at the Park for several days!"

"It had occurred to me to warn them about today's meeting, but thank you for reminding me of the storm."

"Thank you also for the treat, Lord Rohampton," said Ardith's companion.

He bowed. "You are quite welcome, Miss Fremby."

With a grin at Ardith, he left the room and she whooshed out a long breath. "I am so glad he reminded me to warn John and Owen not to speak of the snowstorm. They might have said something and then the questions would fly!"

"So they would, my dear. Will you have another cup of tea?"

"Tea?" Ardith looked at her half-filled cup. "No, I've had enough. Shall we go?"

The sun was behind the trees when her coachman pulled up at the Hawkes' front door. Ardith's sister was in the hall as she and Fremby were bowed in by the butler. Cecilia rushed forward to embrace Ardith, looking up into her tall sister's face searchingly. "It wasn't my idea," she whispered.

"It? How are you my dear?"

"Me? Oh. Fine. We are all fine. Truly, Ardith, I had nothing to do with it! I must speak to you."

"Well, show us up to our rooms, dear, and you may speak to me as much as you like. If the footman would bring that portmanteau, I believe it has the gown into which I'd like to change. I assume I am to be in my usual room?"

"Yes, but you don't know how complicated it all is. Terrance and Maud brought along guests without warning. *And* their servants, of course." Cecilia looked as miffed as any hostess might under the circumstances. "Then Clarence forgot to tell me his aunt wrote. She is coming. And . . ."

"And you don't know how you are to put us all up. Perhaps Fremby and I could share a room?" Her sister nodded, her frown smoothing slightly. "Then there is no problem, is there? Sharing will not upset us a bit."

The room was as usual except for a rather messy bouquet which stood on the dressing table. Miss Fremby's eyes twinkled, but Ardith looked a trifle irritated and her sister tut-tutted and ordered it taken away.

Cecilia apologised for allowing the men in the family to choose Lord Rohampton as god-father. She was soothed and left to do the next thing required of her as hostess. Alone with Miss Fremby, Ardith asked, "Who could it be, do you suppose?" She picked up a stray petal from the bed.

"Whoever it is, he's persistent, Ardith."

"I don't like it. It isn't natural. Look! On the pillow. A note."

"What does it say?"

Ardith spelled out the rough lettering. "Later."

"You'll tell me later?"

"No. That's all the note says. *Later*. What can it mean?"

For a moment the two women puzzled over it, but time was passing and it was necessary to change for dinner. The note slipped Ardith's mind as she and Miss Fremby joined the others. Ardith glanced around the drawing-room, noted the scowling face of Cecilia's aunt by marriage, and walked over to join the old lady. Ardith had always liked the old woman, a tartar who frightened her poor sister to death. She immediately asked after the health of the lady's overfed pug and settled down for a blow-by-blow account of its every wheeze and cough during the miserable winter. When the woman paused for breath, Ardith offered a receipt which might help. The woman, pounding her cane on the floor, demanded Cecilia's presence.

"Yes, Aunt Meresdon?"

"I require pen, ink, and paper. At once."

"At once?" Cecilia glanced at her sister who was choking back laughter. "But dinner . . ."

"Lady Meresdon," Ardith suggested, "perhaps I could write it up later and give it to your woman?"

Lady Meresdon glanced around the room, noted the butler hovering by the door. "Your man, there. Is he waiting to announce dinner?"

"Yes, Aunt Meresdon."

"Then tell him to do so. I'm sharp set. Does my system no good at all waiting around like this when I'm hungry."

Rohampton, as the highest ranking peer in the room, was required to take his hostess into dinner. He did so without grumbling, but the fact Ardith was seated somewhere in the middle of the table as not only the youngest lady present but also the only one unwed, was an irritant. Cecilia, noticing how often he glanced that way, determined that proper or not she would seat Ardith on his other side at the next meal.

Cecilia didn't approve the trick her father had instigated in suggesting the two be made god-parents and had wished for the courage to write Ardith and warn her. But it seemed to have been a good plan. At least Ardith had not boiled over and rated her father up one side and down the other, which was the *least* Cecilia had expected. At worst, she'd wondered if her sister would order out her coach and turn back for home as soon as she was given the news.

The evening passed pleasantly, but as time to go up to bed approached, Ardith remembered the badly lettered note and found herself growing nervous. She gave herself a lecture, reminding herself she had Miss Fremby in the room with her. Nothing would happen. She could sleep in peace. She *would* sleep in peace.

No matter how she lectured herself, she lay awake a long time wondering why she felt so uneasy. Then, the coals in the fire barely glowing, she heard a click, turned, and stared, wide eyed, towards the door. It was opening. The case she'd casually placed near it tipped over with a crash, and Miss Fremby sat up on the other side of the bed.

"Ardith? What was that?" she asked in a sleepy voice.

"It's all right," Ardith said loudly. "I believe a draft must have blown open the door. I'll just close it." She got out of bed and, looking out the door, saw a part of a hairy leg and bony bare foot whisk around the corner at the end of the hall. She shut and locked her door. A frown creased her brow as she climbed back into bed.

Suddenly the small gifts she'd found over the past couple of years, the ribbons and flowers and cheap fairings weren't touching little tokens as she'd once believed them to be. A man didn't try one's door in the middle of the night merely to leave a love token behind. Who could it be? Since she'd only discovered such tokens when the whole family was gathered together, it had to be someone who moved with their master and mistress. One of the grooms, maybe—or a valet? A valet would have more freedom to move about the house. Why had she assumed the gifts were innocent?

Oh drat. Wouldn't she have a lovely time trying to explain to her father why she'd not told him of them long ago, why she'd not asked for assistance in discovering who left them for her to find!

Another question entered her head. Why, in any case, was *any* man so persistently threatening her? With her odd looks and beanpole figure? It simply didn't make sense. Either the man was mad or a blithering idiot.

The next morning Clarence told a heavy-eyed Ardith he had a new lady's mare he wished she'd try for him. Ardith was agreeable and after eating returned to her room to change into her riding habit.

Looping her skirt over her wrist she made her way downstairs, carrying the jaunty little hat which went with the stark blue-black habit. She was met in the hall not only by Clarence but also by Rohampton. She ignored him except to nod and made no objection when he followed them out of the house.

St. John and she walked all the way around the mare. They glanced at each other, similar expressions of distaste in their eyes. "Well," said Ardith, "if I'm to ride her, I suppose I might as well get on with it."

Rohampton moved to help her mount. "Why don't I escort Lady Ardith, Hawke? As host you can't really wish to desert your guests for this."

Clarence winked suggestively. "As you say, although it is family except for those hideous friends Maud drug along. Don't hurry back," he added. "Take as long as you like." He watched as St. John and Ardith set off, waving them on their way.

Ardith waited until they were beyond hearing before speaking. "I'll have Lively delivered for Ajax just as soon as she's ready to be bred again."

"What?" St. John laughed. "Yes, Ardith. You do that. I forgot our wager, didn't I. But I had reason. Holding one's tongue between one's teeth concerning that mare would make anyone forget, don't you think?"

Again they looked at each other, then at their respective mounts. "I knew Clarence was a slow top, St. John, but this is terrible. I apologise for him. You will find yourself crippled, crossing that bonesetter."

"Will you be in better condition?"

"What? You think I might find this creature's gait requires more energy than my rocking chair? Shame on you, St. John. Don't embarrass the poor creature!"

"I suggest we curtail this ride out of sight of the house. You had something on your mind when you came down to breakfast, did you not?" She compressed her lips tightly. "M'dear, you need a confidant. That is obvious. Whatever else you think me, I am safe in that role."

It was the truth and she admitted it. Still, could she tell him? But if not St. John, then who? Her father? Oh, yes, certainly. She must. But the very notion of going to him and enduring a quite justified tirade made her ill. She conceded St. John victory, and while trying to get up courage began in a round about way. "You read me much too easily, St. John, to have guessed I've a problem. What's worse, I feel a fool. How I could have been so convinced of something so utterly beyond all bounds of civility, I don't know. Obviously my wits have wandered off into—"

"You are chattering in order to avoid telling me, Ardith."

She sighed. "I suppose I am."

"Well?"

"I fear I've been a veritable fool."

"I promise I won't laugh."

"I should think *not*. It's no laughing matter."

They reached a quiet walk through the woods and St. John dismounted, tying his gelding to a convenient branch. He came to her side and lifted her down. Ardith wondered at herself, waiting that way for him to come to her. She hadn't required help to dismount for years—or ever? She couldn't *remember* waiting for a man to help her off a horse.

"Now," he said, looking down into her face, his hands loosely around her waist. "Will you tell me?"

She did. Even about that awful fear she'd felt last night when she'd realised that someone had come to her room with the intention of ravishing her. "I can only think it one of the valets, St. John."

"There are six of them here at the moment. Mine included, of course." St. John frowned down at her. "I think I can find out from him about the men's sleeping arrangements. It is common, you know, for them to share a single room under conditions such as these. Not Clarence's man, of course. He'll have a room of his own. If I can do so without arousing my man's curiosity, I'll see if any of the others slunk out and back in. And," he smiled, "Glickson is the least curious man I've ever met! So I think perhaps we might be able to determine your villain and then . . ." He frowned again. "What then, Ardith? He mustn't be allowed to try again. Will you take your father into your confidence?"

She slumped under the hands he'd moved to her shoulders. "I must, of course, but I dread it. *He* won't refuse to call me the fool I am. I shouldn't have assumed the gifts were innocent."

"Would you like me to deal with it?"

"How can you?"

He grinned. "Do you think I cannot?"

He could. And going to her father . . . no. The nausea returned as she thought of it. Her father would *not* be tactful or considerate of her feelings. But how would St. John deal with the culprit? Ardith decided she didn't want to know except . . . "How can you be certain you have the right one?" she asked.

"I don't jump to conclusions. If Glickson hasn't the information I require, then I can do nothing and we'll make plans to trap your would-be ravisher. It's a good thing I didn't try the very same thing myself, isn't it? Why, he and I might have met in the hall on our way to your room!"

"You are not to bam me that way, my lord."

"Ah. I see I am once again reduced to 'my lord.' In that case I think it time we returned to the house."

"I'm a trifle chilled so I won't argue that point, my lord."

"Any other woman and I'd consider that an invitation, Ardith."

"Invitation?"

"You are cold. I should warm you, should I not?"

St. John proceeded to do just that, keeping himself well

in check the while. But both were trembling when he lifted his head. Their eyes met, hers searching, his warm and smiling.

"That was quite lovely, my dear. May I do it again some time soon?"

"I . . ."

She turned towards the mare and, fighting her foot clear of her skirts, placed it in the stirrup.

"Ardith, you did not answer."

"You really must not do that, my lord!"

"Must not?"

"It is wholly improper."

"Yes." He nodded, a judicious expression pursing his lips. "Most improper—of both of us. Me for kissing you and *you*, my love, for responding so sweetly."

She stared down at him, a worried look in her eyes. "St. John, will you misunderstand if I apologise for accusing you unjustly for that fiasco in London five years ago?"

"I don't know. How should I interpret such an apology? Incidentally, are you apologising?"

"Yes. I believe you now, but," she said as she backed the mare away from his reaching hands, "now it is too late. Things have changed. A great deal."

Her words came quickly and at the last moment halted his prowling, dangerous-appearing approach to her.

"I think you'd best explain, Ardith."

"I am no longer that innocent girl, St. John." His eyebrows flew up and her skin burned with mortification. "No! I didn't mean *that*! I meant I am not so young. Nor am I dependent on my father as I was then. Things are different."

He nodded. "Yes. I can understand that having had a taste of independence, you can't like the idea of giving it up. Are you certain I would require you to change?"

"I could continue running my stables? My breeding scheme? You'd not argue if I were needed again as a midwife?"

His expression stilled at the last and he stared through her, his eyes blank and unseeing. "I see."

"Do you?"

"I think I do. Ardith, would you think I've changed my mind about you if I tell you I must think about this?"

"I would find you very strange if you *needn't*."

"We will discuss it again, my dear." His eyes held hers, and after a moment she nodded. "But now we must return this poor excuse for a mare to her stable and I must talk to my valet about your problem."

"Discreetly."

"Very discreetly, m'love."

Clarence was waiting for them when they returned. "What do you think, Ardith?"

"The mare?"

"Of course the mare. What else could I mean?"

"Well," said Ardith with a straight face, "so tied in the knees as she is, she'll never make it into a canter." She glanced at her red-faced brother-in-law and went on hurriedly. "But she *is* for my sister, is she not?" He nodded. "Then she'll suit very well since Ceci prefers something resembling a nursery rocking horse and has been known to fall off when her mount changes gaits. Since this poor lady is nearly incapable of changing gaits that shouldn't be a problem." Ashamed of herself, she smiled kindly at Clarence who huffed impotently once or twice, sounding very much like his father-in-law. To distract him, she asked, "What happened to Merry?"

"Ardith, do not tell Cecilia"—the red deepened across Clarence's ears—"but Merry succumbed to a cough last winter along with our eldest daughter's pony and one of my hunters. I thought I might find a replacement before I confessed it to my wife."

Ardith's hand flew to her cheek. "Oh, poor Ceci. She loved that animal. She's had her for nearly twelve years and she'll never have another like her, I think. Why, Merry was perfect for Ceci. It didn't make any difference what Ceci did with her reins, Merry knew best and did what she was supposed to do anyway!"

"Doesn't Cecilia like to ride?" asked St. John.

"None of my sisters could be said to *like* riding. Ceci has neither the seat nor the hands for it. Maud is intrepid enough but no one has ever managed to teach her not to yank at her reins, and every horse she rides ends with a bad mouth. Ellie has good hands but the worst seat I've ever seen. All, of course, ride. Father insisted."

"You are severe," scolded Clarence.

"Perhaps I am. But, as it is my only accomplishment—my ability to ride well—I must make the most of it by denigrating my sisters' ability, must I not?"

She stalked into the house leaving St. John laughing uproariously and her brother-in-law more red faced with anger than ever. "She is impossible!"

"She is a delight."

"She has just insulted her sisters. *My wife* included."

"She was, you fool, being sarcastic at her own expense."

Clarence was silent for a moment. "She was?" he asked cautiously.

"She most certainly was. I wish I could lay hands on whomever gave her such a poor opinion of herself."

"Ardith? Why, she's the most . . . the most . . . She has *far too good* an opinion of herself!"

"No, you are thinking of that sharp tongue of hers. It is a defence she uses against being hurt, as she has been far too often."

"Ardith?" asked Clarence again, completely confused. "Who would dare to hurt her when she gives as good as she gets?"

"Whoever convinced her she has no beauty, that she is inferior to her sisters in every way."

"But she *is* inferior to a lovely womanly woman like my Cecilia!"

St. John gritted his teeth.

Clarence proceeded to step deeper into trouble: "How can you say that long meg has beauty? And she's far too intelligent for a woman! Why she's . . ." Clarence blinked as St. John stalked by him and into the house. He scratched his head. "I believe Cecilia must have the right of it. Rohampton is in love with Ardith! Only love could make a man so blind!"

He went to tell his wife of his discovery and didn't understand *her* reaction either. She smiled and patted his cheek just as she did one of their daughters when the child did something particularly intelligent.

— 5 —

"LORD ROHAMPTON? Of course he may come in. Well?" Lord Arthur Winters scowled at his valet. "Well? Must you keep him waiting? Well, Marvin? Open the door!"

The valet bowed and opened it, allowing St. John to enter. The man then walked towards a chair near the fire and turned it slightly, holding the back in a silent suggestion the visitor be seated and stay out of the way. Lord Winters' valet was annoyed at the interruption to his lordship's toilet and did not bother to hide that fact.

After Lord Winters' cravat was tied and while his evening coat was forced onto his shoulders, the men talked of commonplace things. St. John held up the quizzing glass hanging on a ribbon around his neck.

"Like it, Rohampton?"

"Fine as a fivepence, sir," he said dryly. "Very well tailored."

Arthur laughed heartily. "You never like the way we popinjays rig ourselves up, do you? Not that I do it often, much to Marvin's chagrin. Eh, Marvin? Well, Marvin? Isn't that all, now?"

The valet puttered a bit longer, laying out fobs and rings and a second lace-trimmed handkerchief, which was to be tucked into Lord Winters' sleeve. He looked around the room, bowed to the two men, and left.

"Well, well. Now we can be cosy. Come to tell me you and Ardith have fixed things up, have you?"

"No, I have not."

"But you're as close as two birds in a pie! Whyever not?"

St. John crossed one leg over the other and opened his

snuffbox. He offered it to Lord Winters, studying the man as he did so. "You know, occasionally I've had reason to doubt you've any sensitivity. This is an example. It would please me if you would leave me to deal with your daughter. No teasing her. No ordering around. Just ignore the situation."

Lord Winters' eyes widened. He huffed. Huffed again. "Well, that's an odd thing to say to a father!"

St. John nodded, a slow judicious movement. "Yes. I see your point. But do you see mine? Ardith has, as you've said often, a very odd twist in her make-up. She's an unusual girl in all ways."

"She's m'daughter. She'll do as she's told."

"As she did five years ago?" Lord Winters' face crimsoned. "Don't push her. You'll only set up her back and she'll turn from me again. As it is, we are speaking. We are slowly finding our way back to the trust and friendship we once shared. I believe she will eventually become my wife but *not* if you interfere and her pride takes control again."

"She's female," blustered Winters. "Needs a man to take care of her."

St. John's brows climbed his forehead. "Do you really believe that?"

"Of course I do."

"And Lady Sibley? Did she, too, need male advice and support?"

Winters' face reddened. Again. "Here now. You aren't saying m'daughter takes after that half-mad woman, are you?"

"Some of her philosophy has rubbed off on Ardith, I'd say. Mostly those aspects which are good."

"Good!" exploded Lord Winters. "There was nothing *good* about that eccentric old witch. Why, she wouldn't even let *me* see Ardith for months and months, and when I did she was there the whole five minutes. *Five minutes*. What can a man say in five minutes?"

"Yes, Lady Sibley was too protective, but she also taught Ardith a great deal and left her a very neat property which you, of all people must know, gives Ardith something more than a tidy income."

"Income!" Lord Winters blustered. Then he frowned. "Income? Beyond the three percent Aunt Sibley left? Never really thought about it. The farm rents, y'mean? Not her horses. I know she buys and sells and plays with those horses day and night, but an income?"

A quizzing glass swung in a lazy arc from the string held between St. John's fingers. "I did some calculations from the gossip I've picked up from members of my club. I estimate she made a very good living last year just from stock sales and stud fees. The two farms attached to Summersend bring in something. Then there's her work with the sick. I doubt that pays her in money, but I've seen local people handing in produce at the gate." St. John paused, noted Winters' goggling eyes. "I doubt," he went on, "if she has much in the way of expenses, excepting wages, tack for the horses, and repairs, of course. But even there some of the men whose families she's physicked offer their services in payment."

Lord Winters stared at him. "What's this? She goes out doctoring people?"

"You were unaware that Lady Sibley passed on her medicinal lore?"

Lord Winters rose to his feet and stalked back and forth across the room. "It must be stopped! *At once.*"

"Why?"

"Why! 'Tisn't proper, that's why!"

St. John mentally kicked himself for making such a mistake, and thinking quickly how to repair the damage, responded, "I see nothing improper in the lady of the manor helping the poor and needy. The practice has a long and hallowed tradition behind it."

Lord Winters blinked. "Well, put that way, it don't sound so bad, but . . ."

"You just leave Ardith to me. *No interference.*"

Lord Winters hesitated, then sighed. "If that's what you want, but I can't say I like it."

"I'm certain you do not, but, believe me, it is the only way. Enough of that. It isn't why I came here for a private moment." St. John paused to order his thoughts. Still irritated, Lord Winters demanded he open his budget. The marquis formed a tent with his fingers and said, "There is a problem which you *can* help solve, if you will. It will require a bit of trickery to accomplish, however. I can do nothing without your help, and something must be done."

"Now what?"

"Some man has developed a passion for Ardith."

"What? For *Ardith*?" Lord Winters snickered, noticed the icy look in St. John's eyes, and sputtered to silence. "Well, well. How amusing. *Ardith* with an admirer."

"She has had an admirer in *me* for years."

The cold hard look froze Lord Winters. He didn't move for a long moment. Then he chuckled weakly. "Aye. I keep forgetting. Never understood it, you know. Now if it had been my Cecilia. Or Maud. Yes Maud, with her love of the pretties and liking for parties, then 'twould make sense. Maud would make a great thing of being marchioness. Must admit I never saw what you see in my Ardith. *I* like her. Think the world of her. But y'must admit she ain't a beauty like the oth—Lord Rohampton . . ."

St. John leaned forward, his hands tight around the arms of his chair. "Open your eyes and *look* at Ardith, you fool! She's far more beautiful than those pasty-faced dolls you admire. Ardith . . ." St. John controlled himself with a gasp. In a calmer but still dangerous tone he went on, "I once told Ardith I'd like to horsewhip the person who gave her such a low opinion of her attractions. Now I find *you* as guilty as I'd believed that silly twit you hired as governess to the girls. I cannot whip my future father-in-law, but don't ever again imply by word or deed you think Ardith unattractive!"

"You are impertinent, my lord."

"I am angry. If she'd had more self-confidence when she went to London for her Season, we'd have married long ago. She would not have assumed my proposal a cruel joke, that those two idiots and I were roasting her."

Never having heard the full story, Lord Winters gaped. "What idiots?"

"Never mind. If she'd understood her own style of beauty, had known herself attractive, she would have believed me.

I was unaware just how deep her feeling of insecurity ran. And you know the result." St. John ran a hand over his brow, hiding his eyes for a moment. When he looked up he found Arthur clutching the arms of his chair, his eyes starting from his head. "My lord?"

Lord Winters swallowed. "You seriously believe her a *beauty*?"

"I do. She is."

"But . . ."

"We need not agree. Tastes in such things differ. But you must not denigrate her person. Don't you see how you have damaged her? How you've made her believe no man could want her? Leave me to convince her otherwise. Do nothing to interfere. Now, this other thing. The man must be stopped. Last night he actually opened the door to her bedroom. She is sharing the room and the two women speaking scared him off."

"He came to her room? Why didn't she come to *me* about this?"

"I can't say," said Rohampton gently, seeing that Lord Winters was feeling genuine hurt. "This morning I knew something was troubling her and forced her to tell me or she would have said nothing to me either. We have guessed it is a valet, but which one? She would not allow me to suggest *all* be sent packing, because the innocent would then suffer unfairly."

St. John rose and paced the room as he continued. "I talked to *my* valet in hopes he noticed who left their room last night. It seems my man, who is awakened by no more than a whisper, slept like the dead. He heard nothing from the time he laid his head on his pillow—a head which felt full of cotton-wool when he woke. He believes he was drugged. So, as I said before we got off the track, I need your help to trap the man. He's become dangerous, I think. I had something like this in mind. . . ."

The two men spoke for some time, Lord Winters eventually agreeing to St. John's plan.

When Ardith and Fremby arrived in the salon, her father and St. John were not there. Ardith wondered if they were discussing her, but put it aside as she noted Ellie was as skittish as a mare in foal, her eyes turning towards Bertram again and again, her skin paling whenever *he* looked at *her*.

Ardith moved across the room, speaking briefly to those she passed. "Ellie, what is it? You look worn to a thread."

"Oh, Ardith, I cannot oblige him. I *cannot*. I'm *afraid*."

Ardith reran that in her head and turned to look at Bertram. "I see. Father's absurd offer to buy a grandson, I suppose. Then you are not *enceinte,* my dear?"

"Oh, no." Ellie blushed at the notion of telling her unmarried sister she'd not yet allowed her husband back into her bed. "Bertram agreed I could see the doctor first. Perhaps I am well enough I need no longer fear childbearing . . ."

"Well?" asked Ardith when Ellie didn't go on.

"I haven't seen him."

Ardith blinked. "Whyever not?"

Ellie glanced at her husband and back to her sister, a tic twitching the corner of her mouth. "I told him Dr. Baile was very busy, you see, and I couldn't ask him to come to me when he had so much to do."

"Well?"

"Bertie insists I see him when we return to London. Or . . ." Ellie's neck turned a mottled red.

"I understand, I think. Bertram won't wait to come to you any longer."

"Yes." Ellie hung her head. "You understand."

"Our dratted father should be flayed."

Ellie looked scandalised. "Ardith, you should not say such things. You really mustn't. I know you are only jesting, but if anyone were to hear you! Oh, Ardith, do mind your tongue. Please do."

"I love him, Ellie, but I cannot approve of this . . . this . . . *offer* he's made. Perhaps if I tried calmly and carefully to explain to him . . ."

"I *tried* talking to him. He only pooh-poohed my fears and told me it was my duty. You know how he is when he gets a notion into his head. He wants a blood heir to whom he may leave his private fortune and he won't be moved from that."

"There he is now. I wonder . . ."

"Ardith, you look quite angry. Please," Ellie hissed, jerking at her sister's skirt, "do calm down, dear, there are *strangers* about!"

Ardith once again scanned the room. The strangers were guests of Terrance and Maud, a couple as wild as they and with tongues which wagged at both ends. No, she could not cause a scene now. But Ellie's situation was serious and her father and her husband should be made to see it.

The evening continued as such evenings did. Dinner went smoothly even though Ardith, much to her surprise, found herself seated next to St. John. *That* divergence from custom would be an *on-dit* once the others returned to London, but she had nothing to do with London. So why care what was said?

Later Cecilia played for the party. Then the woman Ardith didn't know sang. She had a rather thin but not unpleasant voice, much better than Ardith had feared. Then it was time for bed. Tomorrow the christening and then home. Ardith longed for home.

There was only one surprise. Her father gathered his family in the salon the next afternoon after the celebration in which the countryside had joined and announced that he was planning a celebration of his own.

"I'll be sixty m'next birthday. I've a wish to make it a day to remember. And I want all of you there for it." He glared around the room.

"You'll open the townhouse ballroom, Father? I'll help plan it."

"Not a ball, Maud."

"Not? A *soirée*, perhaps? No? Then what had you in mind?"

"An old-fashioned country *fête*," said Lord Winters with satisfaction. "A barrel of home brew and a feast for my tenants. Games on the south lawn for the brats. You know the thing. Then a country dinner and, I guess, dancing for the gentry. So there's your ball after all, Maud, m'dear."

"*You intend to hold a party at Winters Hall in the middle of the Season?*" Maud stared at him. "You're mad."

He huffed, saw Rohampton shake his head in warning,

and scowled. He controlled his ire and said jovially, "Nice break from all the rush-rush you do in town. You can go down to Winters Hall early and help."

"I'll do no such thing." Maud pouted. "Terrance, tell Father I cannot leave town in the middle of the Season. All our invitations! Our little parties! Oh, no, I cannot do it!"

"Your father wants you there, you'll go, you fool," hissed Terrance.

Maud stared at him. He made a movement of sliding his thumb across his fingers. She blinked. "Oh. Oh, well, if I must I suppose I must."

Lord Winters also noted the hint and laughed sourly. "Aye, I'd guess you *must*." There was more sarcasm in his tone than Ardith had ever heard.

St. John cleared his throat, bringing Lord Winters back to the topic at hand.

"Hum? What? Oh. Yes. You, Ellie, you'll be my hostess."

"Of course, Father. I would enjoy the whole. I will come down to Winters Hall whenever you wish." Ardith noted the genuine smile and was reminded Ellie wished any excuse to escape her husband's attentions. Was the whole world gone mad? Or was it merely her family that got itself in such pickles?

"I, too, will be glad to help if you will not mind my bringing the children, Father."

"That's a good girl, Cecilia. Happy to have them. But you need your rest before your next child and may come just in time for all the pother. We'll open the nursery and Ellie can bring her girl, too." He swung a black look around the room. "That reminds me. Anyone got any news for me?"

"You'd be the first to know, Father, I'm sure." Ardith was no sluggard herself when it came to sarcasm. Then she felt small for indulging her propensity in that direction. "What part am I to play in your plans?"

"You, Ardith? Well," her father hemmed and hawed a bit. "Well. I don't precisely know. What *can* you do?"

"My sisters left Winters Hall some years ago so my part will be to make up the guest lists. I'd enjoy planning the *fête* for the tenants as well."

"Well." Her father was nonplussed. Since he never thought of Ardith as having any of the skills required of a gently bred miss, the notion she could plan such an occasion made him blink. "Do you think you could?"

"I have done so each year for my tenants and your cottagers. They appeared to enjoy it a great deal."

"You have? They did?"

Ardith trembled with anger, felt a hand on her shoulder, felt it tighten around it, then relax. She relaxed as well and thought before loosing the bitter words on the tip of her tongue. Her response was firm but within the bounds of civility. Just: "Yes, they did." Ardith turned on her heel and left the room. If she stayed her control would slip and she'd boil over. She didn't need still another roaring argument with her father. Upstairs she found Fremby packing. The days had lengthened and there was to be a nearly full moon that night. They would leave now, she decided, late as it was. "About done, Fremby?"

"I'll finish in no more than a moment."

"Good. I'll order around the coach."

"I thought you might wish to leave tonight and took the liberty of having it up from the stables at five, Ardith, if that is satisfactory."

Ardith looked at the clock on the mantel. "It is nearly that now. I suppose I can wait."

"Another bout with your father?" Miss Fremby's voice held sympathy.

Ardith laughed. "No. I'll leave in order to *avoid* going a round or two with him. He rouses my temper faster than anyone I know. Even St. John can't make me so angry so fast."

"Even St. John? Do you fight with him as you do with your father?"

"Not so often. Well, he is not a relative, is he? Perhaps I control myself better around him."

"No, I think *he* controls the situation. He does not allow a disagreement to get out of hand."

Fremby folded the last gown and wrapped it in tissue as she spoke. Ardith didn't respond, thinking of that hand squeezing her shoulder and cutting off sharp words. Yes, he'd made her think before opening her mouth again. And she'd managed to leave the room knowing someone understood how she felt—that very understanding dissipating her hurt and anger.

How strange. The thought that *anyone* understood her filled her throat with incipient tears. Only Aunt Sibley and Fremby had done so before; no other had ever expressed the compassion and empathy they gave her. Oh, she was *glad* St. John had come back into her life. Now—she bit the end of her finger—she only had to figure out how to deal with him. Safely, that is.

The weeks following the christening were peaceful. Her father and St. John were in London as were nearly all the families of any standing in the area. A letter from her eldest sister—crossed and re-crossed until she could barely decipher it—told her something of their doings. It also hinted that Ellie had once again put her husband off until she could have Dr. Baile to see her. Ardith busied herself with her lists and plans and spent hours and hours with her beloved horses.

Lively's foal showed great promise, and one day when out exercising one of her youngins she caught a glimpse of St. John's new stallion. One of his more intrepid grooms was exercising the beast. She almost drooled at the thought of the foal her Lively and his Ajax would produce.

About two weeks before her father's birthday Maud was driven over from the Hall. She entered the neat hall of Summersend, her expression one of curiosity. "Why don't I remember a thing about this house, Ardith?"

"We were rarely here as children and you have not visited since."

"It's a very nice residence, isn't it?"

Summersend was not as large as Applewood, Terrance's country house, but was better kept and far more welcoming. Jealousy welled up in Maud's heart but she suppressed it. After all, her sister was a spinster, definitely on the shelf, and no spinster was to be envied. "I suppose we'd best get on with it. You have the list of guests ready? You didn't forget?"

"They are here. Did you bring the cards?"

"Of course. I ordered them ages ago."

Maud followed Ardith into the back parlour where ink and pens were arranged on a highly polished, marquetry-topped table. Again Maud had to quell a feeling of jealousy. It was a lovely room filled with attractive colors, the hangings and carpet and upholstery obviously new, and the lovely old furniture well polished. So welcoming. So comfortable. How could *Ardith*, who lacked all those inclinations necessary to a woman, have achieved such style and comfort?

Miss Fremby bustled in. "How are you, Lady Maud? Such a nice day, is it not? You'll want refreshment before we begin so I've asked Amy to bring in a tray. Ardith? Did you get the message from the blacksmith? His lad seemed to feel it important."

"Another burn, Fremby. He's the most awkward man for a smith. Luckily I had the salve by me."

"That's good, and here is Amy. Set it there, Amy. We'll serve ourselves."

"What is this about a salve, Ardith?" asked Maud, choosing a lobster patty and a fruit tartlet.

"A medicine Aunt Sibley taught me to make. I keep it by me for emergencies of this sort. Now, tell me what you've ordered in for the party. I suppose you went to Mr. Gunter for the biscuits?"

Maud explained the contract she had made with Gunter for the catering. Ardith foresaw problems with her father's French chef but forebore to speak of them. Finally Maud asked, "The feast for the country people? You have that in hand?"

As Ardith outlined her plans for the afternoon *fête* it became obvious to Maud her least-admired sister had the organizational skills of a general. "Well," she said, her eyes wide. "You amaze me, my dear. All that just for a pack of tenants."

"Don't scorn your tenants, Maud. You'll deal with them far better if they know you appreciate their efforts."

Maud frowned. "I don't understand. It is their duty to serve us."

"Is that Terrance's philosophy? And what about his duty to them? To see they are well housed and have the implements they need for their work, and to offer aid in time of trouble?"

Maud bit her lip. She remembered riding past one of her husband's tenant farms and wondering at how slovenly the tenants were, the weedy yard and broken fence, the chimney which needed repair. Was Terrance responsible for that? Should he see to such problems? But he had an agent, didn't he? And wasn't the agent to do that? Of course he was. She felt better. "We leave it to Terry's agent. That's what an agent is for."

"Who checks on the agent?"

Maud bridled. "Why have an agent if one *can't* leave it to him?"

Taking a deep breath Ardith forced herself to give a pacific response. "There are good agents and bad. I hope Terrance's is a good one, Maud, if you leave him to his own devices."

Ardith set down her cup and moved to the table. She'd noted the stricken look in her sister's eyes. Not that she thought her little lecture would do any good, but who knew? Given that they were forever under the hatches, perhaps Terrance would look into things just to discover if the man was stealing him blind!

They finished the invitations reasonably quickly. Ardith flexed her hand as Maud reached for a sheet of paper. "What now?"

"You did very well as far as it went, Ardith, but you know no one in London. I'll just make up a list of those Father would wish to come." She worked spasmodically, chewing on the end of her pen or staring into space before adding each new name to the growing list. "I wonder if the Regent could—"

"The *Regent*? Have you discussed this with Father? I thought he'd conceived this as a local do."

"How utterly boring, Ardith. Of course he'll want his London friends. My goodness, I know one must do one's duty by one's neighbours, but can you imagine how dismal if *only* the dowdy and dull were invited? Perhaps *not* the Regent—not along with the locals."

"You'd better go over that list with Father before we write more invitations," said Ardith sharply, but was pooh-poohed.

"Don't be such a marplot, Ardith." Her sister brightened as she thought she understood. "I see. You don't wish to deal with modish folk. You'll feel awkward. We'll shield you from the worst of it, dear." Maud returned to her list, not noting the fire flashing in her sister's eyes.

As she was leaving about an hour later, Maud had another thought. "I almost forgot. I've ordered a dress for you, Ardith. I'm sure you have nothing suitable for a party such as this one will be. It'll arrive by the end of the week along with mine and I will drive it over."

"How generous of you." Ardith had ordered her gown weeks earlier. It hung in her wardrobe as they spoke.

"Oh no. The modiste will bill Papa. It is for *his* party, after all, and he would not wish his daughter to look the dowd. I'll bring my dress to show you. It will be perfect, I assure you. A lace overskirt and short train. A low décolletage decorated with matching lace and ribbons. *Three* flounces, love. A *delightful* design."

And expensive, thought Ardith. "I hope you chose something less elaborate for me. I look a guy with too much decoration."

The comment was ignored, but a faint colour came into Maud's averted cheeks as she drew on her gloves. "I had to guess your measurements, of course, but she put in plenty of seam in case any must be let out."

Ardith clenched her jaw, relaxed it carefully. "Very thoughtful."

Fremby spoke quickly when Maud was gone. "That woman wants conduct. You'll wear the delightful gown *you* ordered. It suits you very well."

Ardith laughed. "You are correct, of course. Why do I let Maud's comments rub me up the wrong way? Why can I not just laugh? Maud is so tiny and well formed. Then there is my tall slab of oddly padded flesh. It is really a good joke, isn't it? Three lovely Winter roses and then poor Father had *me* dumped on him! One should really feel sorry for the poor man."

"One should have one's head examined for thinking oneself in any way inferior to those feather-heads, that's what one should do!"

"Are you angry?" Ardith tipped her head. "But why, Fremby?"

"I'm angry because you run yourself down when you have beauty and style and intelligence." Ardith shook her head. "Just because you are tall and dark does not make you ugly, m'love. You were brow-beaten into believing beauty comes only in small packets and that one must be blond and milk and water. But, Ardith, that is not true. Will you let me dress your hair for the party?"

Ardith saw the pleading look in Fremby's eyes. Why not? If it would give her friend pleasure. She smiled. "You may try if you will, my friend, but don't be disappointed if you cannot make me fashionable."

Fremby turned away before she could reveal her satisfaction. Her fingers had itched for *years* to take that magnificent head of hair in hand. Ardith, poor dear, was in for a surprise. Fremby wondered how the young woman would cope with the discovery she was a match for her sisters any day.

Ardith grumbled through the following days as more and more of the actual organisation of the birthday celebration fell into her lap. Fremby was of course an able second-in-command, but she would not make decisions. All too often Maud—or Ellie, who had arrived on Maud's heels—would tell their father's housekeeper or steward to go ask Ardith, or worse, give contradictory orders to the chef which Ardith was then required to mediate.

"My schedule for schooling the horses is in *shambles*, Fremby!"

"You know very well the lads follow your every order. They know their work. As they should. You trained them, after all."

"It is not the same. I wish to observe and help. I hate this, Fremby. I will be so glad when it is over."

"Was your father put out when he discovered Maud invited all her friends from London?"

"He was. At first he blamed me, but I pointed out I didn't know a one of them and couldn't have invited them if I'd wished."

"I'm sure Maud is in a pelter."

"Of course she is. It is my fault, as you'll guess. I'm informed I shouldn't have told Father I advised against it."

"Your sisters do not treat you well, Ardith. They never have."

"Little more than a week ago I'd have argued with you, Fremby. I've had so little to do with them the past few years, I'd forgotten, remembering only the good things." She sighed.

"Don't fall into the dismals, m'dear. Families are rarely all one would wish."

Ardith stared at her friend. "I'm sorry, Fremby. Your own was nothing very special, was it? What would you have done if I'd not needed you?"

"As the youngest I was expected to stay home and care for my father. I would, I think," said Fremby, a twinkle belying her words, "have run away with Father's verger. He wasn't so very ancient, after all."

"Fremby!"

"Ardith!"

Chuckling, they walked arm in arm to the dining-room. They'd just finished when Ardith's footman entered. "Lord Rohampton is at the gate, Lady Ardith." Tomlin wore a vaguely wary look. The orders to deny Lady Ardith had never before been contravened, but servants' gossip had led to this breaking with convention. He was obviously relieved his mistress showed no anger.

"My lord requests to see you, milady."

"I wonder why." She blushed when Fremby chuckled. "Oh, dear. Do order it opened for him, Tomlin," she said as she realised how her incivility must have sounded.

St. John's first words on entering their presence were not particularly polite either. Certainly not the phrases usual to the situation. Instead of wishing them good evening, he said, "Ardith, that gate-keeper of yours is the most uncivil man I've ever met. It is embarrassing, I tell you, to stand there arguing with the clodpole and have a ragged little red-headed urchin gallop up on the most broken-down nag I've ever seen and see the boy admitted while I stand there cooling my heels."

"Red hair? Oh." Ardith rose to her feet. "That must be Martha's little brother. I told them to come at once when I was needed. You'll have to excuse me, St. John." She disappeared out the door as she spoke.

St. John blinked. "How uncivil of her. What's to do, Miss Fremby?"

"I suspect Martha has been confined."

"Martha?"

"She married the son of one of Ardith's tenants a year ago and the boy came with her. Her husband asked long ago if Ardith would help at the lying-in."

"So, no sooner do I walk in the door than she walks out."

"You do not seem particularly upset, my lord."

"Surprising, is it not? I've come to the conclusion that if I'm to have her, I'll have to take her as she is." He seated himself at Fremby's gesture and settled back. "Do you believe she will be long?"

"There is no way of knowing." Fremby had a tray set before her and poured coffee into a cup, asking Tomlin to pass it to St. John. She poured her own but barely sipped it before setting it aside. St. John chuckled knowingly and she smiled. "I will not stand on ceremony with you, my lord. I do not like it and I don't believe I ever shall. Tomlin, please order me a pot of tea, if you'd be so kind." The footman nodded and left the room. "Now that we're alone perhaps you'll tell me why you've come? I am sorry Ardith was required to leave."

"It can't be helped. I came because, as you've most likely guessed, I could stay away no longer. I thought I'd manage until her father's party but . . ." He shrugged slightly. "Miss Fremby, I know you are close to her. Very likely you are the only real friend she has." He met her eyes. "Are you for me or against me?"

"That is blunt, my lord. I'll be equally blunt. I believe you the man for her. Since I wish for her happiness, I must be for you."

St. John, that hurdle crossed, nodded. "Then have you any advice? I've waited so long for my darling termagant. Once I believed she hated me and I left her alone. But she doesn't." Miss Fremby nodded agreement. "Now I know that I want her leg-shackled and installed in my home just as quickly as I can manage. It's the managing I find difficult."

"I believe patience is the key, my lord. She tells me little, but I think there will be a happy outcome if only you can go on as you've done since the storm brought her back into your orbit. She seems quite relaxed in your company, which surprised me, I'll admit, given all I'd heard."

"It surprised me, too. I suspect it is the fact she is older, that she has developed a great deal of self-confidence of which she is not yet aware. I must discover how I might make that fact clear to her."

Fremby opened her mouth, then closed it as her tea was carried in. "That will be all, Tomlin." When they were alone again, Fremby asked, "Lord Rohampton, are any of your special friends coming to Lord Winters' party?" He looked startled. "Oh," laughed Fremby, "you had not heard? Maud extended the guest list far beyond the initial conception of this affair. One might say, with justice, it has grown into a gala."

St. John chuckled. "Poor Winters. He has been thrown into the middle of a bumble-broth, has he not? And all my fault! I must remember to apologise."

"I don't understand." Her curiosity aroused, Fremby forgot the point she'd meant to make to the effect that the behaviour of his friends, and their attentions towards Ardith, might go a long way towards proving to her she was *not* unattractive. St. John sobered. "Will you tell me?"

He pressed his lips together, undecided. "You can have no notion of the real reason for the party, it's true."

"You and Lord Winters haven't plotted some shenanigans to bring her up to scratch, have you?"

"Oh, no. Not that. It has become, I'd guess, a far more expensive plot than intended. Nothing may be done about that now. It will have to go forward. Do not feel concerned, Miss Fremby," he added as her frown grew. "I believe I can trust you but think I'd best not so that you will act naturally. All will be explained once the trap has closed."

He firmly turned the conversation to unexceptionable topics, only occasionally looking towards the door. Miss Fremby smiled as he did so for the fifth time. "I believe it will do you no good to wait, my lord. Ardith is likely to be gone hours."

"Hours?" St. John thought back to Mrs. Martin's confinement and shuddered. "Does she expect problems?"

Miss Fremby chuckled. "I see you are ignorant of the most ordinary facts, my lord. But why should you be aware of such things? This is a first child. They are often very stubborn about coming into the world. I'd be much surprised if we see anything of Ardith until well into the night, or perhaps not until sometime tomorrow."

St. John sighed and rose to his feet. "Miss Fremby, thank you for a delightful evening, but I fear I'm intruding and had best take myself off."

"Nicely said, my lord."

Noting the twinkling eyes in Miss Fremby's otherwise sober face, St. John grinned. There was, as he'd suspected, a sharp mind behind the middle-aged features, and just now she'd caught him out when he'd offered polite platitudes as his reason for taking his leave.

He reached for her hand and held it. "Miss Fremby, you'll never know how much I appreciate the fact you've stood friend to my stubborn and lonely love." He bent and kissed the air above her wrist.

Very much in charity with each other, Miss Fremby walked him to the door. They chatted about nothing in particular while they waited for St. John's mount to be brought around. She waved him off, closed the door, and for just a little, leaned against it. After a long moment's thought, she nodded briskly, and after checking the candles were out and the fires well banked, took herself off to bed.

— 6 —

As Ardith approached Summersend the next morning, she was tired but pleased at the happy outcome. It always made her feel good when a healthy new infant entered the world, and although the delivery had been long both mother and child were doing well. The euphoria faded, however, when she rode around the last curve to find an altercation going on at her gates. Lord Winters' voice rose over the low country growl of the gate-keeper.

Ardith liked the privacy achieved by the irascible old man trained by her aunt to keep her neighbours at bay. Therefore, she'd made no effort to change the rule that no one be allowed through without explicit instructions from the manor. Except the poor and sick, of course.

"Father? I had no expectations of seeing you today."

"You tell that Friday-faced old man that when I come to visit my daughter he is to open the gates to me! Demmed old fool!"

"Don't say such a thing, Papa. I'm sure you are not damned."

"I meant . . . !" He tossed a suspicious glance her way. "Don't you roast me, m'girl. I'll not have it." Ardith nodded at Hubert, who ostentatiously unlocked the gate and, much more slowly than need be, swung first one aside and then the other. He took off his cap to his mistress, but made no effort to hide his glower as he bent slightly towards Lord Winters.

"Insolence! How can you put up with the man?"

"Hubert is not insolent to me, Papa."

Lord Winters grumbled the whole way up the lane and handed over his horse to Owen, who followed his mistress. Ardith dismounted with difficulty, her tired body not obeying the commands she gave it. She spoke quietly to the groom and then taking her father's arm, leaned a bit heavily on it.

"What's the matter with you? Now I look at you, you look burnt to the socket!"

"Nothing is the matter a few hours' sleep won't put right. I have had a time of it recently and mostly your fault."

"My fault! I've not seen you since the christening!"

"I refer to this party you tossed in our laps with too little warning. It is monstrous difficult putting together such a complicated celebration with so little notice."

"And that, missy, is why I'm here. You're needed at the Hall, m'girl, and no havering. Maud and Ellie between them have the servants all in a dither. One gives an order and the other changes it. There is no peace. Last night my dinner was well-nigh inedible. So, you order your trunks packed and come home right this minute, do you hear?"

"Hear you? I should think they hear you in London. But now? I think not. I will come tomorrow and straighten out any tangles, but this instant I want nothing more than a bath and my bed. And I won't be packing. I'll stay here and ride over each day."

"You'll pack your bags and return to your home, do you hear? You'll do as I say."

"You forget." Ardith's back straightened despite her fatigue. "*This* is my home. You have no authority over me now. I'll bid you good-day and will see you early tomorrow."

"You listen to me!"

"No. *You* listen, my lord. I am exhausted and would be no help if I were to come. So I will do exactly as I said—bathe and sleep and that is that." She turned on her heel, passing Fremby, who, standing near the stairs, gave her a commiserating look. "See him out, will you, Fremby?"

She heard her father swearing as she climbed the stairs and was glad his voice faded when she shut her door. The hip-bath was ready for her and she heard steps in the hall.

Her father's voice rose when she let in the servants with hot water, faded out again when she closed the door behind them. A shuddering sigh ripped through her, and she stripped off her clothes, letting them fall where they would. Twenty minutes later she was in bed and asleep.

Lord Winters' next visit was only slightly less frustrating. He entered Rohampton Hall, his voice preceding him through the door. "Where's your master? Must see Rohampton. At once, d'you hear?"

St. John strolled out of his library at the loud voice. "I should think the whole county could hear. Is there something wrong?"

"You're demmed right! There's a deuce of a problem. Do you know what that daughter of mine plans? Do you know?"

"Come into the library, Winters, and I'll pour you up—well, a little early for brandy—some claret perhaps? You sound as if you need it."

"Servants a bunch of prattlers, are they? Don't want them listening, eh? Well, can't say I disagree."

St. John exchanged a wry look with Ransome and led his guest away. Not until he'd poured up a glass for each of them and insisted his guest be seated did he allow Lord Winters to speak. "*Now* you may tell me."

"She says she ain't coming to the Hall. She says she'll ride over each day! Do you know what that means, m'boy? Do you? All this demmed nonsense for nothing! The expense of it, too. And for nothing, do you hear?"

"I heard the first time. I suppose you rode over and ordered her to the Hall. Will you never learn you must not give Ardith orders? Would *you* react well if treated so?"

"Me? Me? What has that to say to anything. She's m'daughter!"

"So she is. Very like you in some ways. Stubborn and proud, for instance. She is also a very independent lady."

"Tell you what, Rohampton. You marry the wench and beat that out of her. Don't do for a woman. It ain't right."

"Since her independence is one of the things I like about her, I most certainly will *not*." Rohampton sipped his drink and met the gaze of his visitor, who spluttered a few times and was still. "Yes, I know. It is very odd of me. However, it is also none of your business how I treat my wife or what I require of her."

"I assume, m'boy, you require the usual!"

St. John repressed anger at the leer which accompanied the words.

"Much prefer a cuddlesome little armful myself, but no accounting for tastes. Couldn't bear to take such a long meg of a woman into my bed. Why would be like . . . like making love to a giraffe!"

The anger grew. "You are disgusting."

"Here now! That's not nice."

"Neither, my lord, are you. Again and again you insult the lady I love. Your *daughter*, no less. I'm sick of it. I thought I told you to leave her alone."

"Well." Lord Winters tugged at his cravat, finding the harsh look on Rohampton's face rather unsettling. "You asked for m'help on this thing and look where it's gone. Right up in smoke if you ask me."

"You, as usual, went about it wrongly."

"She's m'daughter!"

"You keep saying that, but you treat her as if she were . . . were . . ." St. John could come up with no metaphor which pleased him. He sighed. "We have a problem. We will not discuss how it arose. What we must do is discover a way of getting her to Winters Hall." He slipped down in his chair, his legs extended and crossed at the ankle. Staring into his glass he spoke slowly. "It would not do, of course, for her to be there before myself, so the fact she isn't there now is all to the good."

Lord Winters looked chagrined. "Hadn't thought of that. Just want my home back in order," he muttered. "That Maud and Ellie are, between them, turning it into Bedlam."

St. John raised startled eyes to his lordship's face. "And you think Ardith capable of turning it into an ordered household?"

"Of course."

"Seems a bit contradictory, my lord. I thought you despised Ardith for having none of the usual feminine tricks and no skills at keeping house."

"Well. Well . . ."

Lord Winters huffed once or twice. He did not like being told he had contradicted himself. It forced him to think. Why had he assumed Ardith would make sense of the situation he'd escaped that morning? Without hesitation he'd ridden straight for Summersend, quite certain she was what was needed to bring peace to the chaos surrounding him.

"Well, well," he said more calmly. "I suppose I've simply assumed a horse-mad hoyden would have no wifely qualities. But I've heard enough to know she runs a tight ship over at Summersend." He thought about that and looked up, inspiration solving the contradiction. "More likely it's that Fremby witch."

"Miss Fremby is an excellent housekeeper, Winters, but she does not assume an authority she does not have. I assure you, Ardith is mistress in her own home."

"Well, well. If you say so. Maybe she isn't the ramshackle I've always thought her."

"I thought her your favourite."

"So she is. So she is," said his lordship. "But not because of her looks or feminine tricks! I like her spirit. Always have. The only one of them with a smidgeon of spirit!" He frowned. "Not that it's right. Should have beaten it out of her when she was young enough for it to take. Women shouldn't have it. Wouldn't want any woman of mine to have so much."

St. John sighed. It was obvious Lord Winters would never understand the inconsistencies in the things he said. "You are again insulting my bride-elect, but I will ignore it." He sipped again and sighed. "Perhaps it is for the best. Ardith would not like our doing things behind her back. I will see her and explain to her, and you, my lord, will keep your distance when she arrives at the Hall."

"If you say so. But no need to hurry off. She said she was for her bed and I'll admit she looked peaked enough." On a surprised note, Lord Winters added, "She actually had difficulty dismounting. Very stiff. Never seen her so awkward."

"Explain." St. John straightened in his chair.

Lord Winters described his arrival at Summersend with far too much animadversion on the behavior of the gate-keeper. The relevant information he inserted here and there told St. John that Ardith had just then returned from the delivery to which she'd gone the evening before.

"I see. I will ride over later. Well, I'm sure you have things to do, my lord." St. John rose to his feet.

Lord Winters rode home with the vague feeling the younger man did not exhibit the respect he should have for an older and wiser man. On the other hand the marquis would, or so Lord Winters hoped, marry the last of his daughters and make her respectable. 'Twasn't respectable, her living there at Summersend like she did. Not at her age, even if that frump of a companion was there to give her consequence.

So, until then he'd put up with Lord Rohampton's arrogance. But no longer. The pup must be shown that Lord Winters was *not* a man with whom one trifled. That Rohampton's title outranked his own was irrelevant. The age difference alone meant St. John owed him a decent show of respect!

A man of a totally different cut from his future father-in-law, Lord Rohampton made no demure when the gate-keeper sent a message up to the house. Instead, he smiled. The old servant's brows beetled in response. St. John spoke softly. "I am glad you look after your mistress so well. She is a good woman but she is a woman. She needs someone to care for her."

The gate-keeper opened his mouth to respond tartly but, startled, shut it. His glower softened to his normal spiteful expression—which was quite enough to curdle milk in any case—and, when word came the visitor was allowed entry, he actually doffed his cap as St. John rode by.

"Well, Ardith, you are up to your old tricks, I see," said St. John without preamble when he was shown into the back parlour, the most comfortable and most used room in the house.

Ardith shook her head as if to clear it. "Tricks? What in

heaven's name do you mean?" Enlightenment dawned. Or so she thought. "If going to the aid of a woman in childbed is something to be ashamed of, then I'll just have to learn to feel shame."

He laughed. "Not that. Never that, Ardith. I am assured you are excellent help at a confinement and we would not like to lose your services for the neighbourhood, now would we?"

She frowned. "If not that, what have I done to put up your back?"

"Certainly not that, although I resent how tired you become in behalf of others, you know," he said gently.

"Oh, come now! I am not tired."

"But you were this morning when you arrived home, were you not?"

She felt her cheeks heat and looked away. "I recover quickly."

"Good girl."

The soft words brought her gaze to meet his, and there again was that warmth, that pride and approval which always turned her inside out. "I am?"

"You didn't deny you were tired, Ardith. You didn't dissemble."

"Why should I?"

He chuckled. "May I sit down?"

More flustered than ever by the discovery that their argument had caused her to forget common civility, Ardith gestured to the wing chair across from her place on a small sofa. He ignored her silent suggestion, seating himself beside her. Suddenly Ardith realised her father had been to see him and, her emotions cooling at the thought, said, "But that has nothing to do with why you are here, does it, my lord?"

"No. I'm on an errand."

"My father sent you to whip me into line?"

"Don't use that tone to me, m'love. I offered to come since it was obvious he'd made a mull of it. Ardith, you must go to the Hall." He touched his fingers to her lips when they opened to argue. "Not, however, until the house guests arrive. It is essential you be there that night."

"Of course I'll be there. Having had to plan this thing from one end to the other, to tactfully head Maud off from her more ridiculous starts, to soothe Ellie whenever Maud set up her back. And the servants! You've no notion! Having done all that, do you think I would miss the celebration?"

"Of course you will attend the functions you've planned. What I mean is that you must stay that night and perhaps the next." He touched her brow, running his finger down her nose, on to trace her lips. "However, if you continue to tempt me with that delicious pout, I may forget why I came, and explanations can go to the devil."

Ardith jerked her face away from his touch and drew in a deep breath. Her heart pounded and she hoped he did not notice. Nor did she wish him to see into her eyes just then. "I will listen, my lord."

"My lord, is it? Ah, well. Explanations are so dull, but if it is explanations you wish, then that is what you'll get. You see, Ardith, I made a plan to catch your . . . admirer. But if you are not sleeping at Winters Hall, then how may my plan succeed?"

Her temper rose in a flash. "You would have plotted to catch him without informing me of the plans?"

"I had every intention of informing you. Not, however, until the ball was nearing its end. You have a great deal of responsibility to contend with without the distraction of worrying about this as well, m'love."

She searched his face, the anger flowing out of her. "I believe you'd have told me eventually."

He grinned, "It would have been necessary, although not nearly so pleasurable as if I did not! However, I don't believe your father would allow me into your bed with you still in it, would he?"

She blushed deeply. "No," she managed to say in an even tone. "He'd not approve. It is a good plan." She frowned, thinking. "If I were to have my old room with the connecting door to the next which was once Cecilia's, and you that one, then I could enter my room and go through to yours, exchanging rooms with you."

"It is just as compromising if I'm given a room with a door

connecting it to yours! Your father will have that room, giving up his own to the Duke and Duchess of Ware. He'll wait there with you for our plot to be fulfilled."

"I see. Do you really believe he and I can be within the same four walls for however many hours it takes and not come to blows?" she asked idly.

"I note your sense of the ridiculous has returned."

"There is nothing at all ridiculous about my relationship with my father. He can rouse my temper more easily than any other."

"It is because of the deep affection you hold for each other." St. John's tone was soothing. "That, coupled with his lack of understanding of you as a woman, leads him to say and do things which set up your back."

"I wonder. Do I love him? Sometimes I think I detest him. This thing of desiring a grandson for instance. Has he no conception of how his sons-in-law will treat his daughters, their greed overcoming all sensitivity to the women they've promised to love and cherish?"

"Is that supposed to make sense?"

Ardith bit her lip, eyeing him from under lowered lids. He grinned at her and she smiled. "I suppose I can trust you. I expected to tell you when we were caught at Rohampton during the storm, but forgot."

St. John laughed during part of the story but sobered towards the end when she told him that Ellie was not to bear another child. "Why are you concerned for the others?"

"Oh, not Maud. Her wish to have no children is completely selfish, although I believe there, is some fear there, too. But Cecilia is worn to the bone, St. John. She needs a long rest from childbearing."

"Does she complain?"

"No, but I was taught to look for the signs. Another child will weaken her terribly. She has never been strong. But she would not dream of disobliging Clarence." She stared at St. John, bewilderment obvious in her expression. "I don't believe she particularly wants to. I can't stand the man, but she seems content with him."

"You look as mazed as a duck on ice, Ardith."

"Well, how *can* she love that pompous ass?"

"*Ardith,*" he scolded, "you allow your tongue too much freedom. Clarence Hawke is not a pompous ass." He watched her temper grow and as she was about to rebut him, he grinned, adding before she could speak: "Merely an ass."

Ardith, meeting his eyes, covered her mouth to keep back an unladylike chortle. "You, Lord Rohampton, are a complete hand."

"So I am. Such a burden to my friends." This time her laugh broke out, and taking her hands in his he joined her with a few chuckles of his own. "Oh, my dear, you are such a delight. Your mind so quick and lively. You always understand. I will never be bored in your company."

Flushing, Ardith pulled her hands from his and rose to her feet. "I am glad I entertain you, my lord. I must make myself a cap-n-bells."

He rose, too. "Fool," he said softly. "It was no insult. Our minds work as one, Ardith. We find interest and humour in the same things. Do not you, too, find that a delight?"

She turned away. "I enjoy our battles."

"Good. It's a beginning anyway."

"Please, do not go on."

"I have no intention of continuing. Having made a step or two in the right direction, I will certainly retreat at this point. It is not late but you are still tired, m'dear. If I leave, will you go to your bed for a long night's sleep?"

"Yes. I must go to Winters Hall early tomorrow. Such a nuisance. This celebration couldn't have come at a worse time for me. All my young stock to school! Ah, well. A dutiful daughter should not repine, I suppose."

"Repine away, m'love. No one's accused you of being a dutiful daughter!"

She turned on her heel, noted the twinkle in his eyes, and smiled. "I think you have had the last word, my lord. Does it please you?"

"Of course. I keep score, and you my lovely nemesis are far ahead in the count!"

"Lord Rohampton," she said, forcing her face into stern

forbidding lines, "you have a long ride home and will suffer all the dangers of the night air unless you leave immediately. I wouldn't wish you to endure a rheumatic complaint, so perhaps you had best be off before the light is gone."

"And so decrepit as I am, I suppose I might succumb to a quinsy, as well, an' I do not obey. Good-night, Ardith."

"Good-night, St. John."

She watched him go, a tight band of reluctance to see the last of him, fighting with the desire to keep him at arm's length. She feared those feelings he roused with his lightest touch. She raised her fingers to her mouth, touching her lips as he had done. An echo of the longing his touch induced returned—but only an echo. He hadn't tried to kiss her. Would he have done so if she'd given him a hint of encouragement? Ah, but it would be dangerous to encourage him. Give that man an inch and he'd take an ell! As he'd proved on more than one dearly remembered occasion. But, the sensations he had taught her to feel had an insidious life of their own, she thought, as she prepared for bed. They demanded more, that they be fed again and again until . . . "Until what?" she murmured, braiding her hair as she gazed through her window towards the dark silhouette of trees on the near horizon.

Until what indeed. As if she didn't know where such behaviour led. A flood of red stained her cheeks. She'd been fourteen when she'd stolen out to the barns against her father's express orders to watch her mare being bred. When her older sisters whispered about what happened between a married couple, it occurred to her that men and women behaved in much the same way. The notion embarrassed her. She'd never told anyone what she suspected, and as an unmarried girl no one discussed such things with her. That is, no one until Aunt Sibley set her down and described how babies were made.

Her aunt finished, stared at her great-niece, and laughed. "This is no news to you, is it, Ardith?"

"Well, not exactly. I've long known the process of making colts!"

"You may be told by unhappy women the process is disgusting. Don't believe them. It is not."

Aunt Sibley had never again raised the subject and Ardith had had no reason to ask questions. It occurred to her now that Sibley never explained how *she*, a spinster of great age, knew lust needn't be disgusting!

Disgusting? There were those feelings, those sensations which Lord Rohampton's lightest touch roused. Was it that to which Sibley referred? But to marry for that alone would be naïve and lacking in foresight: men were notoriously incontinent. Once St. John had an heir, would he remain faithful to her? Ruefully, she wished her aunt were alive and available for her to consult.

There was an alternative, of course. Not to marry him, but to become his mistress. At least then she would retain her independence! Ah, it was too much to think about when she so badly needed her rest. She'd need all the patience she could muster to deal with the problems at Winters Hall on the morrow. So, sensibly, Ardith pushed it all away and allowed the familiar feeling of lassitude and a quiet mind lift her towards sleep.

The ball was almost ended when St. John approached Ardith. "I believe a waltz is about to begin. Shall we?" He took her limp hand and pulled her onto the dance floor.

"St. John," she hissed, "I *can't*."

"Of course you can," he said with a smile which warmed her clear down to her toes. "I know you've been taught."

"If you are referring to last night, Maud bullying Terrance into making the attempt to teach me, it didn't serve. His feet couldn't take it, he said; he'd be unable to dance tonight if we didn't give it up."

"We'll try."

Ardith was lucky in that it was one of the slower waltzes and unlikely to turn into the sort of romp for which the more quickly paced music could occasionally be blamed. She concentrated desperately, counting and forcing her feet to move just as they were supposed to do. But she could not forget St. John's hand was warm at her back, that her hand was held closely in his. "I warned you," she said, embarrassed at treading on his toe for the second time.

"Relax. Listen to the music." He hummed it, softly emphasising the beat, and much to her amasement Ardith found it worked. "See?" he said as he chanced a more elaborate step which she followed.

"Perhaps," she said, thoughtfully, "it is that for the first time I'm trying it with a man tall enough to see over my shoulder."

"Well, Ardith?" he asked some minutes later when they'd circled the floor without mishap.

Finally believing she would not step all over his feet if she stopped thinking on her steps, Ardith raised her eyes from the level of his cravat. "The day has gone very well, I think. Am I wrong?"

"You are not wrong. The garden *fête* for tenants and villagers was a great success, as you know. And look around you—are there long faces now?"

"No, although if some of them knew of the last-minute disaster in the kitchen, they might well stare!"

"I did not hear of that. Tell me."

"The cook tasted a sauce and discovered too much salt. He threw a temper tantrum which came near to ruining the rest of the meal! It was a lucky chance which had me in the housekeeper's room and near enough to hear the row, or our dinner guests might well have dined on the leavings from the *al fresco* meal we fed the afternoon lot."

"You are joking, I hope."

"Oh, no. You have no conception of what a woman must deal with in the kitchens, St. John! A temperamental cook can be the very devil, and when joined to the caterers ordered down from London by Maud before I knew what she was about, it had the makings of a riot!"

"But why?"

"Antoine's nose was out of joint that Maud thought caterers were needed at all. Then his pride was touched when it was discovered the sauce was ruined. All the makings of a farce, but when one has forty guests sitting down to dinner in an hour I assure you I felt not one bit like laughing."

He chuckled before saying, "This is the last dance, Ardith. Already many guests have left and many of those staying the night have gone to their beds. Are you ready for the final act in this long day?"

"Is that why you cajoled me, nay, *bullied* me into dancing, my lord?"

"I bullied you into dancing, my dear, because it is a more or less socially acceptable way of getting you into my arms. You noticed that Maud had the tact to wait until most of the local gentry was gone before asking the waltz be played? Many tabbies call the dance a sordid display of what should be kept private. I'm surprised Maud talked her father into allowing it."

"He didn't know anything about it. I'd guessed she might, given my aborted lesson, but forgot to warn her against it. There were simply too many last-minute details."

"I'm glad you didn't. Disgusting or not, I'm enjoying this very much." He chuckled. "I so like raising a blush in those lovely cheeks of yours. It is very becoming, you know."

"With my dark skin, you can't possibly tell the difference."

"You have magnificent skin, Ardith. It begs to be touched."

So it does, she thought, ruefully. But I must not let *you* know that.

"What are you thinking? For once I cannot read what is in your eyes."

"Oh? I can keep a few secrets from you? I had come to believe you read my mind, my lord."

"There is no pleasing you, is there?" he laughed. "I'm reduced to 'my lord' again."

"If you will spout such nonsense, how can it be otherwise?" she insisted.

The music drew to a stop and Ardith, feeling a need to escape the warmth in his eyes and the feel of his touch, backed away and curtsied. She moved on, joining her father at the front door where the few late-stayers were collecting wraps from tired servants and making their *adieus.*

Lord Winters was in a surprisingly jovial mood, and when

the door was finally shut, he turned to Ardith, hugging her. "I do believe it was a success. I think I will make it an annual institution," he said.

Ardith stared at him. Annual? She would be required to go through this every spring? Oh, no. She shook her head and backed away. "Oh, no, Father. You will not. No, you *will* not." He stared at her. "I will not go through this ever again. Not for anything. Don't you *dare* suggest such a thing!"

"What is the matter with you? You are hysterical."

"Hysterical?" She laughed. "Yes, perhaps I am. The thought of having to plan and carry through another such occasion is enough to send me straight to Bedlam. Don't even *think* of making this an annual occurrence"—she had a thought—"unless you are willing to find yourself a bride whose duty it is to take on all the horrendous details of it!"

"Here now, get married?" His eyes bugged. "Again?" He shook his head. "You mean me?"

"Why not, my lord?"

"Can't. There's your mother. Mustn't forget her."

"You are a widower now. Mother has been dead for well over a year. You are not exactly doddering and decrepit, so why not?" She had a thought. "Besides getting yourself a hostess, perhaps you might get yourself a son as well and could stop concerning yourself about a grandson," she suggested with a certain slyness.

About to object again, he reconsidered. "A son? Hadn't thought of that." Lord Winters touched his chin, rasping the slight stubble there. "Sometimes, Ardith, I think you an intelligent and thoughtful daughter. I wonder why it hadn't occurred to me to remarry and take care of that small problem," he mused. "A son. Perhaps I'll look about me."

Ardith raised her eyes to heaven and noted St. John leaning on the balustrade surrounding the landing on the floor above. Their gaze met and, her temper fading, Ardith chuckled. "You should do that, Father. The Season is not so far advanced you will have difficulty finding a bride."

She made her way up the stairs to where St. John awaited her. Looking back into the foyer below, she saw her father talking to his butler, the man looking as if he'd succumb to exhaustion at any moment. "I must remember to tell the servants how well they did. Father will never think to do so, and they deserve compliments. Perhaps I can convince him to pass out *pourboire* to each of them. They deserve that even more."

"So they do. You'll make an excellent mistress of a large estate." Ardith quickly banished from her mind the other meaning of "mistress" which more and more filled her thoughts. St. John continued. "Your sort of understanding and your thoughtfulness make people much more willing to put out the effort required of them."

"The vicar did more than teach me Greek and Latin, my lord. He interspersed practical lessons drawn from what we read. That people work best when they know their work is appreciated was only one of them."

"I think I've not valued our vicar as I ought. Perhaps I should get to know him better." St. John laid his hand on her arm when she yawned widely. "You are tired. Go to your room and, as soon as you have changed for the night, through to the other bed. I will wait for your father and we will take care that no one sees us enter. I will go straight through to your room and your father will bear you company."

"Do not treat me as a child, St. John. You explained all that before, and I assure you I find my orders quite clear."

He chuckled. "At least you called me by name that time."

"So I did. Good-night."

The halls were rather dark as Ardith walked to her room. Most of the candles had been snuffed, only a very few still lit for late-comers such as herself. The servants had been told to go to bed and let the last few gutter out, which they would very shortly. She heard snores behind a couple of doors and behind one, where the lady given that room should have been alone, giggles and a gruff voice speaking too softly for her to distinguish words. She felt her skin heat and hurried on.

Ardith was soon in the adjoining room, covered from her chin to her heels by a voluminous robe of lightweight wool challis. She built up the fire and waited. Some minutes passed before a light tap at the door preceded its opening.

Ardith stood up to meet St. John's glowering eyes. She pouted. "*Now* what have I done to displease you, my lord?"

"You? I am not angry with you but with myself," he whispered. "I made a sad mull of it just now. Your father suggested a last drink. I demurred and ordered him to accompany me up here. *Ordered*. Of course he took snuff and walked off to his library forgetting every detail of our plot. You'll have to wait alone, m'dear. Will you be all right?"

"Of course I will." She reseated herself, a little uneasy that he didn't immediately remove to her bedroom. "But what of you?"

He grinned, his teeth white in the light from the fire. "Don't worry. I'm a match for a man the size of any of our suspects!" He started for the connecting door, switched directions, and came to the fireplace where he leaned over her, his arms straight on the arms of the chair. "Shush, love. I know this is outside of enough, but you can't have any notion how delectable being *en deshabille* makes you."

She pushed back as far as she could. "I am smothered in cloth, far better covered than in what I wore at the ball!"

"Did I tell you how lovely your gown was?" he whispered, his voice husky. "It's exactly the right style for you. I must remember that when I'm in a position to buy your gowns."

Ardith giggled, suddenly nervous. "Tell Maud. My sister was quite out of patience with me. She ordered a gown I refused to wear. She denigrated my choice as dowdy and so plain I'd be mistaken for a servant!"

"She was wrong. I can see the sort of thing Maud would choose. Lots of lace and ruffles. Just the style she and the other Winter Roses are flattered by, but quite wrong for you. I believe they are as blind as your father that they cannot see what a jewel you are."

She blushed. "I've told you to not pitch the hammer my way, St. John. I hate flattery."

He drew in a sharp breath. "There you go. Pouting again." He leaned the last little bit and took her lips, tipping her head until he could deepen the kiss. Her mouth opened to his teasing tongue, and taking full advantage he didn't stop until he felt his knees weaken.

"You mustn't do that to me!" she said rather breathlessly.

"I shouldn't," he agreed, "but I suppose I will again and again until you understand how much I love and need you, Ardith." She stared at him but could find no words. He nodded and stood away from her, an act obviously requiring willpower. "I will go now. I suggest you get into bed and try to sleep. There is the possibility he'll not come tonight since it is so late."

St. John closed the door between the rooms and stared blankly at nothing in particular before removing his coat and cravat. He laid them on a chair out of sight of the hall door and sat down on the bed to pull off his dancing shoes. He tossed one and then another towards his other clothes and, unbuttoning a few buttons at his throat, pulled back the bedclothes. For a moment he stared up at the canopy over his head. A smile crossed his harsh features as he studied the frilly pink silk. Was it Ardith's choice? Or had someone chosen it for her? He'd bet on the latter. He must ask sometime. He folded his arms above his head and, snuggling into the pillows which for years had cradled his love's head, he dozed lightly.

Ardith remained by the fire. She knew she'd never sleep. She was wound up from the responsibility of the day and—more pertinent—that dance, and after. She'd understood St. John perfectly when he'd explained why he'd forced her to take the floor with him for the waltz. She'd felt the same way. She smiled, a soft wondering smile her family would not have recognised as she relived the kiss St. John had stolen before removing himself from her presence just now. Thank heaven her father had gone off in a snit!

She waited, listening carefully for any sound from the hall. The clock ticked quietly on the mantel and, once, the coals settled, sending up a shower of sparks. Why couldn't she allow herself to help St. John to a seduction, allow herself to become his mistress? The sensations he called forth demanded more. Much more. Was it a silly maidenly fear of the unknown? St. John would care for her. He'd know she needed patience and tenderness, wouldn't expect her to be an expert in love, but would teach her all she should know!

It wouldn't be that difficult to meet secretly. Their estates marched together, although it was quite laughable to compare her acres to his! Would Fremby, perhaps, guess what she was up to? Ardith chuckled softly. Fremby might guess but she'd never raise an eyebrow if Ardith *did* bring herself to do what she longed to do.

A frown pulled at her brows and she touched the mole beside her mouth. She'd forgotten the problem of pregnancy. Could she bear the ostracism if she were to bear a bastard child? Suddenly she remembered how she'd felt as she held the most recent of "her" babies, the infant warm and cuddly and so very, very tiny. She'd *like* a baby of her own. A child which would grow and learn and find the world an exciting, interesting place in which to live.

The frown deepened. "Interesting?" Yes—until the child reached an age which needed playmates. Not even the cousins would be allowed to play with a bastard. Ardith knew all too well how bastards were treated: she'd used her whip one day to break up a fight in the village. The local whore's boy had been unable to put up with the taunts and gibes of his peers one moment longer. The lad worked in her stables now and was doing well, but he was sullen even with her, suspicious of any kindness or compliment.

She sighed. It would be unfair to bring into the world a child who would find only cruelty. So, it would be stupid to chance that she might. Ardith felt tears pressing at the back of her eyes. Would she ever have the love she wanted? The closeness that love implied? Of course she would if she married St. John.

Once married, her possessions would become his, be under his control, and she would be expected to dance at his whim. A rueful smile twitched the corners of her mouth as she remembered his startled expression when she'd asked if he'd put up with her midwifery and her stable management. It hadn't occurred to him she'd want to do so, of course, and that told her all she wanted to know about his expectations. She couldn't see herself submitting to his wishes so *that*, she sighed, was *that*.

Her thoughts were so deep that the muttering in the next room didn't immediately disturb her. When it did, she pressed her ear to the door.

"Finally, at long last. Oh, my love, my voices told me to be patient."

The body of a man crossed St. John's, and, startled by the strange words, he didn't immediately move.

"Oh. My dearest. They were right. They were right. You realise this is fated, my jewel? Your father's offer proves it. We'll have money. The only thing lacking and it was provided. You have been given me . . ."

"I don't think so." St. John put long fingers around the man's neck, lifting him away as he sat up. "Now, let us see what we have here."

The valet struggled violently, gagging when St. John's fingers tightened. When the body slumped, St. John changed his grip and forced the man off the bed onto his feet. He followed and pushed his captive towards the nearly dead fire. "Sit down and don't move, do you hear?"

The valet glowered. "You don't understand. This is wrong. I've been so patient, just like they said. I've waited and waited. Why are you here? What has gone wrong? When money was offered for a boy-child, I *knew*. She's mine, I tell you. They told me she's mine!"

"Just sit and be silent. We need light."

The valet, shaking his head, sat as ordered, St. John's tone the sort he'd been taught to obey, but he moaned and rambled on and on about his "voices" and Lord Winters' offer while St. John kindled a candle from the dying coals and lit the others standing on the mantel.

"It's over now, so pull yourself together. You've been caught and that is that."

"No, no!" the man shrieked. "She's mine. They said she was mine. They told me and told me . . ."

He sobbed into his hands. Suddenly, with no warning he launched himself from the chair, and St. John caught off guard recovered just in time to land a punch that laid the valet flat on the floor. He looked around as the connecting door opened.

"It's all right, Ardith. I had to give him a facer, but it's over now."

Ardith ran to St. John and he pulled her trembling body into his arms. She looked up at him, her eyes wet with tears. He held her close, rocking her. Turning her head, she glanced down at the felled man and shuddered.

"Shush. Don't think about it. The man is crazed, Ardith. He carried on about voices telling him you were his. He'll have to be incarcerated somewhere for fear he gets such notions about another woman."

Ardith nodded and tucked her head into the convenient space where his shoulder met his neck.

Her father burst into the room, having at last remembered to join his daughter. "What is going on here? What are you doing with my daughter, Rohampton? Let her go at once!" Lord Winters' voice rose to a roar. "You will marry her as soon as I can acquire a special licence, you viper!"

St. John felt Ardith stiffen. He smiled down at her. "Shush, love. I would willingly marry you if you'd agree but I know you would not. Not under these circumstances."

"Stop that whispering at once, do you hear? Ardith, come away from the scoundrel." Ardith, preparing to do just that, gritted her teeth. Suddenly her eyes widened, and reaching for St. John's neck, she pulled with all her might, lifting her feet from the floor as she did so. They fell in a heap and the tongs, meant to connect with the back of St. John's head, whistled through thin air.

"You will not have her. She is mine." The voice rose to a shriek, the valet's eyes rolling in his head. "They promised me. She is mine. You will not have her!" St. John rolled them away as the implement crashed down just where they'd lain and scrambled to his feet, backing from the crazed figure preparing to swing once more.

Lord Winters' eyes bugged. "My God, I did not believe there *was* a man! I thought it was the imaginings of a spinster mind!"

"Perhaps," said St. John, never taking his eyes off his assailant and ducking as the tongs once again swung viciously, "if you are done exclaiming, you might come to my aid?"

Lord Winters, listening to the filth pouring from the valet's mouth, stood gaping at him, but St. John's words finally registered and roused him to action. Between them, they subdued the creature.

"He is quite insane, you know," said St. John once the valet was bound and sobbing as if he would never stop. "He spoke of voices and how they told him what to do. He said your offer of money for a grandson proved he was to have her. The money would support them, you see."

Ardith looked towards the door where several people, robes hastily pulled over nightclothes, crowded each other and gaped at the goings-on. She reached for the neck of her robe which had fallen open in the struggle.

St. John looked at the beaten figure. "What are we to do with him?"

"Send him packing," said Lord Winters.

"So he may prey on some other innocent woman?"

Lord Winters harrumphed a couple of times. He hated it when St. John spoke to him in that sarcastic way.

Ardith stared at the still figure, the ugly sound of his sobbing finally stilled. "He must, of course, be put where he will do no one harm," she said. "I can almost feel sorry for him." She remembered his attack on St. John and shuddered. "Almost."

"You are generous as always with your pity, Lady Ardith. It is unnecessary to make a decision at this moment, but he cannot be left here on the floor of your bedroom. Lord Winters? A store room, perhaps?"

The man was placed in safekeeping, and at St. John's suggestion Cecilia was asked to stay with Ardith that night. Ardith didn't argue. She had a premonition she would have nightmares for some time to come!

"Well," she said drowsily just before she went to sleep, "this is one party the ton will not soon forget. How many hosts offer up a crazed man attacking a daughter of the house as part of the entertainment!"

Cecilia chuckled, already half asleep. "Trust you to think of that instead of the danger you were in."

"I don't think I'll ever forget. But it is ended and I must try." Ardith reached for her sister's hand and, with it clasped in her own, allowed herself to go to sleep.

— 7 —

TERRANCE RAISED A row late the next morning when his valet did not answer his call. Lord Winters was allowed no more than the bald news before he was interrupted.

"Dead? Impossible. He was perfectly healthy last night."

"Your man hanged himself."

"Hanged himself? Nonsense. Why would he hang himself?"

"I presume because he had just enough sanity left to realise what his future would be in a bedlam."

"My valet was not insane."

"He was. Never mind that. Not that it can be kept a secret when half the demmed household came gawking and the other half will not rest until they know the whole," said his lordship bitterly.

Terrance calmed down enough to demand Lord Winters open his budget. When he understood his valet had truly been mad and was now dead, he paced his room, his hands clasped behind his back and his brow in tight ridges.

Lord Winters watched him pace. "I see you are upset knowing you had in your employ a man who might have done *anything*, but it's over. Calm down. All is well."

"Well! *Well*! How can you say all is well? The idiot died without revealing his secret for polishing my boots! I'll never again find a valet with his touch. Blast the man!"

Even Lord Winters, insensitive soul that he was, found this a trifle out of line and did not forbear to say so.

"Ardith's all right, ain't she? He was thwarted?"

"Yes."

"Ardith! Well, I suppose that proves he was insane. I mean, *Ardith*!"

The two men looked at each other, and Lord Winters remembered that Rohampton insisted Ardith was a beauty. He was glad Terrance did *not*. Terrance's opinion meant he need not change his own, which was a relief, for he did not like new ideas.

"Anyway, that isn't important. I must leave for London at once." Terrance's forehead creased again. "Maybe I can bribe Howorth's valet from his service, although I've heard he's well suited and has turned down all offers. Then there is Morton's man. He has a good way with a cravat. Here," he turned on his father-in-law, "loan me Marvin, will you? I must be on my way. Tell Maud we leave within the hour."

Lord Winters described this scene to St. John sometime later and was outraged when Rohampton laughed heartily. "Well, really, it seems he might have shown some concern for Ardith's ordeal."

"So he might. She'll love that tale."

Lord Winters goggled. "You will not *tell* her."

"I most certainly will. She'll see the lighter side of things and if the circles under her eyes mean anything, she needs something to give her thoughts another turn. We are men, Winters. I do not think it is possible for us to know what a woman threatened as Ardith was threatened must feel."

Lord Winters tried to imagine. "Terribly frightened, I suppose. Or, perhaps not, an innocent who has no idea what to expect, you know."

St. John glanced at Lord Winters. "Do not get it into your head that Ardith had no idea what might have happened to her. She is innocent in the sense she has not experienced the love of a man, but she is well aware of what goes on between the sheets."

"Don't speak foolishly. She was cosseted and protected like every other woman of our class."

"And she has been her own mistress for five years. Lady Sibley, I'm sure, did *not* cosset her. Also she breeds her horses. Do you believe she has no knowledge of how that is done?"

Lord Winters' eyes started from his head. "My God, Rohampton, you are not saying she has actually *watched* . . ." His voice failed.

"Knowing Ardith, I suspect she's done so from an early age. You may think forbidding that one to *do* a thing is enough—as I suppose you did. But you should know by now that forbidding Ardith something is exactly the way to make her do the reverse!"

Winters flushed deeply. "She is my daughter."

"So you say any time you have no other argument. Your first three spoiled you. You expect Ardith to behave in the same missish pattern. Yet you aided and abetted her in every way imaginable so that she be utterly different."

"I did not!"

"You did. You enjoyed the way she'd stand up to you and argue with you. Fine. I'm glad you did. Then, miffed when she went her own way and refused to sew samplers and practise the piano, you sent her for the sort of schooling reserved for males. That gave her a mind which works with what is considered an unfeminine penchant for logic. Again I thank you. But that you allowed her to roam the neighbourhood, the veriest hoyden, and then insist she obey you like a little mouse, and, more, *assume she will,* is the height of folly."

Lord Winters rose to his feet, huffing again and again. "You've gone your length, Rohampton. You will leave this house and you will drop all pretensions to my daughter's hand. I'll not be treated *so* by any man!"

"I don't apologise. Nor will I give up hope that Ardith will someday marry me." St. John smiled tightly. "Forbid her to do so! *Do*. I hope you will. As I've told you before," repeated St. John, with a dry chuckle, "she tends to go contrary to orders."

He walked out of the room. He ordered his valet to pack and return to the Park before searching for Ardith, whom he found in the great hall. She was supervising the servants who were clearing away all evidence of the previous day's entertainment. Guests appeared, a couple who'd heard the most intriguing rumours and wished to quiz Ardith. She deftly moved them out and into their carriage, suggesting the rumours were the product of a disordered mind instead of the result of one!

When they'd gone, St. John asked for a few moments alone with her. They strolled towards the rose garden which was just coming into bloom, tight buds unfurling in the warm sunshine.

"I have been ordered from your father's house, Ardith. I told him once too often exactly what I thought of him, and I can't blame him for taking snuff. Will you forbid me entrance to Summersend?"

"I don't suppose so. After last night I owe you a great deal. Besides, St. John, you know I will not allow my father to interfere in my life. He has not accepted that yet, but eventually he will." A doubtful expression fleetingly crossed her face. "I hope."

"Hold to that and you will be fine. He is, by many lights, a good man, Ardith, but he doesn't understand you."

"You think you do?"

"I'm certain I do."

She faced him, holding his eyes for a long moment. "As well as anyone does, I'd guess. You had many years to study me and you did. That is the difference, I suppose. He has never bothered his head with the reality of me, although I'm not sure that communicates what I mean."

"He has put you in the same little box labelled 'daughter' in which he placed his others. As far as he is concerned you are all exactly alike."

"Which is nonsense. We are none of us like the other. Poor Ellie is a mouse. Maud is a pleasure-loving little butterfly, and Cecilia is simply a very nice lady. I am by far the oddest." She sighed. "I will be glad to get back to Summersend. Thank heaven this nonsense is over."

"I will give you a few days to rest and come visit you for a game of chess. Will that suit?"

"I would enjoy it."

She watched him mount and ride off. So. He was to remain at the Park, then, not return to town and what remained of the Season. She remembered he was still worried about his friend. If he heard Colonel Westman had recovered and returned to his regiment, he would return to London. In the meantime she would enjoy what she could of his company. It would be little enough, unless she discovered she were even odder than she thought.

The beguiling notion that she might become his mistress recurred with disturbing regularity! But she had decided, she reminded herself, it was not to be—a disturbing thought all by itself. She shouldn't have *had* to use logic in this case. Becoming St. John's mistress was so far outside acceptable behaviour it should never have crossed her mind as a possibility in the first place. Indeed, it was simply wrong.

Two days later, while dining with Miss Fremby, she asked, "What would you think of me if I invited Rohampton to dine with us sometime soon?"

Her companion met Ardith's bland gaze with a placid look of her own. "Are you asking what I'd think or what the county would think?"

"You know me too well. It would be outside of enough, would it not? I have by the skin of my teeth—given my eccentricity—managed to maintain my reputation. But if I were to have a man other than my father eat at my table, even with you in attendance, I would have stepped beyond what is permissible." A thoughtful expression and a tipped head alerted her companion to listen closely: "How do women who cuckold their husbands get away with that which is far more outrageous? I'm only suggesting he *dine* here, not sleep in my bed!"

When she stopped laughing, Miss Fremby stared at her charge. "Really, Ardith, the things you say!"

"My wretched tongue. It is a cross I bear that it runs away with me all too often. But what is wrong with inviting a friend to dinner?"

"If he were only a friend perhaps you might succeed in doing so."

"But he *is* only a friend."

"Ardith, those wide eyes don't look at all innocent to me. The ton still wonders why for years you refused to have anything to do with him. If you suddenly turn around and allow him to run tame at Summersend, it will open up the scandal all over again."

Ardith bit her lip. Hard. "Fremby, have any of your correspondents told you what is believed to have happened?"

"Oh, all sorts of suggestions run their course. That he seduced or forced you are the most outrageous, but not widely believed thanks to the fact your family does not snub him. But that he insulted you in some way is widely held to be true. The problem with that is that no one can guess the sort of insult which would lead you to putting him out of your life."

"It is suggested that he raped—oh, I cannot believe the gossips would be so cruel!"

"Of course you can believe it," said Fremby calmly. "You spent only a short period in society before hiding yourself away here at Summersend, but you are not stupid. I'm sure you know exactly the sort of things which are whispered over the teacups and in the clubs."

Ardith's lips received more punishment, guilt growing that she had subjected St. John to such a nauseous situation.

"I, too," went on Miss Fremby with a hint of laughter, "have been guilty of speculation. Oh, only to myself of course. You never explained to anyone, did you?"

"No. I do not think the true story ever made the rounds. St. John must have threatened those idiots within an inch of their lives. And," she added thoughtfully, "if he did more than tell my father he'd bungled a proposal, I have not heard it."

"Lord Rohampton proposed?"

"Oh, yes. I assumed you knew that much."

"My dear, *will* you tell me? I'm agog with curiosity."

Telling the whole to Fremby—with all the verve and drama of which she was able—Ardith finally saw the humour in the situation. They stopped laughing and she continued. "I'm older now. I know I misjudged him and have told him so. I felt such a fool having to do so, but . . ." She shrugged.

"But knowing you were wrong, and being the woman you are, you plucked up your courage and did so. I know."

"It wasn't as difficult as I'd believed it would be."

"Lord Rohampton has a strong sense of justice. I'm sure he put the misunderstanding down to that overblown insecurity you hold to your bosom like a shield."

"I don't know what you mean."

"You have a bad view of yourself, Ardith. Your aunt did what she could to instill self-confidence in you, and in many ways it took, but not when you think of yourself as a woman."

"St. John said something similar. But then he suggested I was more beautiful than my sisters, so absurd a tarradiddle it doesn't bear thought, so I didn't take him seriously."

"He did not lie, Ardith. You *are* more beautiful. More important, you have the sort of beauty which will only improve with age while your sisters are already fading and becoming commonplace."

"No, please, not you, too!"

"Ardith, think of Ellie. She is, what?—thirty? thirty-one?—and already she becomes fubsy-faced. Maud is growing hard and, with it, unattractive. Cecilia is not that much older than yourself and is content. She will hold her beauty longest of the three. You must recognise the fact that just because you are something other than small and blond and mild tempered, that does not make you ugly. I watched you at the ball. You were disconcerted by the men who gave you compliments, were you not?"

"Very. I wondered if St. John had put them up to it!"

"I'm quite certain he would do no such thing. In the first place, he would not like to draw attention to you. One of them might convince you to marry before he does himself!"

"I simply don't understand it. I'm a long-legged hoyden with a ridiculous figure and a complexion which will never be properly white. Thanks to you, my hair was surprisingly flattering—did I thank you for that, by the way?"

"No. And you aren't thanking me when you put it up in that ugly knob at the back of your neck, either. I assumed you did not like it looser, with waves over your ears, the rest wound into a neat roll."

"It isn't that. It's that I can't do it myself. I tried."

"Then I will do it for you. And teach you to do it yourself."

"Only when we have reason to. It took forever, Fremby. I haven't time for such nonsense on a day-to-day basis."

"Well, we have gone far beyond your original question, have we not?" Fremby chuckled when Ardith looked totally blank and questioned her as to what she meant. "You asked if it would shock me if you invited Lord Rohampton to dine. The answer is that I wouldn't mind at all. You must decide if you can put up with the talk if it gets around you have done so, that is all."

"I will think about it."

And she did. That and other things. Her head groom found her distracted when working with the stock being prepared for sale. He wondered if the social whirl at Winters Hall had gone to her head and if this most sensible of young ladies was to become as frivolous as any other he'd ever known. When he asked a question about the breeding program and was told to use his own judgement he was convinced of it—only to find, the next day, his suddenly erratic mistress was poking her nose into every corner of the stable and working longer hours than ever with her favourite horses.

"Women," he said to the undergroom when, as dusk closed in, Lady Ardith finally walked away towards the manor.

"They's all flibbertigibbets. What can un expect?"

The head groom stared down his nose at his second-in-command and, after reducing the man to a quivering lump, told him to hold his tongue.

The groom stared after the older man. " 'Taint just women what gets a flea up their—" A stable lad chuckled and the groom turned on him. "Here now, get that feeding done. You won't get yer own 'til it is."

That evening St. John waited patiently for permission to enter the gates. He carried a gift for Ardith, a chess set his grandfather had purchased in Italy when on his grand tour. It was an unusual present for a young woman, but flowers or a fan or a book of poetry, a trifle of the sort a courting man gave a woman, would not have done for Ardith. As he waited he spoke with the gate-keeper about country things, and the old man thawed a trifle more.

"Good evening, Miss Fremby. Good evening, Ardith." He handed the latter the case and told her he could not remember if her aunt had a set, so had brought her this one.

Ardith set it aside, asking him to be seated. She wasn't quite certain why, but she found herself uneasy and slightly flustered by his arrival. Not that she hadn't looked forward to it. She had. But now that he was here, she didn't quite know how to behave.

St. John sensed her unease and spoke with Miss Fremby, asking how her days had gone since all the bustle and urgency of the party was ended.

"Quietly enough for myself, my lord. Ardith, I fear, has worked harder than she should. She's out from dawn to dark with those horses of hers."

St. John looked into his love's face, noted the dark circles under her eyes, but refrained from commenting. He talked on for another fifteen minutes or so, introducing innocuous topics of conversation whenever the conversation lagged. Then he rose and held his hand to Ardith. "I've looked forward to our chess game. Shall we begin?"

Ardith set up the board at the table in the window while St. John arranged candles to give them better light. They seated themselves, and Ardith's nervous response to his arrival dissipated as the battle for advantage on the board became more tense. They finished the first game with a stalemate, and St. John immediately set the pieces back into place.

Sometime during the second game he noticed Miss Fremby quietly put away her mending and leave the room, but said nothing. If Ardith's chaperone felt he was to be trusted altogether she was wrong, he thought, losing his queen due to the distraction. But if she merely believed he'd not go too far, then she was quite right. He was, he believed, too close to success to chance ruining all by frightening Ardith with the passion he felt for her. Not that she hadn't revealed, more than once, that she was beginning to feel it as well, but it wouldn't do to push her too hard. Ardith could *not* be pushed. Led, yes. But not pushed.

They finished the game and Ardith hid a yawn. "I'm sorry,

St. John. Despite that early advantage when I took your queen, I seem to have given you an easy game."

"I think Miss Fremby was correct in her assessment. You've been pushing yourself too hard to make up the time lost organising things for your father. Your mind wandered now and again. I'd hoped for a third game, but I will leave and let you get your rest."

She moved a hand in a distracted manner, as if she'd urge him to stay but capitulated when another yawn opened her mouth wide. When she opened her eyes he had stepped close to her, his hand coming to her chin and holding her steady to his gaze.

"Ardith, it isn't the hard work, is it? I feared you'd sleep badly after our experience with the madman. You've had nightmares, haven't you?"

"A few." She twisted away.

"It is to be expected, I suppose. I only wish you'd call Miss Fremby to comfort you. He did not attack you, but I know how excellent an imagination lurks under that magnificent hair. I won't suggest you forget it, because I know that's impossible, but I wish there were something I could do to help."

"Thank you. I'm sure I'll put it behind me soon." She closed her mouth tightly, fearing she'd reveal the content of those dreams. Again and again she'd awaken just as that awful man was about to slam the tongs down onto St. John's head. She'd find herself shaking and tears running down her face. And there was nothing she could do. Except, as she'd said, wait for the fear to pass, which she'd felt for him in that awful moment—when she'd looked into the valet's face and seen the hatred there. She looked at St. John, noted he seemed to expect more of her. "I tell myself he is dead," she added, "and can never again be a problem to anyone, but I still dream."

"He *is* dead. Tell yourself that very firmly before you go to bed, and perhaps it will help."

"Perhaps," she said doubtfully.

"Perhaps this will give your thoughts another direction," he said softly as he drew her close. He was slightly surprised when she didn't struggle. Putting the thought from his mind, he reached for her face, tipped it up. Her eyes were closed and again he wondered, but as she was relaxed in his loose embrace, the growing temptation to kiss and caress her was too strong for questions of any sort.

"I shouldn't allow you to do that, St. John," she said when he lifted his face from hers.

"I know. Nor should I behave as I do. But it's nice, isn't it?" He smiled down at her.

Nice? He thought it only nice? She sighed inaudibly. She'd known she was inexperienced and ignorant, but if that was only nice, then she had far more to learn than she'd believed. Carefully, she extracted herself from his arms, both relieved and contradictorily chagrined that he let her go.

"It is late. Thank you for the games, my lord."

"*Now* what did I do?"

"My lord?"

His mouth twisted in self-derision. "Never mind, Ardith. I will come again if that is all right with you?"

"I enjoy chess."

He laughed. "Yes. We both enjoy *chess*. Good-night, Ardith."

In a moment he was gone, leaving Ardith staring at the closed parlour door and wondering just what he'd meant by that last exchange. He'd done nothing—well, nothing to make her angry—so what had led him to ask what he'd done? Her mind wouldn't function and, deciding she was more tired than she'd known, she took herself off to bed.

The spring lambing had ended weeks earlier. Ardith had come to check on her young shepherd and flock not because she needed to, but because she wanted to. She loved anything young and new, and the lambs were such fun. Ardith had only a small flock, just large enough to mow down the lawns, the rides in the small homewood attached to Summersend, and the edges of the fields. Nearby the shepherd lad and his dog watched her joy in his youngest charges, an indulgent smile forming now and again at her antics.

She was cuddling an orphan when they were interrupted. Ardith was deeply reluctant to respond to the message that she was needed, but Fremby would not call her away from one of the more pleasant of her duties for a triviality.

Rebelling, she delayed long enough to ask, "Well, Sam, do you think all is well?"

"Oh, yes, m'lady. We'd a good year, didn't we now?" The youth looked over his charges with pride.

"A very good year. Send for me if I'm needed, but I doubt it'll be necessary." She took one last look at the frisky lambs, and smiled. "I suppose I must go." She strolled towards the barns through the yard area and in by way of the back door where she left her pattens and a man's old garrick, wondering again where her aunt had acquired the ugly but useful mantle. After washing her hands she entered the small parlour and stopped short.

"Maud!"

"You don't sound pleased to see me, Ardith." Maud pouted, but her gaze was wary.

Ardith looked to where Fremby was unpicking the hem of a sheet which was needful of turning. "Well, of course I'm pleased to see you, but why are you here? I'd think the Season would hold you in London."

Maud waved a hand and spoke with airy nonchalance. "I found myself bored. One party after another and all exactly the same. You are wise to remain in the country, Ardith. It is so tiring, London, but if one is there, there is simply no way to slow the pace."

"You are welcome, of course, but you are not telling me the truth." Maud bit her lips, indecision obvious. "Are you?"

Realising Maud would not speak in her presence, Fremby rose from her place and, telling Ardith she would see a room was prepared and that Cook knew there'd be an extra for dinner, left the room.

"Well, Maud? The truth with no bark on it?"

Maud dithered, but meeting her sister's steady gaze she gave in and spoke with some heat. "If it is necessary to satisfy your curiosity, then you must know I had an argument with Terry. I will not be treated *so*."

Maud's pout was joined by eyes sparkling with unshed tears, and Ardith found herself feeling a trifle sorry for her sister. "Was he an awful beast?"

"Oh, you cannot *know*, Ardith. Simply terrible. There was nothing I could do or say or . . ."

"Or?"

"Well, never mind. I have come and you'll not mind my remaining awhile, will you?" wheedled Maud, her voice sweet, almost syrupy.

"No," said Ardith slowly. "But you know how it is here at Summersend. We do not entertain. The country is thin of company right now, so you cannot even visit old friends. I don't know what you will do with yourself."

"I'll manage." The pretty little face firmed and the eyes hardened. "Besides, it matters not what I do. You must not allow Terrance to know I am here, Ardith. I will not see him until he apologises."

"Apologises for *what*? Besides," Ardith tried humour, "how can he apologise if you will not see him?" Maud turned away. The weak joke had no effect. "Maud, how long do you think we will have the, er, pleasure of your company?"

Maud turned, her big blue eyes filled with tears which rolled down her pretty cheeks one after the other. "Oh, Ardith, do let me stay. Do not turn me away. And," again the rounded little chin tipped dangerously, "do not allow that beast to know where I am! *Please*, Ardith."

The smaller woman ran across the room and flung herself against the much taller, much fuller form of her youngest sister. Ardith could do nothing else but hold her, make soft encouraging noises, and wonder just what Terrance had done to put her sister into such a state. It had always seemed to Ardith that the two had a better understanding than most couples, both involved in nothing but a constant seeking for pleasure and somehow managing to scrape together the needful—although always, it seemed, on the edge of financial disaster.

"There, there, Maud. You may stay as long as you like."

"And you will not let Terrance find me?" Tiny hands shook her older sister's arms. "You promise?"

Looking into her sister's pleading eyes, Ardith felt she could do no other. "I promise."

"What do you mean she is not here and you haven't seen her?"

Terrance stared at Lord Winters' butler. His wife had run off more than a week earlier and, assuming she'd go straight to her father's house, he'd decided he'd let her fret and when she'd had time to calm down go and get her. If she had *not* come to her senses, he'd shake some sense into her. She *knew* how badly dipped they were, how the ten thousand was needed.

But this! If she'd not come to Winters Hall, then where was she? A touch of fear entered his soul. It had not occurred to him his wife could be so upset she'd hide herself from him. And where would one such as his wife hide? All her friends were in London. He was sure they'd believed his lies she was indisposed and gone to the country. Small gifts of books and other trifles had been left for forwarding. Notes of encouragement and concern had been written. Cards left. No. Word had not gotten around Maud had left him, so where could she be?

Terrance ran a hand through his neatly styled hair, ruffling it as he never did—his concern for his looks and dress that of the dandy who followed Brummel's lead and that of the other bow window dandies. It was a sign of his distraction that he did not think of the ruin his fingers caused.

"Ardith! She's gone to Ardith."

That settled, he ordered the butler to prepare him a room. He could not stand another long drive at this point and, besides, would arrive at an unconscionable hour if he were to go on. So he'd stay here tonight and ride over in the morning.

Morning brought further frustration: Ardith's gate-keeper insisted Ardith was not receiving visitors. That, in fact, she was from home.

"And my wife? Is she too from home?" The gate-keeper looked at him blankly. "Lady Maud, you looby!"

The "looby" stared.

"My wife!"

The gate-keeper scowled. "Lady Ardith gave me m'orders. There's no'un ta home." Hubert turned his back and stalked off.

Terrance, angry his easy solution to the problem of his wife's whereabouts was not yet proved, threw his almost new beaver top hat to the ground in a temper. Then he looked around sheepishly, found no one watching him, and dismounted to retrieve the as yet unpaid-for article of clothing.

"Now what?" he asked a bird singing lustily in a bush near where he dithered. Then the fear he'd felt the evening before returned. Surely his wife had not gone off on her own! She did not know the dangers which faced a woman alone in the world. His heart filled and he blinked back the moisture in his eyes before mounting, turning his hack, and cantering off.

Something had to be done and the only thing to occur to him was to write his father-in-law and ask his advice. How he was to explain why he'd made no attempt to trace his wife immediately he didn't know. Then it occurred to him the cause of their argument could be laid at the feet of Lord Winters, and his mouth twisted into a sour smile. If worse came to worst, he'd tell the man so. Not that that would help find Maud.

Ardith's gate-keeper had not lied. The ladies were not at home. Once a month Ardith and Fremby made a tour of her tenants and her father's cottagers—not that the latter were any responsibility of Ardith's. But Sibley, at the death of her mother, had taken on the duties of the lady-of-the-manor, not relinquishing them to either her sister-in-law or her nephew's wife when their respective husbands had risen to the peerage—and now with no woman at the Hall, Ardith had inherited the role.

Maud had expected to find little interest in the duty visits, but discovered it was otherwise. The surprise of that kept her silent for over a mile. "Ardith, you say you do this regularly?"

"Yes. Father's steward is responsible for the cottages. However, there are things I, as a woman, am told which would never be raised with a man. Then, too, I look over my property and parts of our father's, since his agent does only the minimum he must for Father's pensioners. I always order the needful."

"We leave it all to Terry's man of business," said Maud. "I'm sure I don't know what I could do if *I* were to visit his people. I envy you Summersend. You have a steady income from it. Ours is so erratic." She sent a quick look towards her sister. "Not that we're in the hands of the cents-percents, of course, but occasionally I wonder how to pay the bills."

"I've noticed," said Ardith casually, "that those estate owners who rely completely on their agents don't do so well as those who take a personal interest. If you and Terrance were to spend a little time talking to your tenants—"

"Terry," interrupted Maud, "says they'll only want a lot of expensive repairs and equipment and we can't afford it."

"Think of this, Maud. If the equipment wears out and the buildings deteriorate, your tenants will go where the landlord *does* care for his property and the land will cease to produce even so much as it does now."

Maud's cheeks paled at the thought of reduced income. Could it be true? Could the condition of the estate decline more?

"Notice Rohampton's land." Ardith gestured to their left where a well-kept hedge bordered an equally well-tilled field. "St. John tours his property both here and in the north several times a year. He checks with his agent on all points and has an eye for detail you wouldn't believe."

"You know him well, don't you?"

"I suppose so."

Ardith's pretended indifference aroused Maud's curiosity more than if she had simply said yes. Knowing Ardith, however, her sister mulled over her suspicions and decided she was a fool. Ardith was far too well bred to become Rohampton's country convenience. Yet the notion was not totally lacking in merit. At the christening, much to everyone's surprise, the two had been on easy terms. The trick played on them had not only *not* caused a row, Cecilia's prediction, but had revealed their relationship was not one of antipathy as all had assumed.

So how close were they? And how had it happened without anyone knowing? And most important of all, what would be the result? Maud had not realised until this visit how jealous she was of her youngest sister. To have inherited Summersend was an undeserved honeyfall—one resented by all Lady Sibley's hopeful heirs. At worst and by rights, it was thought, the property should have gone to their father as Lady Sibley's closest relative.

Then Rohampton! A *marquis*. If Ardith were to become Lord Rohampton's bride it would be outside of enough! Why, she'd not only have Summersend, but she'd be raised to a social position far higher than anyone so lacking in sophistication deserved. It wasn't fair that the ugly duckling among the Winter Roses should walk off with such a prize on the Marriage Mart when those who deserved it far more had not.

The women were silent, each occupied with her own thoughts. Only the gate-keeper's laconic message that Sir Terrance had put in an appearance turned their minds elsewhere. He also mentioned Lord Rohampton had stopped by, but had gone on without leaving a message.

Maud reiterated her insistence Terrance not be allowed entry to Summersend. Ardith found herself surprised Terrance had even remembered the existence of his unpopular sister-in-law. Fremby was not at all startled. Her only curiosity was that it had taken the man so long to conclude his wife was with her sister.

Ardith felt a grim premonition her quiet contented life might never return.

The women were settled at the tea table late that evening when the gate-keeper's daughter arrived with word another visitor waited in the road. This time it was Ellie, and Ardith—the premonition growing stronger by the minute—told the girl to run back and have her admitted at once.

— 8 —

THE NEXT MORNING Miss Fremby and Ardith met in the breakfast room. They were alone for the first time since Ellie's arrival. "Lady Rambeth," Fremby spoke with gentle concern, "seemed greatly agitated when she arrived. Did you manage to calm her, m'dear?"

"Ellie is as close to being demented as I've ever seen her. If I were her brother I swear I'd take a horsewhip to Bertram!"

"Can you tell me or are you under vow of silence?"

"You are aware of that absurd offer father made for a grandson?" Fremby nodded, her mouth twisting in distaste. "Bertram has been rather patient, actually, but he came to the end of it when he discovered she'd made no attempt to see a doctor as she said she'd do. So *he* called in Dr. Baile, who repeated what they'd been told after my niece's birth: Ellie should not attempt to have more children."

"So?" Fremby went on when Ardith didn't. "I presume there is more?"

Ardith sighed. "Bertram has some bee in his bonnet. He told her, doctors never know what they are talking about and to prepare herself for a visit from himself that night, regardless. Then he slammed out and walked off to his club. Ellie, as you may have noted, arrived with no more than a band-box stuffed with odds and ends of no use at all. Which is why I raided your room for a nightdress, Fremby dear. Nothing of *mine* would fit. I'll ask Maud, who arrived better prepared for a visit, to share with her, but last night I couldn't leave Ellie so long as it would take to argue Maud into such generosity." Ardith sighed. "I swear my formerly placid existence was a boon I little understood. Do you remember my telling you I'd felt restless and unsettled and *bored* during our long winter? I have come to the conclusion I prefer boredom to this constant upheaval."

To say nothing of the responsibility—a point she didn't add to her tirade. She didn't want to feel responsible for her sisters. She wished she had someone to whom she could talk about it. A fleeting vision of St. John crossed her mind, but she dismissed it and reminded herself to send him a note to the effect she could not allow him entry to Summersend for the nonce. She berated herself for having not done so when Maud arrived.

The note was sent and St. John received it with a fast-beating heart. He had stayed away from Summersend, not wanting to push his luck too soon and now wondered if she were inviting a visit. Yesterday he'd stopped by hoping they might go for a ride. He was missing her more than he could express. If she missed him half so much, then his plans were going well.

He waited impatiently for the door to close behind his footman before running a finger under the drop of wax sealing the folded page. A cold shiver raced up his back at the single blunt sentence: Ardith was sorry, but, for an unknown period of time, she could not welcome him to Summersend. That was it. He crushed the bit of paper into his fist. There was no explanation, not even a signature, let alone words of apology for forbidding him to come.

The first feelings of rejection and hopelessness turned to anger and, calling for Ajax to be brought around, followed by a curt demand for his valet, St. John took the stairs two at a time, removing his coat as he went. He had stripped and was fastening his buckskins before his valet, called from the laundry where he'd been overseeing the starching of his lordship's cravats, could reach him. "My boots, man. And where did I put my crop?"

"If his lordship had mentioned he was riding this morning, I would have had his things laid ready."

"Stubble it. It is not *your* fault. Hurry, man."

The stallion waited at the door, a groom having serious

difficulty holding him. "Fresh is he?" St. John eyed the rolling eyes and tossing head with a grim look in his own. "All the better."

He took the reins and, barely settled into the saddle, took off like a flash. The groom stared after him. Not only did his master make no attempt to hold the stallion in, he didn't even head down the lane. They jumped the first hedge, kicking up the highly pampered sod, and then took a stone wall as if out to win a steeplechase by as many lengths as possible.

The groom wondered what emergency had set Lord Rohampton racing away in the direction of the village. He turned a questioning look towards Ransome who also had a perplexed expression on his face. "Ye'd think all the hounds in hell were on his tail, now wouldn't ye?" questioned the groom in a soft country voice.

Ransome looked down his nose. "And if they were, 'tis no business of *yours*." Ransome closed the door with a snap and hunted Mrs. Lander.

"Very strange," they finally agreed.

The note had come from Summersend, of that Ransome was very certain. But if Lady Ardith was in a hobble, then why had Lord Rohampton ridden off in quite the wrong direction?

St. John's black mood lightened only slightly by the time he realised he was running Ajax into the ground. He eased up and patted the sweating animal's neck, ashamed to have treated such a prized beast so badly. Luck alone had kept the poor creature from stepping into a hole or straining a knee. It was iniquitous to let one's temper harm another living creature, a blameless animal. St. John rode on more gently to a country lane and a ford where he'd find water for his mount. By the time he reached the crossing, the stallion was cool enough for a drink. He dismounted, leading the black towards the stream.

He was standing there staring into space when Bertram Rambeth tooled up in a curricle and pulled in his pair. "Rohampton." Bertram's voice held accusation. "Didn't expect to see you here."

"Your surprise is nothing to my own. After all, I am in residence at the Park. Has Lord Winters returned to the Hall?"

"No. Saw him in town last night." Bertram looked flustered. "Just tooled down to look around."

St. John's eyes narrowed. "Several stages just to look around?"

Bertram's face turned red. "Needed a repairing lease. That's it."

"At the Hall?"

"Oh well." Bertram waved a hand. "Needed a change."

"I see." Except he didn't see at all. Bertram Rambeth had a perfectly good country estate of his own. Rambeth was proud of his acres, and unless he'd had reverses no one knew of and had rented it out, why had he not gone there?

"Can't smoke you, can I?" Bertie sighed. "I've gotten myself into a fix. Well, not exactly, but I . . . well, I . . ."

"Been gambling beyond what you can pay, Rambeth?" St. John asked the question kindly, but Bertie looked startled at the very idea.

"Egad, *no*. Never outrun the carpenter at the tables. You know I don't play for more than chicken stakes. Never understood those who did. No, it's Ellie."

"She's ill?"

A shamed look crossed Bertie's face and he looked away. St. John remained very still. A suspicion as to the meaning behind Ardith's terse note crossed his mind and, his heart beating fast, he wished it confirmed. Not wanting to interfere with any confidences which might come his way, he waited, hiding impatience.

Bertie sighed. "I've been a selfish, greedy fool, Rohampton, but I've come to my senses. A shock you know, to discover one is less a gentleman than one thought oneself to be. Nicest little lady in the world, my wife. I *like* her. Fact is, I'd miss her if anything happened to her. And yet, I didn't stop to think of that. . . ." His words trailed off, his eyes blind.

"Could this possibly have anything to do with Lord Winters' generous offer of money in exchange for a grandson?" The blunt question was uncivil as St. John very well knew, but it looked as if Rambeth had no desire to unburden himself beyond generalities.

"You know about that?" When St. John nodded, Bertie got down off his curricle and tied the reins to the whip stuck upright in the well. "If you know that I guess I can tell you the rest. Need to talk to someone. Feel such a fool, you know, and you're a safe confidant."

He'd not quite asked the last and seemed reassured when St. John nodded. The stallion was also tied and the two men strolled beside the shallow stream. This time St. John's forbearance was unfeigned. He was too good a man to cram his fences now. Finally Bertie opened his budget.

"You see, it's this way. Nice little property to the west of my land. Good tenant on the piece who does things the way I like 'em done. Wanted that land for ages but never thought I could get it. Then I heard it was up for sale so went to talk to the owner." Bertie sighed and shook his head. "Should have known the old screw would ask the earth. 'Specially since he knew I wanted it. Couldn't swing it. Not without serious retrenchment. Almost given up all thought of it when Winters made that offer."

St. John prodded. "Would be nice to have a son, too, I suppose."

Bertie nodded, his eyes sad for a moment. "Yes. Gave up all thought of it after the girl. Nice enough child I suppose, but a man wants a son. I suppose that tipped me over the edge, the thought of a son *and* the money."

"Except there is no guarantee a child will be a boy."

"Thought of that. Last night when I got home."

"Got home?" At last. Now he'd discover if his guess was correct.

Bertie nodded again. "Not proud of myself. Not proud at all."

At last, had he told himself? St. John tried again. "When you got home . . ."

"Yes. All my fault. Know that. I'm a total fool."

St. John tightened his control over his impatience. "I suppose every man makes a fool of himself now and again."

Bertie nodded and sighed lugubriously.

So much for patience. "Am I to suppose Ellie left you?"

Bertie flashed him a glance. "Don't know how you guessed. Thought she'd have gone home. Wasn't there so thought she'd come to the Hall. Didn't. No one there but Terrance, and he's too distracted about something to be a bit of help. Not that I wanted to explain m'problem to him. Not like you, you know. He'd have thought it a good joke, Ellie running out on me that way."

"Templeton is at Winters Hall?"

"Said so, didn't I?"

"But what is *he* doing there?"

"How should I know?"

"Has *he* outrun the constables?"

Bertie blinked, wondering for the first time why Templeton *was* in residence in their father-in-law's house. " 'Tis a bit strange, ain't it? I mean, Maud in the country recuperating from an illness. You'd think if he were going to rusticate, he'd go to Applewood to be with her. Come to think of it," Bertie added, suddenly feeling ill-used, "I'll bet a monkey that was a canard Terry put around when *his* wife ran out on him, and Maud is as healthy as you or me. Now why would he be staying at the Hall?"

St. John realised that, if Ardith *was* hiding her sisters, he had no right to interfere with her plans and closed his mouth on revealing words.

"Maud hates the country. Was surprised she'd gone away from town to recuperate." St. John didn't comment. "I think I'll just go back and have a word with Terrance." Without so much as a good-bye, Bertie swung on his heel and strode back to his rig. St. John followed more slowly, wanting Rambeth on his way before *he* rode off to warn Ardith. Since his love didn't want him at Summersend, it would be best he decided if he skulked around and approached her stealthily. It was a nuisance both of Summersend's gates were kept by gate-keepers. Accordingly, nearly half an hour later, he set his stallion at a stone wall very few riders would chance.

The grim expression on St. John's face creased and hardened as Ajax approached the wall. He gave his mount all the aid he could. Safe on the other side he heaved a sigh and wondered at his own stupidity: what good would it do Ardith if he'd broken his fool neck or—very nearly a more serious thought—maimed his horse. In some ways, his perverse love would find it harder to forgive him the latter than the first!

He rode on cautiously, reaching the homewoods without seeing a soul. He made his way into the stand of trees and dismounted, tying Ajax with enough freedom he might nibble at available grazing. A very little later he found a sheltered spot which looked over the manor and surrounding barns and paddocks. A rueful smile crossed his face at the silly game he played, but considering the quirks of Ardith's mind, he deemed it necessary.

There was too much activity for a straightforward approach. He searched the workers until he found Ardith working a young gelding with excellent lines and interesting markings—the tail and mane being considerably lighter than the black coat. He made a mental note to find out if it was for sale and how much she wanted for it and then set his mind to find a means of approaching her.

The gelding was turned over to a lad, and Ardith moved on to the next. St. John watched her lift each hoof and run her hands up each leg. She paused in front of the mare and held out her hand. The mare nuzzled her palm, obviously picking up some treat, and lifted her muzzle to push gently against her mistress's shoulder. St. John felt his body tighten at the sight of Ardith, laughing joyfully, her head back. The sound, almost a dream-echo because of the distance, affected him still more.

When she mounted the mare and rode off, he went back for Ajax.

When he reached the point where he'd hoped to intercept her he swore softly: she was just disappearing over the next rise. St. John bit his lip and thought further. She was simply hacking. It was probable she'd return by much the same route. He found a secluded spot near the top of a low hill and, hiding his horse amongst some bushes, settled himself to wait.

He'd almost given up, deciding she'd gone home by some

other way, when she reappeared. He looked carefully over the countryside, discovered there were no observers anywhere in view, and stepped into sight. He knew exactly when she saw him by the start her horse gave thanks to the involuntarily tightening of her reins. She shifted directions a fraction and, frowning, rode up to him.

"Rohampton?"

"Well, at least I'm not reduced to 'my lord'."

The frown deepened. "Why are you here? I thought my note made it clear I could not see you for a while."

"It made the point clear, but not the reason why. If it is because one or possibly two of your sisters are at Summersend, I can understand you'd not want to feed their hopes of a final rapprochement between us. But if that is so, why could you not say so?"

"How the devil did you know?" She closed her mouth with a snap, her eyes narrowing. "My lord, just what do you know?"

"There's that 'my lord' again." He grinned but she didn't smile back. He repressed a sigh. "Do you think you might dismount so I needn't get a crick in my neck? The sun, too, is in my eyes."

She hesitated, but did as he asked, holding the reins and not approaching him. "What is this all about? How did you get on my land?"

"Over the wall, and precisely because I thought it possible you'd prefer I find you alone. I met Rambeth on the shortcut to the toll road. He came up to the ford where I watered Ajax and there was no missing he was upset he'd been seen. To cut the story short, he told me his wife was missing. Then, given Templeton is at the Hall—ah, you *knew* that much, did you?—Bertram concluded Maud is not sick, but that she has also bolted and for a similar reason. I thought you might want warning."

"I thank you for thinking so," she said, still frowning, "but Hubert has his orders and will not open the gates for anyone. Ellie will be quite disturbed Bertie is on her trail so quickly, however. She practically fell into hysterics when she arrived last night."

"Ardith, I believe Rambeth is ashamed of his behaviour towards her. It has to do with needing money for some land he wishes to buy. That added to the desire for a son, of course. He went on at some length about what a fool he'd been and mentioned he actually liked your sister—seemed quite surprised by the notion—and hadn't realised how much he'd miss her until he came home and found she'd gone."

Ardith stared at him. "Do you believe him? Will he give up pressing Ellie for another child?"

"I think so."

"I wonder. Can I convince Ellie of that? You couldn't guess how awful she looks. She's lost weight and has a strained looked around her eyes."

They stared at the view. Finally, not looking at him, she asked, "What should I do, St. John? I sympathise with my sisters, even Maud, but I admit I feel a trifle guilty keeping their whereabouts secret and an even more guilty desire to have them gone and out of my life again!"

He laughed. "I love your bluntness. It is refreshing and so likable."

"Such attitudes are not at all likable. I should *not* wish my sisters to the devil. It is wrong of me."

"I don't know why. They have homes of their own. They have a father on whom they should be able to call for help. Why shouldn't you resent their landing themselves and their problems in your lap? It seems reasonable to me."

"A fine rationalisation, but it will not serve. I'm not an admirable character, I fear." She grimaced. "I suppose I'd better go back and pass on your information to Ellie. I don't know if I can make her believe me, but I'll try. St. John, you will not let the cat out of the bag, will you?"

"That your sisters are here? No, I won't. But your people?" He shook his head and heaved a sigh of pretended chagrin. "No, not they. Ardith, how *do* you keep your servants from gossiping all over the county? You are the only person I know who can trust your people to keep their collective mouths tightly shut. My own are loyal to me, but news of this sort—that I had a pair of runaways in my house, for instance—would be instantly passed on to trusted friends and from them to others. I wish you'd let me in on the secret."

"We stay very much to ourselves. That includes my people, St. John." She frowned, obviously thinking. "Another thing which helps is that my servants, those connected with the manor, at least, are almost to a man or woman without nearby relatives. Either they simply don't have any or they are from farther away. Except Amy," she added as an afterthought, "And since her family isn't speaking to *her* she's no problem."

"Ah, yes. Amy."

"St. John, you are not to say a word against Amy. It was not her fault. She did not encourage the man in any way. Why should she be ostracised because she happened to be in the wrong place when a man was in rut—" the choked back laugh he struggled to suppress didn't stop her for an instant "—and not strong enough to fight him off?"

"Are you finished?" She coloured and nodded. "I had no intention of saying a word against Amy. I was merely thinking it was another evidence of your kindness and objectivity. She is a good worker and, I suspect, particularly loyal to you because you took her in."

"Nonsense. I hired her because I needed a servant."

St. John reached for her chin. "Don't lie to yourself and don't lie to me, m'girl."

"I don't think I am."

"You didn't feel at all sorry for her, in her situation?"

"Of course I did. Anyone would."

"Oh no. Very few in our station of life would, let alone this 'anyone' of whom you speak."

Ardith sighed. "It is very strange, isn't it? Why are people that way, St. John?"

"Why? I don't know and we haven't time to explore the subject now. You've been gone overly long as it is and soon a groom will be sent in search of you. So, while I can, may I make a suggestion about Ellie?"

"Of course." She grinned up at him, and the twinkle in her eyes made his breath catch. "I do not promise I'll take

your advice, but I'm always willing to listen to it. Besides, I asked for it, remember?"

Determinedly he put a rein on his passions. That groom *would* soon be searching for her. And if he were to kiss her now, here where he had absolutely none of the usual restraints put on a man's ardour—not even the trappings of a civilised household with servants somewhere out of sight—he might not be able to control the situation.

"St. John? You were going to say something about Ellie?"

With a supreme effort St. John restrained his instincts and said as evenly as his feelings would allow: "Why don't you let it alone for a few days? Let Rambeth brood. At the moment he is remorseful. Let him be, without knowing for certain where his wife is. Let him worry about her. I believe he'll swear to anything to get her back if you wait even a day or two. Make it too easy for him, and he might be tempted to change his mind. Now, off you go, m'dear, before *I'm* tempted beyond bearing."

She took one look into his eyes and, blushing, turned to mount. St. John struggled with his conscience, gave himself just a little leeway, and after tossing her into the saddle, lay his hand on her thigh. She was too shocked to push it away.

The look in his eyes promised things she couldn't be expected to understand, only that they left her breathless and excited and wondering what their future would be. Oh, if only he'd receive news about his friend. Good news! Then he'd return to London and she could relax, not be pulled one way and then another, as confused as a chit in her first Season confronted by her first innocent affair of the heart. It might help, she thought ruefully, if she could believe all this *was* innocent, instead of a serious emotional and dangerous physical situation!

She was still considering the problem of St. John when she met a worried groom. She soothed him and rode on, turning the mare over to him near the back door. She climbed the service stairs and changed into more appropriate dress. Having her sisters in the house made for all sorts of minor inconveniences—changing clothes so often not the least of them. She was in no good humour when she went down, knowing she could not possibly desert her guests again that afternoon, which put her work that much further behind. She was not pleased to find Ellie and Maud squabbling.

Ardith paused in the doorway. "Really, I swear it reminds me of the schoolroom where I listened to this sort of thing again and again." She stared at first one open-mouthed woman, then the other. "I will not put up with it. This is my home and you will behave as gently bred women and not as shrews who haven't a care who hears them imitating the hen-wives they are not." She didn't add the obvious: "Or leave."

Maud's surprise turned to anger. "You will not speak to me that way. I am older than you. You will apologise."

"I will? I think not. You complain that I behave like a hoyden. I believe that is better than pretending you are a lady, but behaving like something quite other." She watched Maud retreat, her nose in the air. The door slammed and Ardith sighed. "Do you, too, demand an apology?"

Ellie blushed. "No, Ardith, for you are correct. We have not behaved well. I don't know why it is, but Maud and I cannot seem to be in the same house for more than a few hours without descending to nursery behaviour."

Ardith laughed. "Well, if she puts up your back again, as she will, simply walk away. She is bored, you know. It makes her cross. I fear you, too, will be bored here at Summersend, Ellie."

"Oh no. It is very pleasant. I quite enjoy the peace. I've asked Miss Fremby if I might help her with the mending—she is turning out the linen room, you know—and I will find much to occupy myself, I'm sure. It is soothing to do plain work, don't you think, and I like it."

Like it? Ardith, for whom it was penance to pick up a needle, didn't argue. She knew very well she had no womanly qualities and here again was proof of it. She sighed, wondering how anyone could really *like* mending and making. Shaking her head—confusing the footman who was serving her a slice of ham—she thought, once again, of her inadequacies. Finally it registered she had not been served and she turned slightly. "Tomlin. I requested the ham, did I not?"

The footman, thus ordered to serve Ardith, raised his eyes to heaven and consigned all guests to the hottest locale in hell. It was obvious that company turned his mistress into a feather-witted female.

"Well?" Lord Winters glared from one son-in-law to the other, neither of whom seemed willing to explain the note a groom had brought him at his London club. His lordship was particularly angry at being called away because he'd just discovered a comfortable little widow in straightened circumstances who was neither fubsy-faced nor too old to do her duty by a husband. He believed he was making progress in his courtship, but there was a retired major also in the running, and although an earldom would weigh in the scales, he was not certain the widow didn't prefer the major's younger and less, er, mature figure. It was beyond anything to be called away in such a havey-cavey way, but then to find no explanation at the end of his journey into Kent was beyond even that. "Well? Have neither of you anything to say?"

"It's all your fault," grumbled Terrance into his brandy.

"My fault? Mine? How can a note brought by *my* groom *from* the Hall *to* London *to* me be my fault?"

"I think he means it's your fault we're in this fix." Bertram mumbled his words almost as much as Terrance had done.

Lord Winters raised both his fists and his voice. "One of you, *now*, in words of one syllable, explain this hugger-muggery."

Terrance looked at Bertram, who shook his head. Rising to his feet, Terrance went to the fireplace and leaned against the mantel. "In words of one syllable, then, our wives are gone."

"Gone?" Lord Winters goggled and dropped onto the sofa which luckily was just behind him. "Gone, you say? Both of them? But how did this happen? Were they together? A carriage accident, perhaps? Oh, I say, brandy. I need brandy. Gone. Just like that. Snuffed out."

"Not dead!" Bertram hastily handed Lord Winters the required brandy. "Gone. Disappeared."

Terrance turned and mumbled again. "At least I pray Maud isn't dead."

It was always difficult, once Lord Winters got an idea firmly in his head, to change it and so it took somewhat longer than necessary to explain the situation the men found themselves in.

"My fault? I'll not have it. How dare you say it is my fault!"

"Because you knew when you offered the ten thousand that greed if nothing else would lead us to act contrary to behaviour required of a gentleman," said Bertram with gentle dignity.

Lord Winters stared, surprised at what he saw in the younger man's face.

"If I can only find Ellie and explain to her. I have," Bertram said in a sad voice, "discovered I love my wife. I never thought about it before, you see. I'd like the chance to tell her."

"Love? Love? What has love to do with marriage?" His lordship was truly bewildered. "Well, well, it makes no odds, does it? The problem is to find the women before something untoward comes to them. What have you done?"

"I assumed Ellie returned to our home. When she wasn't there I came straight on to the Hall. She is not here. Terrance tells me he, too, believed Maud to have come here. But," Bertram added with the faintest of spiteful notes, "his wife has been gone much longer than my Ellie."

"Longer, you say?" Winters turned on Terrance, who paled beneath the glare. "Longer? How long?"

"Over a week," said Terrance. "I was sure she would come to her senses. I was positive she'd be here. Well," he blustered when the glare only became more fierce, "how was I to know she'd be such a buffle-head as to simply disappear? Do you think I am not worried about her? I am. But," he added, "I now believe her to be with Ardith. I think they *both* are with Ardith. I can't get myself admitted to Summersend and I presume it is because my sister-in-law is protecting her sisters. Which is why I wrote you to return to the country: she cannot keep *you* outside the gates, my lord."

"So you'd think," muttered Lord Winters and didn't notice the exchange of startled looks between the younger men. "Well, well. 'Tis too late to do anything tonight. I believe you are correct that Ardith is hiding your wives. I'll have a thing or two to say to her about such behaviour, you can trust me for that. Good-night." Lord Winters, wondering just how he was to get within range of his rebellious youngest to deliver that lecture, wandered from the room.

"He will go to Summersend tomorrow, will he not?"

"Yes. That is, I'm sure of his intention, but I'm no longer certain of the outcome," said Terrance, his rounded shoulders echoing his weary mind. "When I sent for him I thought that would settle it, but when he said *that*!"

"I find it strange Lady Ardith should refuse entry to her own father."

"But then our sister-in-law *is* a strange one. If she were not a lady, she would long ago have been admitted to Bedlam. How dare she keep the whereabouts of my wife a secret?"

"We do not yet know that she has. I believe I will write a letter to Ellie so his lordship may deliver it tomorrow—just in case. He can hand it in at the gate if he gets no farther." Terrance was struck by the notion, and he, too, went to discover ink and pen and paper.

"Impudence!"

The gate-keeper stared at Lord Winters, a stolid country look behind which a lively mind laughed.

"I wish to speak to my daughter at once!"

"Orders, my lord," was the laconic reply. The old man made a motion towards his forelock, an ironic gesture of respect.

Lord Winters stared down his nose. "Send word that I await her." He fumed, the sun bearing down on his back and shoulders doing nothing to ease his temper. "I will not put up with this. I'll take a strap to her. She is my *daughter*," he told the same bird with which Terrance had recently conversed. For once he said it with an air of bewilderment. Some twenty minutes passed before Ardith cantered around the house. His lordship's eyes widened and, forgetting his reason for coming, he studied the mare with greedy eyes. "Where did you get her, Ardith? Damme if I don't think that's the neatest little mare I've seen in a decade!"

"I raised her from a foal. She's the softest ride I've ever had." Ardith spoke politely, but with caution. She had no doubts about the arrival of her father. Terrance and Bertram had called in reinforcements!

"Well, well. I'd heard you were doing well with your stable. Got a good man running it for you, do you?"

A muscle twitched beside Ardith's clenched teeth. For a long moment she struggled to retain her temper. When she spoke, her voice took on a dangerous sweetness. "Yes. Of course. A very good man."

"Thought as much." Father stared at daughter and the satisfaction he'd gleaned from her words changed to doubt. "His breeding program, of course."

"No." His look forced her to continue. "You taught me all you know about reading blood-lines, Father." Tactfully she added, "I couldn't have had a better teacher."

Irritation struggled with pride. "No better teacher, eh?" He sent a look her way, but Ardith maintained a bland expression and he stilled his doubts. "Well, well. That's beside the point, isn't it? You should have nothing to do with such things, however." He remembered Rohampton's words and scowled. "Here now, you *don't*, do you?" Before she answered, he noticed she'd made no move to have the gates opened. "Where's your manners? I can't be kept waiting out here for ever, now."

"Can you not? I have no desire for company just now. If you'll tell me why you've come, you can then be on your way."

"Came to visit m'favourite daughter," he suggested slyly. "Can't very well visit with that gate between us, can we?"

"I suppose it does seem a barrier. I will join you for a ride."

"Here now, that ain't what I meant. You invite me up to the house!"

But she'd already nodded to the gate-keeper, who opened a narrower door set into the wall to one side. Her head bent low under the arch, she rode through. She was on the outside before Lord Winters could urge his mount nearer. "Shall we ride towards the cottages? There are a few things I'd like to point out to you since your agent refuses to do anything."

She urged the mare to a trot, increasing that to a canter when she heard him follow, swearing under his breath. But Lord Winters was a kind-hearted landlord and knew his agent leaned towards being a skinflint, and he was temporarily distracted from his purpose in calling on Ardith. They inspected the well rope and a cracked wall and discussed remedies.

On their way home Lord Winters remembered his reason for calling on Ardith and sorted out his approach to the subject. Ardith cudgelled her brains as to how to prevent his getting on with what she knew would end in a row. Then she saw St. John hacking along ahead. She called to him and he pulled up, turned, and awaited them. His eyes met Ardith's and her rueful, slightly impish glance told him all that was necessary. St. John manoeuvred until he was between Ardith and her father.

That barrier made it impossible for her sire to say anything out of the way—even under his breath, as she'd known him to do in the past. Once again her eyes met St. John's briefly, acknowledgement of her debt to him obvious in the look. He smiled. There was just the touch of a warning in that smile, hinting she would be expected to elaborate on her gratitude at a later time. The thought of his arms around her excited her beyond reason.

They rode in a silence which finely penetrated her dreams, and she leaned forward in her saddle to see that her father was carrying himself in a stiff posture quite unlike his usual, easy manner in the saddle. Again she looked at St. John. This time a rueful look was in *his* eyes. What was wrong?

Then she remembered his telling her of an argument with Lord Winters and that he'd been banned from the Hall. She sighed softly. Life was becoming far too complicated to bear. Not only was she reprehensibly hiding her sisters from their respective husbands, but she now found what appeared an insurmountable barrier between her father and the man she knew she loved to distraction. What else could go wrong in her little world? Her—until recently—boringly peaceful world!

— 9 —

ST. JOHN SCRAMBLED for a way of breaking the silence which seemed to suffocate him. A glance at the nice little mare Ardith rode reminded him of the gelding he'd seen. "Lady Ardith, before I forget again, are you selling that black with the light tail?" There was a gleam in his eyes which was not altogether devilment.

"The gelding? Yes, he's for sale."

"I liked his action. Is he up to my weight do you think?"

"Yes, but I've not schooled him for hunting," she warned.

"I thought of using him as a hack in town. Well?" he asked.

"Well what?"

"Well, my lovely horse-trader, what are you asking for him?"

Ardith doubled what she knew she'd get if she sent the animal to Tattersall's. "Six hundred."

Her father leaned forward to goggle at her. "Six hundred pounds!"

"Guineas," she said airily, going beyond imagination into fantasy.

"Four hundred," offered St. John.

"Pooh."

"It's more than you'll get in town."

"Who said anything about London?"

"You have a buyer for him?" asked St. John, startled.

"Six hundred." Giving that thought, she repeated, "Guineas."

"Five."

Ardith began to think him serious. "You haven't ridden him. How can you be so sure?"

"I've crossed horses you've trained. A friend swears by your stock. Besides, I know you. Five."

Ardith bit her lip. She'd thought he'd laugh in her face, but he was serious. She tried to put him off. "Let's talk about it another time."

"I want that gelding, Ardith. Five."

"St. John," she said, completely exasperated, "don't be a flat!"

He chuckled. "What's your real price?"

"I'm almost certain he'll bring three if my agent took him to Tatt's. Make that guineas and he's yours."

"Done."

"Three hundred guineas for a *hack*?" Lord Winters shook his head. "You are a flat."

"You haven't seen the horse."

"Once I've seen him, I'll tell you you're a green'un as well as a flat."

Ardith and St. John reined in. They stared at each other, St. John's gaze full of apology. The look also asked, Now what do we do? Both glanced up at the sound of galloping hooves. A lightly sweating roan was pulled up sharply, hunching down onto its hindquarters by the rider's manoeuvre. The Rohampton groom mopped his brow. "My lord! The messenger has come!"

"From Dover?"

"Yes, my lord."

"What word?" The groom looked flustered. "Never mind. Of course you do not know. Ardith, I must go. You understand?"

She held out a hand which he grasped. "I hope he's all right."

"So, m'dear, do I."

Ardith and her father watched as St. John, the groom in pursuit, took off towards the Park. "Well, he might have said good-bye. I've come to the conclusion Rohampton is a rackety fellow. Didn't like to see you encouraging him so. You keep your distance, Ardith, hear me?"

"You change with the wind, Father. When last we spoke on this subject you called me a fool for *not* encouraging him!"

"Finally understood why you cannot like the fellow," said Lord Winters, the sly portion of his mind coming into play. "Too blunt. A wastrel, too, which I never thought. Three hundred guineas for a hack!"

They rode on and Ardith hoped she'd avoided talking about her sisters.

Lord Winters pulled a watch from his fob, a recent purchase from Nicholas Facio, the Swiss, whose watches were considered so fine. He admired it for a moment before opening it. "Thought I was getting peckish," he said, his satisfaction clear. "You'll have to invite me in for a luncheon, Ardith."

I don't *have* to do anything of the sort, she thought peevishly. However, it would be more than uncivil if she did not. "Be pleased," she said, hopelessly, "to join us in potluck, Father."

He beamed. "Good. Very good. Knew you wouldn't send me on my way, nigh gut-foundered as I am."

Ardith pulled up outside her gates and, a trifle loudly, said, "I've no notion what we can serve you on such short notice, but of course you are welcome to dine with Fremby and myself."

The approaching gate-keeper, hearing the warning in her words, turned on his heel. A moment later Ardith watched his granddaughter lift her skirts and race towards the house. She sighed with relief.

"That man," said Lord Winters, "is touched in his upper works. What made him go back when he knew you wanted the gates opened?"

Ardith winked at Hubert. "We all get old if we live long enough." The "old" man's eyes twinkled and she grinned. "Come to the stables, Father, and I'll show you the hack St. John bought."

"Mustn't do that, Ardith."

"Mustn't show you the horse?"

"No, no." He scowled. "Mustn't call him St. John. Must remember the proprieties. Anyone might get the wrong impression if you treat him so cavalierly. He's Lord Rohampton to you, m'dear."

"He is? Strange. I've called him St. John since I was twelve years old and no one has raised an eyebrow."

"Well, well, what has that to say to it? You were a chit of a girl then. Now you're a lady. If you were engaged to him, then it might be all right—but you ain't. Thought I might bring him up to scratch again, but then I discovered I didn't like him. Good thing you're a stubborn wench. Now I don't have to worry about doing the civil to him as I would to a son-in-law."

Ardith stared at her father. Thought you'd bring him up to scratch? Had her father had a hand in St. John's renewed offer of marriage? Ardith gritted her teeth.

Oblivious to the fact he'd just dropped a clinker, Lord Winters said, "So, let's see this famous gelding. I tell you no hack is worth so much."

"Fig out Snowy Charcoal," ordered Ardith, putting her thoughts aside.

"Snowy Charcoal?" Her father laughed heartily, slapping his thigh. "*Showy* Charcoal, more like!" He laughed even harder at his joke, only to break it off to stare at the high-stepping creature run out for viewing.

"Showy, is he? Do you think so, Father? Look at those legs and that chest. And you wouldn't believe how he loves his work."

"Lovely head," said her subdued sire. "Good haunches."

"In a word, worth every pence St. John paid for him."

"*Hasn't* paid for him yet." Lord Winters' eyes narrowed. "Tell you what, Ardith. Give you three fifty for him."

"For a hack? Why, no one pays that much for a hack. No, no. Can't allow my father to make a flat of himself." She felt quite happy at that bit of minor revenge. "Well, best get up to the house. Come along." In company with Fremby her father would not put her over the coals. She had no desire to lie to him, and to avoid it she must avoid conversation about her sisters. They entered the dining-room where they found that her sisters, wearing identical expressions of defiance, awaited them. Ardith sighed.

"Oho!" said Lord Winters. Ardith tried to back from the room, but he gripped her arm and she was caught. "So," he said. "Didn't believe it. *My daughters*. Behaving like actresses in a Cheltenham tragedy! Running away from their rightful husbands! And you, Ardith, hiding them away as if they had something to fear from their menfolk. It was not well done of you, but we'll discuss *that* later."

He glared at Ellie who hung her head in an appropriately subdued fashion. He transferred the glare to Maud who glared right back. Lord Winters blinked at that. Maud? One of his lovely Winter Roses was glaring at him? He expected that sort of thing from Ardith, but *Maud*!

"Well, well. Never does one good to fight on an empty stomach. We'll just set aside our little talk." Lord Winters sent a greedy look at the viands arrayed on the table and sideboard and rubbed his hands together. "We'll serve ourselves. Go along with you," he said to the servants.

Tomlin looked to Ardith, who reluctantly nodded. Then the family—and Miss Fremby—were alone. Ardith brightened. "Father, you are remiss. You've not greeted my friend."

Lord Winters, who'd been seating himself, turned red, straightened, and bowed. "Miss Fremby. Good day to ye."

"Good day, my lord. You mustn't stand on points with me. Pray do be seated. I believe you'll enjoy the lamb, my lord. Cook has a special way with lamb and it is always excellent." She continued talking soothingly, and Ardith sent her a silent thank you as she unfolded her napkin.

The delicious meal was badly spiced with exceedingly desultory conversation. Ellie barely swallowed a mouthful and shoved her food from one side of her plate to another. Maud, too, had difficulty. Ardith, always a light eater at midday, managed better. Only Miss Fremby and Lord Winters had hearty appetites. Why, wondered Ardith, had her sisters decided to face him?

The women removed to the back parlour once everyone but her father had shaken their heads at the apple tartlets served for dessert. He, too, soon arrived and took a stance before the fireplace. He stared from one daughter to the next until he reached Miss Fremby. There his gaze rested, turning to a glare when she met it with a placid questioning look. When she didn't take the hint, he harrumphed. She waited with a patiently polite expression.

"Damme, Ardith," he hissed, "tell the woman to go away."

"I will do no such thing. I have no desire to listen to one of your tirades and I wish her to stay. Her presence will moderate your language."

"I should have beaten you more than I did."

"The beatings only served to make me more outrageous than ever. You wish to blame me for keeping my sisters' whereabouts a secret. Do you deny me the right of loyalty to my sisters? Is it that you wish me to be a sneak? That I should play the Judas?"

Lord Winters, not for the first time, wondered how Ardith managed to put him in the wrong before he'd had a chance to rate her for *her* wrong-headedness. "You should not have abetted their flight from their husbands."

"I was to turn them from my door? Look at Ellie. *Look* at her. She is ill from worry and fear. I'm to admire and trust a man who reduces my sister to such a state?" Ellie made a slight noise of dissent, but Ardith shushed her. "For once face up to the consequences of your actions, Father!"

Lord Winters looked. He was startled at how thin his eldest had grown, at the deep purple shadows under her eyes. Blushing, Ellie hung her head. "Well, well," he said, going to her and seating himself by her side. "Ellie, dear, I did not mean for you to become ill, truly I didn't."

"I tried to make myself accept Bertram back into my bed, but I could not." Her voice was barely audible. "I could *not*."

"No, no. I'll have a talk with Bertram, never fear." Lord Winters remembered the letters entrusted to him. "Here now." He pulled papers from an inner pocket and sorted till he found the one he wanted. "Bertram as much as told me he wished he'd behaved differently, Ellie. You read that and see if it doesn't say so."

Ellie clutched the folded sheet to her breast and looked around. Blushing again, she rose and went out the French doors to the garden.

"Knowing Terrance I'm sure it is too much to hope I, too, have a letter there? Terry hates putting pen to paper."

Lord Winters, whose worried gaze had followed his eldest daughter from the room, swung on Maud whom he'd forgotten in his very real, if belated, concern for her sister. "Aha."

"Do not rant at *me* now. I do not *wish* a child." Maud frowned, no longer sure that was true. Ardith had dumped a cottager's baby in her lap, and she'd been surprised at how cuddly and warm the infant was. "I do not wish to become fat and awkward"—which *was* true—"and, besides, I, too, am afraid. If Ellie had so much trouble, what of me?"

"Think of Cecilia who had no trouble at all," her father stormed, surprising himself that he'd come up with a reasonable response even as he delivered it with his usual bombast.

Maud did think of Cecilia and shuddered. "Even she . . ."

"The pain of childbed is a burden women must endure!"

Maud snorted. "I remember when a horse stepped on your foot. Just how well did *you* bear the pain of *that*, Father!"

He blinked, blustered, harrumphed and, ordering his thoughts, insisted, "It is not at all the same. I was not duty-bound to be stepped on. You have a duty to present your husband with an heir."

"So I do. And am I to be like Cecilia, constantly *enceinte*, until I have? I fear we will both be in our graves before we can buy pretty gowns and go to parties and enjoy ourselves."

"Pretty gowns? Parties? You, m'daughter, are shallow and selfish."

"And if I am? With your example, how could I be other?"

"Me? My example? I'm a *man*."

Ardith looked at Miss Fremby, who touched a finger to her lips. This is as good, said the expression in her bright birdlike eyes, as a play.

"Oh, yes. A man may do as he pleases. A man may waste the ready as he will, may let his lands go to rack and ruin, need not care if his wife starves, and is made to patch old gowns and made to live in rooms! Men may do anything and no one may say a word."

A thoroughly confused Lord Winters blinked, opened his mouth to bluster, closed it, and finally, in a more reasonable tone, asked, "Now what are you on about?"

"I have come to a decision, Father. *Under conditions* I will attempt to give Terry an heir. But there must be something for that heir to inherit, or we'll forget the whole thing." Maud folded her arms.

Lord Winters stared at her, his eyes goggling as they were wont to do when he was confused. He turned to Ardith. "Do you have the slightest notion what she's going on about?"

Ardith thought she did. She nodded. "I believe I do. And more power to her. Stick to your guns, Maud."

"*More* rebellion," said Lord Winters, disgust ripe in his tone.

"Yes, more rebellion." Maud tossed her head. "I will write a letter to Terrance. I presume he is at the Hall?" Lord Winters nodded. "Then, if you will wait for it, you may return with it and give it to him."

"Well, perhaps you should read his letter first."

Maud's eyes widened. "You mean he *did* write? *Terry*?"

"Yes, he did and I don't see why you are so surprised." Ardith and Maud both stared at him until, his cheeks blotched with red, he huffed, huffed again. "Oh, all right, so he isn't much of a hand with a pen."

Maud took the letter and disappeared into the hall. That, thought Ardith, left her quite unprotected from her father's rage. She sighed. Oh for the boredom of the long, cold winter days! Boredom meant peace, and peace was a state of being for which she devoutly prayed. She braced herself to meet her father's anger.

Much to her surprise he did not immediately turn on her. Instead he paced the room, occasionally glancing into the garden after Ellie, and occasionally pausing to look out the hall door. "Ardith, it is not often I feel guilt, but you were right and I was wrong. I should not have made that foolish offer. It has very nearly torn my family apart. I will apologise to my other daughters as soon as I may."

Ardith hid her surprise with difficulty. Having stifled it, she managed, "Well said, Father."

"However, that does not absolve you of guilt."

"No, I don't suppose it does."

"It comes of this life you lead."

"It does?"

"Yes, it does. It is high time you were married. Pack a few things—since nothing you own will do for London—and come up to town with me. We will find you a husband despite . . ." St. John's statement that Ardith was lacking self-confidence because of the sort of words he'd been about to say crossed his mind. "Well, well, never mind that. Just you pack like a good girl and I'll stop by for you tomorrow. This little contretemps with your sisters will be resolved. You and I will take a little run up to London and see what can be done."

"We will do no such thing."

"Now Ardith, it is for your own good. You need a man to guide you and keep you busy and away from that stable and"—he searched for more ammunition—"your *dealings* with the country people. Won't do, Ardith, believe me."

"I am my own woman. You cannot order me about as you did when I was a child. I hate London. I hated my Season. I *am* a country person and here I will stay. I like the life I've made for myself."

"Believe me, my dear, it isn't right. You want children of your own and . . ." He'd been about to add: *your own home*, but realised in time she *had* that. "And company and . . ." He sighed. "I blame Aunt Sibley. I should have made that woman give you back to me, but at the time—"

"At the time," interrupted Ardith, "you were happy to get me off your hands." Ardith spoke more sharply than she'd meant to do. She, too, sighed. "The past is done. It's long over. I would like to be friends with you, Father, but until you accept me for what I am we will only argue." A movement on the lawn caught her eye. "Here comes Ellie. She's been crying. Again."

But as Ellie came closer, again hugging the letter to her breast, they saw she was smiling through her tears. "Oh,

Ardith, you would not believe! I must pack. Oh, oh, oh. Everything's wonderful." Ellie blushed. "We are going away together." The blush deepened. "He says it is time we . . . we got acquainted."

Lord Winters expressed Ardith's initial confusion very well. "Got acquainted! You've been married for over ten years!"

"Good for Bertie," said Ardith, beginning to understand. "They've been married years but how much time have they actually spent together?"

The matron's blush deepened and she ducked her head. Ellie hurried to the door, turned with her hand on the knob. "You will order a carriage to take me to the Hall?" she asked anxiously.

Ardith paused. "You're sure?"

Ellie glowed. "Oh yes, Ardith! I am very, very sure."

After Ardith agreed to order out the carriage for Ellie, the room was absolutely silent for a long moment. "Ardith, please come to London?"

She was torn. For the first time her father asked rather than ordered. "It is too late this Season to accomplish anything." Ardith, feeling a trifle confused by the change in her sire, added by way of explanation, "By the time I acquired a suitable wardrobe, it would be over!"

Over. And he'd not made sure of the little widow. Which would take every moment of his time. Lord Winters made one of his abrupt switches. "Very true. Very true. Didn't think of that."

Ardith offered a compromise. "Maybe the Little Season in the autumn."

"Excellent notion. Ah, Maud. That is for Terrance?"

"It is."

Maud had a certain mulish expression the whole family recognised. Not that she donned it often but when she did there was no turning her. Seeing it, her father eyed her warily. "I will see Terrance gets your, er, message." He didn't need to say that he'd describe that look—as well known to her husband as to her father!

Ardith hid a smile. She knew how this would end: with

Terrance's capitulation to whatever demands Maud made concerning the Templeton lands. Once Ellie left with Lord Winters riding beside her, Maud said, "I did it."

"You did what?"

"I promised to have a child if Terrance would agree to go home to Applewood. I said he could go to races and local prizefights and cock fights for amusement, but we *must* reside on the estate for a full year and he *must* take an interest in it." Her mouth pursed into a hard little pout. "I told him what I said about his heir having an inheritance. I don't know if it will answer, but I am adamant."

"We guessed."

Maud bit her lip. She chuckled. "It would be ironic if he agrees to my terms and it comes about I cannot give him an heir."

"Do you think that probable?"

Maud sighed. "I do not know, do I? Part of me hopes I am barren. Oh, I just don't know!" They walked back towards the house. "Ardith, I told Terry to give me his written word before I'd see him. If he comes to the gates, don't let him in until I tell you you may."

That evening a much chastened Terrance came warily into where Maud was supported by her sister and Miss Fremby. "Good evening, husband."

"Good evening, wife." He bowed slightly in the direction of Ardith and Miss Fremby without taking his eyes off Maud. "I want to speak to you."

"I have your written promise in a safe place. You can't renege."

"Nothing of the sort. Word of a gentleman. It's something else."

"I'll check on the tea tray," said Miss Fremby, rising to her feet.

When Maud nodded, a jerky movement of her head, Ardith, too, rose and moved towards the door. "I will be across the hall in my office, Maud."

Terrance, offended by the notion his wife needed protection from her husband, pokered up. He glowered at the closed door. "That sister of yours needs a trimming. It's outside of enough when a man may not talk to his wife without threats and—" He broke off when his wife giggled. "Maud." Forgetting Ardith, he stared at her, guilt and longing in his eyes. "What I wanted to say. Can you forgive me?"

"I think we need to forgive each other. We were both wrong. And stubborn. And, Terrance?" He took two steps towards her and when she held out her hand settled himself on the sofa beside her, grasping her fingers tightly. "Terrance, maybe we needed this upset. I, well, I think we've been playing at life and not taking it seriously. I'm worried."

"Worried?"

"You've complained about the income from the farms for years haven't you? You keep saying we must have more money, and your agent says it's impossible." He nodded. "What if the farms cannot provide more money?"

"I suppose," he said with a twinge of regret, "we might sell them."

She shook her head. "No. It is *our* fault. We've lived on the very edge of our income ever since we first married."

His cheeks reddened. "Yes."

"It is time we retrench before we lose everything."

"But can you be happy in the country, love? You hate it."

Maud looked around the comfortable welcoming room. "I don't know that I do. Oh, when I came to London for my first Season, I was enchanted. I gloried in the attention. I didn't want to marry—until I met you—because I enjoyed flirting and turning down offers." She bit her lip. "Being one of the Winter Roses went to my head, I think." She put her other hand on his. "Terrance, I told Ardith when I arrived, trying to hoax her, you know, that the Season was tiring. Well," her face firmed, "it is. And boring."

"I've felt the same way. Doing the same things over and over. The same faces. Even the same gossip although the names change from time to time. Do you really think we can do something about the estate?"

"Why not? Father will advise us. Ardith, too," she teased, "if you can bear asking a woman! I've watched her while I've rusticated and cannot believe all she does. Why, when one of her tenants complained about a hedge damaged by a neighbour's runaway team and wagon, she listened, inspected it, talked to the other man, and decided what to do. Would we have done that? If we'd known? We'd have ordered your agent to take care of it. How long has it been since we inspected the farms? What do we know about the condition of roofs and fences and stock and equipment? Ardith checks those things every month. All we know is what your man tells us and I don't believe we've listened to him much, have we?"

"You mean me. Hasn't been your business, now, has it?"

"Terrance?" He looked at her and she met his eyes bravely. "Let's go to Applewood. Let's not even go back to London where we'll be tempted."

"You sure?"

Maud took a big breath. "Terry, I'm sure we can manage if we try."

That night was Ardith's turn to do the rounds, checking the fires were well shielded and candles were out. She paused in the back salon. Slow steps took her across to the French doors looking over the lawn.

The question, the meaning behind "bring St. John up to scratch," had teased her since Lord Winters spoke the words. He'd had a hand in making the pair of them godparents for the latest Hawke child. She knew *that*. Was that *all* he meant? Or had the two men already discussed the possibility of Rohampton renewing his suit *before* Ardith found herself caught in the storm which imprisoned her at the Park?

St. John had proposed five years ago in London. It had not been a wager or a jest to teach her a lesson. She believed that. But would a man wishing a woman for his wife wait *five years* before approaching her again? Long fingers clutched at the drapery, clenched the fabric into a knot. Believing he had actually proposed once—to *herself* with all her failings—could she believe he still wanted her?

Her eyes travelled over the moonlit scene, the neatly kept lawns, the hedges and fields, her horses nodding in the pasture. She'd had a decent dowry when she went up to London. Now she had so much more. But St. John was a wealthy man. Surely he wouldn't agree to her father's urgings because he felt a desire to add Summersend to his acres. Would he? No. Surely not.

When his mouth touched hers, when his hands held her—what he did to her was indescribable. But he'd called their kiss "nice," which hurt whenever she remembered. He knew, however, that she wouldn't be a cold fish when he came to doing his duty and bedding her. Surely that weighed a bit with a man!

But if he could make her feel that way, wasn't it likely he could make any woman? A tear glistened on the end of her lash, distracting her by its glitter, and she wiped it away. If only there was a way to *know* what he felt for her. If he *loved* her, then it might be possible to give up her freedom, her eccentric ways. Love. There'd been so little love in her life.

But she couldn't know that he loved her. That was the end result of her cogitations. And, not knowing, she couldn't bear the thought of trading her independence on the chance he might, not when it was much more likely he did not and that he would, when he tired of her odd ways, find entertainment and distraction elsewhere. Such activity on the part of her husband, commonplace as it was amongst the men in the ton, would not kill her. One did not die of sorrow or disappointment. But it would hurt so badly she'd wish she were dead.

She took one more look over the moonlit fields as she remembered the message the groom had given him that morning. She prayed for his friend. Whatever she felt for St. John, whatever he felt for her, she knew she couldn't wish on him the pain he'd feel if Cameron Westman were to die. Ardith closed the curtains and went to bed.

— 10 —

"WHAT DO YOU mean she isn't at home? Is she really not at home or do you mean she isn't receiving visitors?" Mrs. Rollins, the most inquisitive of ladies, had just returned from London where she'd heard rumours that Lady Ardith's sister, Lady Templeton, was ill. She hadn't believed them. Now her beady eyes fixed themselves on the gate-keeper's face. "She cannot mean to exclude neighbours. Why, I'm just back from town and she will wish news, the latest *on-dits*, and the newest fashions! Go and tell her I'm here."

"Lady Ardith is not at home. To anybody."

"Now see here, my good man. . . ."

"Good day, madam."

"You stay right there. Don't you dare . . ."

Hubert turned back to the gates, but not because of the old besom. The sound of galloping hooves also caught the woman's attention and she raised a quizzing glass. A liveried groom swung a well-lathered horse around and slid from the saddle. "Hubert!"

"Well lad, what's to do?"

The groom extended the paper he clutched in his hand.

"For Lady Ardith?" asked Hubert.

"That's Rohampton colours, ain't it?" interrupted the inquisitive lady, as if she didn't know.

"Yes, madam," said the groom, his eyes going desperately from Hubert to the lady he didn't feel he could insult. He sidled towards the gate.

"Something wrong at Rohampton?"

"Must be, madam. Master said not to spare the horse, madam."

"Lud. *Rohampton* said that?"

The groom held the twist of paper towards Hubert. "For my lady."

The gate-keeper sent off his granddaughter and returned to find the neighbour questioning the groom who, whenever he could, inserted the words "don't know" or, occasionally, "don't know nothin'." Hubert grinned at the gossip's mounting frustration.

"You are wearing Rohampton livery. You must know something. You can't have galloped *ventre à terre* with no notion why!"

The granddaughter reappeared and handed Hubert another twist. "Hurry, man," said the gate-keeper with a wink as he passed it on.

"Right you are." The groom pulled himself back up on the sweating horse and galloped off.

Before the temporarily silenced woman said more, Hubert hurried into the gate-house. No amount of urging or cajoling got him out again.

Inside Summersend an observer might have thought all was chaos. Ardith gave quick orders to three attentive servants, each of whom scurried off in a different direction. Others stood by to see if they, too, would be needed. The activity only *looked* chaotic.

"Fremby, you understand what I'll require?"

"We'll load the gig and Owen will bring me as quickly as can be."

Questions were asked by several servants. "Be quiet, do. I must think." Ardith bit her lip. Did she dare? She glanced again at the paper in her hand, read the part which spoke of putrid flesh and hot dry skin. The poor man was obviously much weakened from lack of water. That was almost more a danger than the decay at this point. Putrid flesh. Did she dare? Did she dare *not*?

Ardith moved down the back passage and out the back door where she picked up her divided skirts and raced towards the garden, her eyes searching for her odd-jobs man.

She found him half-heartedly hoeing a row of young peas. "Harry, something died the other day, did it not?"

He leaned on the hoe and stared at her. Eventually he nodded.

"What did you do with the carcass?"

"Nasty thing that. You wouldn't be wanting a thing like that."

"But I *would*. Oh Harry, please. A man's life is at stake."

The old man looked at her through bleary eyes. "Important?"

"Very important."

"Very well."

With a great sigh the man dropped his hoe and shuffled to the back of the garden and behind a brick wall to the pile of compost. He bent, groaning and moaning, and tipped over some clippings which revealed the decomposing body of what had once been a mole. Ardith dropped to her knees, picked up a stick, and poked at it.

"Good. Oh, drat. I need a container of some sort. Harry?"

Another bleary look and another sigh. "Baccy-tin? Got worms in it," he warned.

"Dump them and give it to me."

An even deeper sigh answered her, but he did as she bade. Ardith bit her lip through the next process, finished, and hugged the old man.

"Here now. Don't you go doing that!" Much embarrassed, he unwound her arms and strode off, forgetting his habitual and only partly assumed pose of decrepitude.

Ardith raced back towards the house. "Do you have everything?"

"I think so." Fremby handed her a saddle bag which Ardith took and a hat which she waved away. "Be careful now," said Fremby. "I put in only a flask of the fluid—so don't break it. I'll bring what's left and the receipt in the hopes we'll need it."

"We *must* need it. He mustn't die. It is Colonel Westman, Fremby."

The older woman watched Ardith mount the fastest mare in her string. "Watch yourself. You'll do the man no good if *you* come to grief."

A quick grin was the only answer as Ardith pulled her mount around and set off cross-country. With any luck she'd catch up with, perhaps pass, the groom she'd sent off with word she was on her way.

In considerably less time than one might reasonably have expected, she turned the mare loose at Rohampton Park's front entrance. She gave fleeting thought to the sweating animal, its head hanging, but pushed its condition from her mind. Ransome would see to her. All her attention was needed inside. A man's life was in danger. The huge doors opened as she raced up the front steps showing an unladylike amount of ankle and leg.

"Ransome. Quickly! Where is he?" she asked on her way to the stairs.

"The first bedroom to the right, Lady Ardith." He spoke to her back as she continued up the broad staircase and, panting slightly, on up the next. She stopped at the top barely long enough to catch her breath a bit before moving on and quietly opening the door to the sick-room. The distressed man by the bed holding his friend's wasted hand didn't see her.

"St. John?"

He turned, a grim look around his mouth, his hair down over his forehead, his forearms bare and his chest—where his shirt was open—bare as well. Momentarily she was distracted.

"Ardith." It was a whisper, and his eyes begged for help.

She blinked away the weakness the sight of him caused. "I came as quickly as I could. Oh, you poor man," she breathed, looking down at the wasted figure whose rasping breathing denoted nothing good. Well, Lord Rohampton, she thought, I'll do my very best to save your friend. She studied the flushed face, the skin which was tight and parchmentlike. Worry creased her brow. I'll try, she thought, but . . .

St. John spoke, his words breaking into her thoughts. "Waingarden was waiting when we got him here. The doctor did what he could but . . . Ardith, he said Cam would stick his spoon in the wall before another nightfall! I sent for you as soon as the doctor left."

She heard the quiet desperation and gritted her teeth, forcing calm. "Very occasionally I've been lucky, St. John. I'll do my best."

"The doctor agreed you were Cameron's only hope." What the man had actually said was that Ardith could do no damage, but St. John could not voice that thought. Sending for her had been the most natural thing in the world.

"Well, let's get busy." She knelt and opened the saddle bag she'd carried over her arm all the way from Summersend. She drew out the flask and set it on the bedside table and unwrapped a strangely designed spoon, a thing reminiscent of a pregnant funnel with a handle. "Help me raise him, St. John. He'll choke if he's on his back."

"What are you doing?"

"He needs liquid. He's lost too much blood. I doubt he was cared for at all properly if he lost consciousness on the boat. They never have enough help and tend to give aid to those they know they can save. More pillows. He must be upright or he'll choke. Yes. Like that. Now. Watch carefully."

She poured a bit of the special broth and herb mixture into the spoon, carried it to the unconscious man's lips and, opening them by pressing on his jaws, she tipped the point of the "funnel" towards the back of his mouth. She rubbed Colonel Westman's throat until he swallowed.

"Just like stuffing a Christmas goose, St. John."

He came around the bed. "You want me to do that?"

"Not immediately. If that stays down, then every few minutes. We *must* get liquid down him. Here."

She shoved the bottle and spoon at him and, hands on hips, studied her sheet-shrouded patient. Her nose wrinkled at the smell.

"Did Dr. Waingarden cut away the dead flesh?"

"What he could. I don't know how poor Cam has survived this long."

"Where is it?"

"Along his right side from just above his knee, up his thigh, and on up into his hip. The only thing I can imagine is a saber, slashing almost straight down."

"Let's see what we have."

St. John gasped as she reached to throw back the sheet, and grabbed at it. "Ardith, you *can't*. We didn't put him into a night-shirt!"

She glared, struggling with him for possession of the linen. "St. John, I have washed male children and changed their nappies. Men can't be any different. Or, only more so! Now do you want me to help your friend or not?"

"It isn't proper."

"Well, what did you think I'd do? Sing a few incantations and throw herbs in the fire? Let go!"

A choked laugh and slowly the sheet slipped from his grip. Ardith, with St. John's sudden descent into an overly nice sense of propriety in mind, draped the sheet back carefully so as to reveal no more than the long flank. The seeping wound made her gag. She'd never seen worse and bit her lip, a frown tightening her brows into a sharp vee.

"Not very pretty, is it?"

"No. It is not." She reached into her pocket for the tobacco tin and, pulling it out, weighed it in her hand. "St. John, Dr. Waingarden doubted if he'd last until nightfall?"

"Yes."

"So, if I were to try something I've never tried before, only heard about, it could do no harm, is that correct?"

"I don't understand, Ardith."

"See if you can get some more liquid into him while I think."

She watched some of the broth dribble down his friend's face. Watched it tenderly wiped away. This was Cameron. St. John had talked about Cam back in the good old days before she'd run from him. Stories. The pranks at Eton. The more serious mischief while up at Cambridge. Very slightly risqué, but well-edited tales about their first years on the town before Cam bought his commission. Was it wrong to try *anything* which might save the man's life? But such an ugly disgusting idea. Ardith's nose wrinkled at the stench from the oozing wound. That, too, was disgusting. The doctor had done what he could, but to cut into living flesh shocked a patient's weakened system and Cam could have died right then and there. But the doctor hadn't gotten nearly all the rot. "Aunt Sibley . . ." she began.

"Something she tried which failed?"

"That's just it. She could never bring herself to try it, although she always wanted to see if it would work. Oh, St. John, I don't *know*."

"Tell me." She did. "That's disgusting. No. You *can't*."

Her mouth firmed into a hard line. She had a fleeting thought that there was something crooked in her that sent her contrary to any order, but let the notion slip. She opened the box and dumped ten ugly white maggots along the wound.

"Ardith! No."

"Don't stop me, St. John. They'll not eat living flesh, only the dead. The dead kills the good healthy flesh next to it. It must be cleaned." She reached for his hand. "Oh, what can it hurt, St. John!" But her stomach churned and, to distract herself, she took the spoon, got another dose of the lightly salted liquid down Cam's throat. She set down the bottle and spoon and wiped her forehead against her sleeve. "God, it's hot in here."

"Well, we built up a good fire and . . ." She strode to the fireplace and knocked the burning coals apart. "Ardith, what are you doing?" he shouted.

She flung open the windows as wide as they would go. "Take a damper, St. John. Damnation, man, he'll *sweat*. We're trying to get water *into* him not take more *out* of him."

He calmed down. "*That*, at least, makes sense." His eyes went back to the wound and he closed them, his mouth twisting at the nauseating thought of what was going on in that ugly strip of rotten flesh.

The room was silent after that. Ardith could feel the strain in St. John as he watched his friend. Neither spoke. Every few minutes she pushed another spoonful of the liquid down his throat, pleased that it stayed down. One fear she had was that he'd vomit, the strain doing him no good.

An hour passed and a quiet tap at the door heralded Fremby's arrival. She eyed the patient. "The poor, poor boy. What have they done to the lad?"

"As you see, Fremby."

"Yes. As one sees. My lord, you should rest."

"How can I?" There was desperation, something close to hopelessness in his voice.

Miss Fremby took his arm. "I understand exactly how you feel but do come sit in this chair, my lord. There. That's better. Now your feet. Yes. That's good," Miss Fremby added, as she slipped a stool under his legs. "Isn't that better? You'll be right here if you're needed, and after all, that's all you *can* do now, isn't it? That and pray."

Ardith and Fremby took turns forcing liquid down their patient. Sometime in the middle of the night she found St. John standing behind her. He pointed. One of the maggots lay curled tightly in the edge of the wound. She picked it up, took it to the window, and threw it out. Returning to the bed, she sniffed. Yes the sickening odor was almost gone. She probed gently, found another maggot, then another. More. Carefully she counted them. One was left. Gently she searched the wound, felt a twitch in the exposed flesh. Had she somehow miscounted? Or was there still, somewhere, a patch of the awful putrid ooze? At last she found it, a pocket of decay in the hip. Her fingers were a mess and she went to wash them. Thoroughly. Then she washed them again for good measure.

"Is he breathing more easily or do I only wish it is so?"

"He truly is. Now, all we can do is wait, St. John."

"Ardith?"

"Yes?"

"I shouldn't have tried to stop you."

"I almost stopped myself. The cure seemed almost worse than watching him die."

He nodded. "I'll sit with him now."

She yawned. "Good. Remember, not too often but steadily. He is still losing liquid through the wound although it seeps less now it is clean." She turned away, then back. "Oh, one more of the little fellows, St. John. Watch for it. Right there. I don't think I'll ever again look at one with quite so much disgust."

"Nor I."

Late the next morning Cam groaned, rolled his head. "Fremby," Ardith spoke urgently, "get St. John. Quickly. Colonel Westman must not start tossing."

"Water." The word was a croak.

She held a tumbler with more of the herbal bouillon to his lips, let him swallow greedily until he'd downed nearly a third of a glassful. "That's enough for now," she said softly.

"Where . . . ?" The word was a breath of sound.

"Rohampton. St. John had you brought here."

"Good." He slipped into sleep just as the door opened.

"Fremby said . . ."

"Shush. He spoke, St. John."

Her patient had awakened, spoken, actually drunk on his own. It was wonderful. But the next days would be hell. That open wound was scabbing, thank the Lord, but would it ever heal properly? And the pain, once Cam was truly conscious, would be awful, unbearable. Poor, poor man.

"What is it, Ardith?"

"I'm thinking ahead, St. John. He must be kept still. I can dose him with laudanum and I will, as I must, but . . ."

"You're afraid he'll become dependent on it?"

"Have you ever seen someone who begged for it?"

"I've heard stories." He stared down at his friend. "He's got courage enough for ten men, Ardith. As soon as he's rational I'll talk to him."

A knock at the door preceded Dr. Waingarden. "Not dead yet?"

"Not dead. Thank you for telling me Ardith worked miracles."

"Humph." The doctor glared down his nose and St. John grinned at him. "Don't believe that is quite what I said. Let me have a look here."

The doctor straightened away from the bed after inspecting the wound and stared at Ardith who blushed rosily. "I'm not going to ask. It is not possible. I don't want to know. So don't even try to tell me." He stared at the sweet-smelling wound. "Damme, Lady Ardith, you'd have been burned as a witch not a hundred years ago!"

"I tried something about which Aunt Sibley had once heard."

"There's another who'd have burned. Maybe she is. God rest the lady's soul!"

"Have you suggestions, Doctor?" asked Ardith, her voice deferential.

"Me? The man should be dead. He is not. What can *I* tell *you*?" He glared, a speculative look from beneath shaggy brows. The look faded and, shaking his head, he repeated, "No. I *don't* wish to know. I'll go now."

The door closed behind the doctor and St. John, who accompanied the man to the foyer. When Rohampton returned he stared at Ardith who appeared sad and perturbed. "What is it, Ardith?"

"I feel sorry for Dr. Waingarden. Sad we can't be friends. We could learn from each other, but he is so jealous. The country people come to me, you know. Not the gentry of course. I hate it, St. John, knowing he despises me as nothing but a herbalist, but at times he recognises that I do more than he can. Not always—not even *very often*. If only he'd teach me what *he* knows."

Towards evening Colonel Westman woke again. He gazed dreamily up at the canopy over his head, his eyes wandering amongst the fanciful birds embroidered in silk thread. "Heaven?" he whispered.

Ardith came to the bed. "Try to drink some of this, please." She held the tumbler to his lips and his eyes held hers as he sipped. "Heaven," he sighed, "and you, an angel."

Ardith chuckled. "More likely an imp o' Satan. Some more now."

He drank, then said. "Too beautiful for an imp."

Ardith smoothed the covers over his shoulders, smiling. "I love flattery as much as the next, Colonel, but please save your strength. I'll have St. John called."

He grasped her wrist weakly. "St. John?"

"You don't remember." It was a statement, not a question. "You woke once before and were told you were at Rohampton Park. St. John had you brought from Dover as soon as the boat docked."

"Hospital boat. Remember that. Delays. Storms." His grasp loosened and his words slurred. "We left port. Big storm in the Bay of Biscay. 'Atsall I 'member."

"You were in sad shape when you arrived, Colonel. I'll get St. John."

He raised heavy lids. "Another drink?"

She glanced at the clock and nodded, giving him less this time. "You need liquid, Colonel, but must drink slowly." He nodded but indicated he wanted more. She let him have another few sips, watched his eyes close. She thought he'd gone to sleep again.

They opened, much more clear and direct than Ardith thought possible. "Black hair. Beauty mark. Know you." His eyes closed again. "Wunnerful," he slurred. "St. John made you unnerstan'."

"Made me understand?" Ardith's heart did a flip-flop. What could he mean? Had he really slipped back into sleep? This time, she resented it.

His eyes opened and again his voice was strong for a moment. "Almost slit his throat when you ran from him, my lady. In a sorry state, he was, my lady." Her patient's lips twitched into a travesty of a smile. "I saved his life and now, methinks, he's saved mine. Or you have."

"I don't understand."

"Years ago," he frowned impatiently. "When he proposed to you." Again there was silence. The man's eyes closed, a faint frown between them. "Then he couldn't see you." The colonel looked up at her. "Wanted to cut his throat, but I stopped him."

Ardith felt her knees giving way and backed until she felt the chair behind her. "I don't believe you."

"True." Colonel Westman moved, restless. His eyes widened in shock. His mouth opened and a muffled scream tore from his throat.

"Oh, dear. Oh, Colonel, stay still." Ardith pressed his shoulders back against the pillows, wiped sweat from his brow. "I should have warned you. Oh, dear." She lifted the sheet away from the wound. It was oozing again from several cracks in the fragile scab and she reached for the basilicum powder, sprinkling it in the open areas. "Now behave."

"I think," he said through gritted teeth, the sweat still forming on his face, "I'd better."

"I'll fix you a dose of laudanum, sir."

He didn't argue, taking the dose neatly. They waited, strain about his mouth and eyes, for it to take effect. Ardith breathed easily only when he slipped into drugged sleep.

St. John had asked that he be called if his friend woke, but how could she have done so? First he was telling her things she needed to hear. Then he'd suffered so. Now, the dose would keep him sleeping for some time.

Besides, better St. John *not* know what his friend had said. Could it be true that St. John had despaired to the point he'd tried to end his life? Or was it only a figure of speech? She'd apologised for thinking that, three sheets to the wind, he'd made sport of her with his friends, but had his feelings for her run so deep as all *that*? And if they had, did they still?

Ardith sat near the window and stared out into the dusk-shadowed distance. Had he truly wanted her for his wife? But why her? She had no beauty, despite Colonel Westman's charming words. She was too tall and awkward, and, at that time, a hoyden with no accomplishments—not a woman St. John should have asked to be Marchioness of Rohampton. All she'd dreamed, when she'd dared dream at all, was that when he married a suitable lady, he'd still be her friend. Then, there wasn't even friendship, which was her own fault, seemingly.

Those first kisses downstairs in the library had raised a storm in her much like that going on outside at the time. The others, since, when she'd so nearly succumbed to his lovemaking—had it been more than just the fact St. John had had no woman around for so long? Oh, how was she to know? And even if he had loved her once, how could he still?

The door opened and St. John paused in the entrance, looking first at his friend and then around for Ardith. There. Why so pensive, he wondered? Thoughtful . . . or tired perhaps? Yes, of course, she was tired. She'd barely left Cam's side since she'd arrived the day before.

Miss Fremby had claimed Ardith was used to it, but she shouldn't be. She shouldn't give so much of herself to any rag-tag and bob-tail that came along. He thought of Mrs. Martin and the child who had died. But the mother had not. Now it was his friend she'd saved. Someone—himself for preference—should care for *her*. He moved softly to the window.

"Oh. St. John. You startled me."

"I'm sorry. Why are you not sleeping? You said you would when I left a couple of hours ago."

"I dozed. I never do more in a situation like this."

"But you woke?"

Ardith bit her lip, looked up at him from under thick lashes. "*He* woke and I had no chance to call you, St. John. He moved and the pain—I am so afraid he'll keep shifting and reopen it again and again."

"We could strap him down."

She shook her head. "He'd fight the bonds. I gave him laudanum. I had to. St. John, I've been thinking. That wound will never heal properly. He'll have a long, thick scar. I'm worried he'll not be able to bend his hip. That side will be more or less rigid. I've heard of cripples who—how will *he* deal with it? Will he wish we'd *not* saved his life?"

"Is this why you looked so deeply disturbed when I came in? You were worrying about your patient?"

Ardith dipped her head, blushing. "What else, St. John?"

"I don't know, do I?" he answered thoughtfully, "But, when you can't look at me, you're lying to me. Ardith?" She remained silent. "Tell me."

"I cannot. Do not ask. Please."

His mind raced over the possibilities. "Did Cam say something to you?"

"He told me he remembers being carried to the hospital ship but that there was a storm in the Bay of Biscay and he remembers nothing after that."

St. John stared at her bent head. Finally he shifted his weight and she glanced up at him, then away. "That alone would not upset you." His voice roughened with emotion. "No, do not say more. You will only prevaricate. Please don't. I cannot bear it when you lie to me, Ardith."

A moan from the bed forced him away and she joined him immediately. "This is going to be a problem. He *must* lie still until the wound heals." She wiped her patient's face and he turned it away from her. She sighed. "You didn't answer my question about how he'll feel once he recovers."

St. John spoke slowly. "Cam, despite being the hell-raiser I was, also loved his studies at Cambridge. I believe he will make a life of the mind for himself if his body is no longer his to command. He will not despair as so many badly wounded men have done." St. John shifted the bedside chair closer to the bed. "I will watch him now, Ardith. You must sleep."

Ardith watched with him for a moment before turning towards the door. She was stopped by an exclamation. "What is it? Has his wound opened?"

St. John chuckled. "No, only my own confounded forgetfulness. I came up with a letter from Summersend brought over by your groom."

Ardith took the folded and sealed sheet from him. She spread it out and gave an exclamation of her own. This time one of pleasure.

"What is it?"

"My sister. Ellie. Now let me see. . . ."

"I forgot they were there. And I took you away from your guests."

"They have both gone. Thank heaven. I could not turn them away when they came, but you can't imagine my relief when they went." She waved a hand, studying the closely written sheet. "Let me see if I can decipher this. Hmm. Yes. No, I can't make out that bit. Such a totty-head. The lake district? Does she mean herself and Bertie? Yes. Because my father is to visit Terrance and Maud at Applewood at the Season's end, or later in the summer if things go as he wishes. I wonder what that means? Oh, no. I don't believe it!"

"What?"

"Do you remember I suggested my father remarry? Drat the man anyway!"

"Ardith, are you suggesting he's engaged to be married?"

Ardith was still deciphering the crossed and recrossed letter. "Yes. At least I think so. Or perhaps hopeful of it. Ellie has fallen into one of her economical moods. She's crossed and recrossed this sheet and I'm lost in the maze." She added, "Oh, dear. He still wants a grandson, even though he's now thinking of a son."

"I don't understand."

"It is perfectly simple and perfectly awful. You remember he offered ten thousand pounds to the man who gave him his first grandson. He regards it as a debt of honour and wants to make sure no one can say that by marrying he is trying to escape the bond."

St. John smothered a shout of laughter. "I still can't believe it!"

"Even my father should have had more sense." She sighed. She looked out the window, a scowl marring her wide brow. "I told him it wasn't fair." Was her father seriously thinking of remarrying? And if so, why not? She nodded. It was a good solution to all their problems. Now if he'd officially withdraw that offer!

"Not fair?"

"Well, Ellie, you know . . ." She sent him a puckish look. "Besides, I'm ineligible."

"I can and will make you eligible, Ardith."

"Don't, St. John. I am too distracted at the moment to be teased."

Her words were an automatic response to his apparently offhand proposal. She registered what *he* had said, what *she* had responded and remembered the colonel's words which had upset her. Could she, should she trust him? But marriage . . . She'd given up all thought of marriage after making a life for herself at Summersend. Her freedom . . .

"I'd not roast you on such a subject, Ardith. And, although a sick-room is no place for a proposal, I believe we could make magnificent sons together, m'love."

"First you say this is no place for such talk and then you

persist." She scowled at him but there was a twinkle in her eyes as well. He saw it and smiled, that smile that always sent her to grass. She turned away.

"Ardith?" St. John rose from his chair and pulled her into his embrace. For once he felt only tenderness and a need to comfort her, holding her close and rocking her slightly back and forth. "Shush, love. I'm sorry."

Another moan from the bed pulled them apart and both turned to look at their patient. "If only there was some way to keep him comfortable, St. John. But I know no safe way to do so. An infusion of willow bark is not strong enough for this sort of pain, although later it will help."

"Time. He *will* survive. Thanks to you. You go to the room prepared for you and sleep." He looked at the tray on the table between the windows and decided she'd eaten enough of it; he'd not scold her. "I will have you called if you are needed, m'love."

She took one more look at the colonel, more distracted than she wanted to admit even to herself, then left the room for the one across the hall. Much to her surprise she did sleep and it was close to dawn when she woke again.

She pulled on a clean gown of her own design, one which made it possible to be presentable in a matter of moments. The neck was loose going over her head and pulled into gathers at her throat with a ribbon which she tied into a bow; the high waist was similarly designed with a drawstring. She opened her door, careful not to wake the footman assigned to sit in the hall, on call day or night. He slept, his head thrown back against the wall. She cracked open the sick-room door and peered in.

"Bad, Cam?" she heard.

"Worse than when it happened I think."

"You'll survive it. I sent off a messenger to your parents. I told him not to kill his horses, but to make good time. Your mother will post south once she gets word, my friend. Can you bear it?"

A weak chuckle ended in a moan. "I love her dearly, St. John, but she's such a fuss-pot when any of us are sick."

"I had to let them know. It would have been unkind not to."

"I understand, but you'll have to protect me when she comes. As she will. Sorry to be such a nuisance, St. John."

"Don't be a fool."

"I seem to remember talking to your wife."

"Wife?"

"Did I dream it? I thought it was your Ardith."

"She's here, but not, more's the pity, my wife. We are speaking again which is a first step. Now I must control my ardour and not frighten her."

"Perhaps it would convince her you love her."

"That I *desire* her, perhaps, but I want her love. Besides, seducing her would be improper." St. John chuckled. "Or perhaps I should. Her father has offered ten thousand pounds to the man who gives him a grandson. Ardith might become my mistress just to spite him! But, since Ardith would not allow her child to be born out of wedlock, I might get her that way. I'll think about it. No, Cam, do not move!" His hands went to his friend's shoulders and held him down, the sweat pouring into his eyes matching that on Cam's face. "Bite that rag, man. Bite."

Ardith, coming out of the dream his words had caused, closed the door. A small smile tipped her mouth. "Bite that rag indeed! I see you learned something while we waited for Mrs. Martin's baby to be born. Oh, St. John. Do you truly love me? Do you?"

The footman stirred. Ardith put a hand over her mouth and hoped the man had not heard her foolish words. Speaking thoughts aloud was a habit of which she must cure herself. Once, she'd only talked to her horses, knowing they were a safe repository for her thoughts, but if she were to begin talking to herself where others could hear, they'd soon clap her up as a Bedlamite!

Ardith watched the footman settle himself, return to a deep sleep. Her thoughts returned to the conversation she'd overheard. Seduce her indeed! She chuckled at a further thought: if she were to have a son it would solve her sisters' problems! A few minutes later she entered the sick-room and spoke softly to St. John.

"Of course you had to give him the laudanum," she answered his worried question. "I did not mean he should have *none*. Only that we should ration the dosage. St. John, I think I can return home tomorrow. I will leave Fremby here, but I believe Colonel Westman is on the mend. It will not be easy. He will need constant nursing."

"Yes. We've a long way to go, but he *will* make it. I can never thank you enough for coming when you did. Cam is like a brother to me."

"I know. I remember how you talked about him. Strange we never met." She approached St. John, studied the sharp lines worry had etched into his face, the dark arcs of colour under his eyes. "It is my turn to order you to bed. You are as tired as I was. The laudanum will keep the colonel still, so go rest while you can do so with an easy mind."

"I believe I must. Especially if you are to leave us. Ardith, I . . ." His hand slid up through his hair, mussing it more than ever. Again he was in shirtsleeves and again his shirt was unfastened almost to his waist. Ardith turned away hoping he had not seen the feelings the sight roused in her. "No. This is *not* the time or place. But you will not bar the doors of Summersend to me, will you? Once I can leave Cam and come to you?"

Her voice slightly muffled by the intensity of her feelings, she said, "I will give orders you are welcome, St. John." The room was silent and she wondered if he'd slipped out without her hearing. She turned and found he was right behind her. "St. John . . ."

"Forgive me, Ardith." There was a sad but determined note in his voice. "I am everything you think me for taking advantage of you at a time like this, but I cannot resist. I need you so."

He pulled her close even as he spoke. For a moment he stared down into her bemused face and was very slightly startled she did not fight him. Then he remembered that Cam lay only a few feet away and his mouth tightened. Ardith would do nothing to disturb her patient. He could do as he pleased with her and Ardith, with Cam on her mind, would let him rather than call for help! Damn the woman! How dare she think of Cam before her own safety?

With that thought flitting through his mind his arms tightened around her, and when she pushed her face into his neck he forced it up, his mouth finding hers more harshly than he'd originally intended, softening when she responded, his irrational anger draining as passion was roused. His hands went to her arms, ran down them and raised them to his shoulders, felt them settle around him before he went on to touch her more intimately.

When she moaned and pressed close to him, he pulled on the ribbon at her throat, allowing the gathers to loosen, the neckline to widen. His hand slid along her shoulder, down. God, he had to let her go! To carry this further, even though she responded so sweetly, was the act of a rogue. His mouth shifted on hers, his tongue running between her closed lips. She tightened her arms around him, one hand running up into his hair.

"Ardith. Ardith." He spoke in her ear, his hot breath causing shivers to run up her spine. "I want you. Ardith, do not pull away from me. Not yet. Let me hold you. Let me have that much."

"St. John!" she whispered.

"Shush. I will do nothing to harm you. Nothing you do not like."

She relaxed and his mouth ran down her neck. Then, a little later, he again went too far, shocking her innocence when one hand found a breast covered by nothing but a thin chemise. She broke away from him, stepped back, her eyes wide, slightly frightened, her hands clutching the bodice up against her.

"Ardith."

"No. No more." Bewilderment made her blink. "How can you make me feel that way!"

"It is love between a man and a woman, Ardith. Not wrong. There is nothing wrong in the way you respond to me. Only in me, that I make you respond when I haven't yet the right. Forgive me."

"I . . . don't know. You make me feel things which frighten me, St. John."

"Don't be frightened. Never be frightened of me."

"It is wrong."

"Not wrong." A wry smile twisted his lips. "Only premature. Or, rather, some years beyond when you should have learned these things of me. I am tired, Ardith. I have been terribly worried about Cam. It is my only excuse for allowing the feelings I have for you too much freedom."

She nodded and pushed the loosened bodice higher on her shoulders. She was unaware a mirror behind her revealed her back to St. John's gaze. Her shoulders and much of her back were bared by the wide neckline falling in a deep arc. She wondered what he thought as he stared over her shoulder for a long moment before giving himself a shake and forcing his gaze back to hers.

"I will go and try to sleep. But if I do, I will dream you are in my arms, m'love."

His eyes held hers and she blushed. She knew she, too, would think of him holding her and felt embarrassed, but also a deep burning elation. He'd spoken of seducing her, of making her his mistress. Would the possible costs be worth the experience? Lord, the things he'd made her feel. "Go, St. John. Now."

Now before she went to him and forced herself into his embrace, before all willpower was lost in the long, hot look he gave her. His eyes flicked over her shoulder, stared, closed, and turning on his heel, he left.

When Ardith finally turned to find out what he'd stared at she found her reflexion, her mouth slightly swollen, her hair in wanton disarray, and the gown, slipping from her fingers, sliding towards her breasts. She flushed hotly, turned, and pushing the dress up again, peered over her shoulder. She moaned in embarrassment. She might as well have been naked!

No wonder he had stared! Oh. How *dare* he? She blushed, then chuckled and tried again to see what he had seen. He *had* dared. St. John would dare anything! Besides, something wanton and unladylike within her was glad he'd seen the long slender back covered by nought but the thin, lowcut chemise. Let him see. Let him find her desirable! One of these days she might even be courageous enough to let him seduce her, let those frightening but exciting sensations take her and hold her and . . .

Her eyes widened. My Lord, what has he done to me? Ardith forced herself to check her patient and, desperately needing to stop those totally improper impulses, picked up the book through which St. John had earlier browsed, diverting his mind from his friend and, not so successfully, from thoughts of Ardith—although she didn't know that, of course. She only knew she must force herself to clear her mind of the totally unsuitable thoughts with which she had badly shocked herself. Giovanni Boccaccio's *Decameron*, with its witty but often bawdy tales was not, she discovered, a means to that end!

— 11 —

LORD WINTERS HACKED gently towards Summersend. He looked at the dusty hedges and browning grasses and thought July would in its way be as miserable as the long, hard winter had been. He was concerned for the crops and the grim look around the eyes of his more thoughtful tenants. A miserable summer following a miserable winter. He must have words with his steward. The man would not take the harsh Seasons into account when it came time to collect rents. Fine man, but a little too loyal to the owner and not quite enough heart, thought that erratically kindhearted and sometimes careless owner.

Ahead were the Summersend gates, closed as usual. Lord Winters' jaw tightened. It was insulting that he must wait at the gates like any jobernowl. A sharp barking laugh fought for release. No. *Not* like any country lad! The countryman could gain immediate access to his daughter!

"Well, Hubert? Send off your messenger."

"'Mornin' m'lord."

To Lord Winters' surprise the gates swung slowly inward. "Well, well. What is this? Has my daughter come to her senses at last?"

"They's been some put on the welcome list, m'lord. You bein' one."

"And who are the others?"

"Family mostly." Hubert clamped his mouth shut and stalked away.

Lord Winters stared after him. "Impudence." He got no response and, given the heat, decided it wasn't worth the bother of rating the man, so let the gate-keeper go. He rode gently up the drive and around to the stables where he was certain to find Ardith at this time of day.

In the paddocks the horses were dusty looking as was everything else. His lordship lifted his hat and mopped his brow and wondered what had brought him to Summersend. Then he remembered the sweet letter which had led to the impulse. London must be unbearable. A groom stepped out of the barn leading the gelding Ardith had shown him on his last visit. "There's that 'showy' Charcoal," he chuckled. "St. John must have reneged."

Ardith followed.

"Haven't sold that showy animal, hmmm? Thought Rohampton wanted him."

Hearing the sly note in her father's voice, Ardith turned. Somehow she wasn't surprised to see him. "I'm boarding him until St. John can take him in hand. All has been topsy-turvy at the Park."

"They're in a tizzy? What happened? Rohampton have an accident?"

"Nothing like that. His friend, Colonel Westman, was badly wounded at Badajoz. Bad weather delayed the hospital ships and it was for ever before he could be shipped home. St. John had the colonel brought to Rohampton. The man was as close to being dead as one can be but we saved him."

"We? We? Who's this 'we'? What hand did *you* have in it?"

"The touch of an angel."

Ardith's eyes flew beyond her father to where St. John smiled at her, his eyes warm and approving.

"Morning, St. John." She found she was breathless. Just the sight of him made her that way. Oh, it was too *much*. Why, when it was the first time since she'd left the Park, must she see him in company with her father? Why couldn't they be alone? She wanted—needed—to be alone with him.

"Come for that showy Charcoal you bought?" Lord Winters chuckled at a joke which was fast becoming old.

"Not yet, although I must remember to give you a draft on my bank, Ardith. You've waited far too long for your blunt."

"I'm not on my last legs, yet, my lord. I know you're good for it."

His brow quirked at the 'my lord,' a question in his eyes, but when she answered his questioning look with one of her own, he relaxed. "You haven't asked about your patient."

She chuckled. "You think I don't know? My informants tell me Colonel Westman has graduated to a chaise longue, but indeed I stopped concerning myself when his mother arrived to take over the nursing."

St. John grimaced. "You were wrong to do so. We had a setback!" She gave him a disbelieving look. "Truly. The woman fussed and fidgeted until Cam could take no more. I forcibly removed her from his room and let her in thereafter only when I could be there as well."

"Forcibly? You exaggerate." St. John shook his head, but he smiled and she guessed it had been difficult to accomplish tactfully. "Oh, dear."

"Oh, dear, indeed. But we weathered it. Cam hasn't tried to walk yet, but he is regaining his strength and there is no longer any danger of the wound reopening." He sobered. "That was the worst, Ardith. Keeping him still until it healed to where it wouldn't crack open at any movement. The pain—well, I needn't tell you. You guessed how it would be."

Lord Winters cleared his throat. "Am I to understand Ardith took a hand in nursing this friend of yours?"

"She saved his life."

"Nonsense. She's a lady. Dr. Waingarden . . ."

"Dr. Waingarden gave up on Cam at once." St. John, remembering his despair, felt his face harden, his eyes ice. With effort he forced back the emotions but not before Lord Winters noticed. "Waingarden predicted Cam would die before nightfall."

"But he didn't. Doctors are not gods. He was wrong, that's all."

Ardith made a motion and St. John, understanding she wished he'd not argue with her father, scowled. "He was *not* wrong, but enough of that. Cam is mending, which is why I am here. Ardith, he wishes to thank you."

"No thanks are needed, St. John. You know that."

"I know. But he and his mother cannot be convinced. I rode over to invite you and Miss Fremby to dinner. Tonight." He looked at Lord Winters. Common decency forced him to extend a further invitation. "I didn't know you'd returned, my lord. You, too, are invited to join us."

"Still an invalid, is he?" St. John nodded. "Then better not overdo the company." Lord Winters went on gruffly. "Know you only invited me out of politeness, but well done of you, m'boy. Maybe, if you'd get a few bees out of your bonnet and come to your senses about a few things, you'd not be such an irritating fellow." He tipped his head significantly towards Ardith.

"If you refer to my opinion of Ardith's excellent qualities, I will not change. Nor have I given up my desire to marry your daughter. I haven't in five years, so why should I now?"

Ardith flushed. How dare he say that so casually and here where all the curious ears of her staff could hear every word!

Lord Winters scowled. "Told you to stay away from her."

"I'll not give up. I've waited too long as it is."

"Will the two of you stop discussing me as if I weren't here?"

"But we are not *discussing* you. We are arguing about you. It is the only way your father knows to communicate."

Ardith turned on her heel and headed into the barn.

"Ardith?" She paused but didn't turn around. "You will come?"

"Yes. Miss Fremby, however, has a summer cold and is feeling pulled."

"Mrs. Westman will chaperone you."

"I'm sure she will."

"I'll be off then."

Lord Winters watched St. John mount and ride off before dismounting and following Ardith into the barn. "Ardith?"

"In the tack room."

Her father found her sitting glumly on a three-legged stool. "I had no wish to make you angry, Ardith." She nodded. After a moment, Lord Winters continued. "I came with news I'm sure will delight you."

"You asked your widow to marry you and she said yes."

Lord Winters beamed. "She did. I want you to meet her."

Ardith forced a lighter mood. "Is she, too, staying at Winters Hall?"

A shocked expression widened Lord Winters' eyes. "Stap me, Ardith, you know well 'twouldn't be right 'til we're married. How could you suggest such a thing?"

"Then how am I to meet her?"

Her father looked flustered and turned to the small window in the far wall. He huffed. "Well . . ."

So thought Ardith, I'm to invite her here, am I, you devious underhanded man, you. She wondered if she would like her step-mama to be. "How old is she, Father?"

His ears reddened. "Twenty-nine." He turned. "Very nearly thirty."

"Oh?"

"Yes. Very nearly. Her birthday is in November."

Ardith chuckled. "Hmmm. Only five months away." And of an age with Maud. "Will I like her?"

He turned back to the window. "I don't know."

"Do *you* like her?"

"Of course I do. Wouldn't have asked her to marry me if I did not."

"Then I will try to like her for your sake." Ardith, having put off the evil moment as long as she could, sighed. "I would like for her to come to me for a visit. Perhaps the end of next week?"

"Very generous of you, m'dear. Didn't expect such generosity."

Oh yes you did you old humbug you! She stared and his eyes dropped. "It's the least I can do," she said gently. "I'll write if you'll give me her direction." She invited her father to lunch. It was a more peaceful meal than the last he'd eaten at her table. Maybe a wife—a real wife—would mellow him. Ardith decided to hold judgement until she'd met the woman, but she hoped all would be well.

The short evening over, Ardith allowed St. John to help her into his carriage as soon as the maid ordered to accompany them was settled into the forward seat. Why he felt he must escort her back to Summersend escaped her, and her ambivalent feelings about having him so near made her wary. "My lord, this is unnecessary!"

St. John smiled as he joined her in the dimly lit carriage. "It *is* necessary. And you've no notion how difficult it was to arrange."

"I see. I'm so tired of the men in my life manipulating me!" Ardith folded her arms and looked out, but could see little, the quarter moon barely relieving the blackness. She hoped St. John's coachman could see his way and would not put them into a ditch.

Rohampton extended his legs and found the maid's in the way. Cam's mother had dithered about accompanying them, coming close to ruining all. Only Cam's quick thinking, that very artful moan which had distracted his mama, had given St. John time to think of asking a maid. A carefully chosen maid at that—one he suspected of harbouring warm feelings for his coachman. Beyond sight of the house, St. John opened the trap and called to the coachman. "Take Annie up with you, Parkman. She is finding it too warm in the carriage."

The maid goggled. He winked at her. She smiled and nodded and, much less stiffly than her forty years might suggest, let him hand her from the carriage.

"More manipulation."

"Yes. At long last I have you trapped where you cannot run from me. I will tell you my side of the farce we played in London five years ago."

"I will not listen. It is long in the past and is irrelevant, my lord."

A short period of silence allowed Ardith to breathe again. Too soon, as it turned out.

"I will, then, simply talk to myself. I've been over and over it. There'd been more trouble at the Horse Guards—another traitor, you know—and I'd been called in. It was late when we finished—too late to attend that party, but I'd forgotten to send excuses and knowing you'd be there, decided to drop in. Our hostess was at the ballroom door bidding *adieu* to a couple so I looked around the room for you, Ardith, as I always did."

Ardith turned her head to stare at him. Had he? Really? She had not noticed, although when she could find the courage, she had watched for him, too. Unfortunately, self-conscious already, she'd rarely had the courage to do so.

"My love was looking quite hagged that night. Unhappy and bored very nearly to tears. I could stand it no longer. I decided right then to do something about it. I'd marry her and take her home to the Park and make her happy again."

He remembered the frilled and highly decorated, lace-covered gown Ardith had worn that night, a pale blue completely unsuited to her form and colouring. He remembered how he'd longed to dress her properly, show off her natural elegance which the inappropriate style smothered.

"Such a stupid and ill-considered notion," he went on. "*Nobody*, who has a modicum of social sense, proposes in the middle of a ball. It contravenes every social stricture, every sensitive feeling, to attempt something so private in such a public place."

"You decided, then, before you ever walked into the room?" Ardith clamped her mouth shut. She was not listening!

"Right then, m'love. My misunderstood and sensitive love."

She didn't respond although he gave her the opportunity. Instead she turned away from him again to stare out the window at nothing at all.

"So," he continued, "I was set on my wrong-headed way. I made my excuses to our hostess as well as I might since, my mouth sealed, I could not mention the Horse Guards. I fear," he said thoughtfully, "I was not my usual glib self, because although she forgave me she did so in a stiff and ungenerous way.

"That is irrelevant, of course. I'd plotted my strategy and looked for Lord Toby. I fear I did not hide my nervousness well and he guessed what was up with me. Later, I also realised he'd been well to go if not jug bitten. But Toby holds his wine better than most, and at the time I noticed nothing."

Ardith began to relax. It was not so terrible after all, listening to St. John bare his soul.

"The next step was to get you alone in the little room I'd been assured would be empty. And I had a notion how I might do that, too."

"You asked me to dance."

"A particularly strenuous country dance. I thought you'd need refreshment once it was done and I'd intended to suggest we find it."

"And then my badly behaved hair fell down in such a hoydenish way you had the perfect excuse to find a private place for me."

"Yes. Perfect. In any case, I was desperate. We danced. The feel of you on my arm increased my sense of urgency. We'd marry and I'd have the right to do more than just hold you, my love!"

"I know what happened next. The fact you didn't object to those fools' behavior was a point against you, my lord. You laughed," she accused. "Sort of."

"Yes. From embarrassment. I had made a complete fool of myself. And of you. But I could also see the humour in it. If I'd only controlled my emotions and waited, done the thing properly, had come to you the next day when you were home!"

"What happened once I left?" She'd always wondered why the story had not made the rounds of London. Now, even in the dark, she could tell St. John felt remembered anger at the wags who had interfered in their lives.

"I sobered them up in a hurry. Then I sat them down and explained exactly how they had wounded a sensitive woman. Then I explained exactly what *I* would do if any hint of their actions became gossip over the teacups or in the clubs. Once I'd finished they knew the wise course was silence. Also, sober, they were ashamed, Ardith. Did you get their notes?"

"Yes. Rambling apologies which insisted you'd had no part in their plot, but I didn't believe it."

"You didn't want to believe it."

"How can you say that?"

"Ardith, for you to have considered yourself worthy of becoming my marchioness, for you to believe now that I love you and want you for my wife, you have to change your whole notion of yourself. Your lack of confidence, your belief you are not beautiful and have no womanly accomplishments—it led you to conclude I was roasting you. If you had had any idea of how wonderful you are you'd have seen that fiasco for what it was, would have been able to laugh at those idiots and commiserate with me in my humiliation!"

Ardith's heart swelled. She couldn't disbelieve him. The sincerity was too clear. But he was wrong. So wrong. Oh, he admired her for her skill in the sick-room, her efforts to help those in trouble. But she had no social arts, knew nothing about running a big house such as the Park. She'd be awkward with his friends and embarrass him. She sighed.

"Ardith? Do you understand?"

She understood. Better than he did. So now what? "Yes. I apologised to you long ago, St. John. I do so again."

She felt him stiffen, breathe deeply, and let the breath out slowly. "Is that all you understand?"

"Don't, St. John. Please don't go on."

"Dash it all, Ardith, I want you for my wife. Will you or won't you?"

"Will I or won't I what?"

The sound emanating from him was very like a growl. There followed a short period of silence. "Ardith, will you do me the honour of marrying me?"

"I am sensible of the honour you do me, my lord, but I fear we would not suit," she replied promptly, using the time-honoured formula.

"That's the wrong answer. You are supposed to say you accept my extremely obliging offer."

"St. John, I am not the woman to be mistress of the Park and your other properties. And what of London? Can't you see me in London?"

"Yes I can. Properly gowned as you were at your father's birthday party with your hair well dressed as it was that night—did I tell you how lovely it looked, by the way? I was glad to see you put it up in the same style for this evening . . . but why are you worrying about that sort of thing? You were too young when you went up for your Season. You had not yet learned to value yourself. But you've matured. Think, Ardith. Did you find your father's party such a terrible burden?"

"Well, yes. Not to the degree I'd feared, but I still have none of the graces others take for granted. I found it difficult to talk to people and I looked no-how when some golden-tongued idiot paid me extravagant compliments. I'm sure it was merely to please my father, but . . ."

He took her by the shoulders and shook her. "You fool you! You looked like a goddess that night! Every compliment paid you was from the heart. Oh, it was phrased in the flowery language the gallants use, but it was sincere and meant to please you." He shook her again. "Damn you, Ardith. You are beautiful." He shook her. "Not in the common way, but . . ."

"Take your hands off me, my lord."

"Ardith, I'm sorry." He thought about that. "No, I'm not. Someone must shake sense into you. You are a lovely intelligent woman. A woman of great passion. A woman who can organise a complicated party and not turn a hair. A woman who is brave and compassionate and . . ."

"And can't sew a straight seam or arrange a decent floral piece or play the piano or sing or do any of the things a woman is supposed to do."

"Those things are not important."

"They must be. Why else is every girl born into the gentry and peerage forced to learn them? I am a failure, a disgrace to my sex, my lord."

St. John calmed himself and ordered his thoughts. "We live in an era which has adopted a million shibboleths. A culture which is, I believe, on the verge of stultifying. Our women are forced into a single mold, a mold many men *do* desire. They want women ignorant and docile. How else may they rule the roost? So girls are raised to be perfect little idiots. Most make marriages of convenience and carry out their shallow little lives, do their duty by their lords, and nothing more. If unlucky enough to be intelligent, they are bored. I don't want that sort of wife, Ardith. I never have. I was nearly thirty when I first asked you to marry me. Was I too young to know my own mind?"

That was a new thought. She had never considered the point. "I have agreed that proposal was real. But the situation has changed, my lord."

"Yes. For the better. You are older and have more self-confidence and have *become* what I, then, only dreamed you'd be."

"The situation." She barely choked out the words through a throat tight with emotion.

"You mean Summersend, don't you?"

"Yes." He understood. "And my independence. I'm not certain I wish to marry, that I *could* marry, my lord."

St. John felt the carriage slow, heard the Summersend gates open and knew he had little time. Once beyond the interested gate-keeper, he turned to her. This time he was gentle but firm as he pulled her close. His kiss was tender, his hand careful as it covered her breast. "There is this, too, Ardith. You know I love you. I also want you. And I think you want me."

She tucked her head under his chin to hide her face. "I've wondered if I had the nerve to become your mistress, St. John. Does that shock you?"

He chuckled. "If that was all I wanted of you, Ardith, I could have seduced you long ago. I want more."

"I fear it is more than I can give, my lord."

The carriage halted before the manor and their precious isolation was at an end. "This isn't finished, Ardith. For my own sanity I must convince you that you are the only woman I can marry. Will you condemn me to a lonely old age? Will you let me die without an heir to my lands and title? How selfish of you, m'love." But the last words were said as trembling fingers followed the line of hair which curved against her cheek. "Help me to find a solution, Ardith." He set her away as his coachman clambered down off his perch.

"I . . . I think I hope you will," she whispered.

"Good. We will think about it. I'll find a solution because I *must*."

The door opened and he climbed out, holding her hand to help her down. Still holding it he walked her to the door, lifted it, and, finding the opening in her long glove where it buttoned at the wrist, placed a kiss there. She wondered if he felt the pounding of her pulse.

She watched as the Rohampton carriage disappeared down the drive. Had she really told him she'd thought of becoming his mistress? Oh, how *could* she have done so? Ardith frowned. Strange he hadn't reacted to her words. Surely a man would have taken her up on them if he truly desired her. Wouldn't he? She shook her head. Not if he respected her and wanted her for his wife. In that case . . .

Ardith had trouble falling asleep that night. She *did* want to marry St. John. But she didn't want to give up the life she now led. Oh, it was impossible. There *was* no solution unless she could become like every other woman and submit to the rule of her man. But could she? A feeling of panic set her heart beating. There was no way she could curb her eccentricities. They were too much a part of her. No. There was simply no solution to the quandary in which they found themselves. None at all. Tears slipped down her cheeks, and her pillow was damp long after she finally succumbed to Morpheus, god of dreams. The god was not kind to her that night.

Lord Winters' travelling carriage pulled to a stop before the entrance. Ardith was awaiting her guest with curiosity and her best behaviour, only a trifle nervous at meeting a London lady. Evidence of that last was that she had allowed Fremby to do her hair that morning. Her father dismounted, reaching the carriage before his groom could and gallantly helped the woman inside to the ground. For a moment Ardith and Mrs. Mallingham stared at each other before the slightly plump features of Lord Winters' bride-elect were utterly changed by a sweet smile.

"You are such a tease, Lord Winters. Why, you led me to believe Lady Ardith was less beautiful than your other daughters. How absurd of you to roast me so, my lord! She's magnificent. Her hair! And so tall. Oh, my dear, if you only *knew* how I envied you those inches."

Ardith blinked. Was the woman serious? It seemed she was. Her father stared at his betrothed as if she'd lost her mind, but kept his thoughts to himself. He stayed for a luncheon before leaving the two to become acquainted, warning Ardith he'd return in the morning to take his betrothed riding. "She's a soldier's widow, you know," he finished *sotto voce.* "Suffered all sorts of deprivations when she followed the drum with him. Must make it up to her. You take good care of her, now, you hear me?"

Again Ardith blinked. "I certainly do hear you." When he'd gone she turned to the woman who was to become her step-mama. "Well. I think you've twined him quite around your little finger!"

Mrs. Mallingham flushed. "I don't wish to do *that*. Why, he's wonderful. So careful of my comfort and so easy to be with. He embarrassed me, those things he said to you. I'm sure he was just . . . just . . ."

Ardith laughed. "Don't try to explain my father to me. I am *glad* you have influence with him. And I think we'll be friends, don't you?"

"Oh, I hope so. I could never hope to replace your mother. Such an absurd notion, is it not, at our ages? I so dreaded meeting you, you know. Your father said you were a stubborn strong-minded woman and told me stories about you, and I'm afraid I was sure you'd hate me on sight, that you'd been *forced* to invite me. I almost didn't come."

Ardith chuckled. "You are here now and I am glad of it."

Later that evening when Mrs. Mallingham had gone to bed, Ardith and Fremby stared at each other. They broke into simultaneous chuckles. "Do you think," asked Ardith, "my father has the least notion he's taking another strong-minded and stubborn female under his wing?"

"I think he'll never know. She'll lead him by the nose, but in such a gentle way he'll never suspect. I like her."

"Much to my surprise, I do, too. She tells me it is a marriage of convenience, *her* convenience." Again Ardith chuckled. "I was surprised at her frankness which nearly surpasses mine. Perhaps it comes of the difficult life she led with her first husband. He didn't leave her well provided for, which is her primary reason for wishing to remarry. But I think she will be a good wife."

"Yes. She knows what will be expected of her. She told me she hopes for children, wants them. I believe she will do very well indeed."

Much in charity with each other, their views coinciding nicely, Ardith and Miss Fremby retired to their beds.

— 12 —

THE FOLLOWING WEEKS were amazingly pleasant. The summer was full of social engagements. Twice, as Colonel Westman's convalescence progressed at a surprising pace, there were small dinner parties at the Park. There were riding parties and picnics as word got around the neighbourhood that Mrs. Mallingham would soon be Lady Winters. Fremby and Ardith laughed in secret at the way the lady managed Lord Winters. She did it so tactfully he'd no idea he was on a short rein.

Lord Winters returned the various invitations with one of his own—a dinner which included all of the gentry of the neighbourhood. He dithered and harrumphed and changed his mind a dozen times, always coming to Ardith for a final decision as to menu and decorations and such things as whether he should provide music for dancing or if tables for cards would be sufficient.

Recognising her father's desire to please his bride, Ardith was more patient than she had ever been with him. Finally, several days before the date, she rode over to Winters Hall and went over everything with his housekeeper and cook, and after that simply soothed him whenever he fell into a dither and feared all would not go off as it ought. In actuality, it went very well. The next day Lord Winters and Mrs. Mallingham, with Miss Fremby as chaperone, officially toured Winters Hall. Their wedding date was set for only a few weeks away.

St. John took advantage of the fact they were gone from Summersend and took Ardith riding. He'd kept abreast of the plans and Ardith's part in them, and now praised her for her organisational skills.

"It wasn't complicated. Merely a dinner for friends, after all. If I were in London and tonish strangers were involved I couldn't have done it."

"Ardith, I know it was your hand which ordered it. Can't you see that is all that is needed for *any* party? You could, I believe, become one of London's premier hostesses if you had that ambition. Which I hope you don't! I wish to spend more time at the Park as I've done the past year. We'd go to London for part of the Season and again in the fall for the Little Season, perhaps, but I've no desire to cut a dash in town. I'm much happier doing as we've been doing. I just wish we were doing *more*."

He accompanied that last with such a droll look Ardith blushed. She, too, wished more and more that she could find herself in his arms, his bed. It was such an unladylike thought she didn't know where to look.

"I've embarrassed you. I'm sorry." St. John thought about that. "No, I'm not. I like it when you blush. It means I can unsettle you as you unsettle me. Ardith, we must find a solution. Soon. Or I might be tempted . . ." He frowned, his mouth firming. "No. I will not succumb to temptation. It would not be right. Somehow, someway, we must marry."

"I do not believe I could submit to you, my lord."

He turned a startled glance her way, realised she didn't refer to his advances and chuckled. "You mean that independence of yours. I *like* your strong-minded ways, m'dear. I enjoy our arguments. I like it that you do not say yes, my lord, and no, my lord, to my every word. As I remember, you never have! I could have found that sort of toad-eater for a wife long ago. I only needed to take up any random young lady presented to the ton at Almack's any year you name. I *could* have married such a one if I'd willed. And been bored to tears before the honeymoon ended! We will never suffer so. Our life together will be full and interesting."

"Do you mean you would not ask me to give up my work with the poor and needy? You'd not object if in the middle of a dinner party word came of a confinement and I left the table? Come now, my friend. Admit you would find it mortifying and impossible to explain to your guests." St. John might speak in terms of "we" and "our" but she could not.

A sensible man, St. John did not immediately deny the charge. "I wonder. Yes, I think I might be a trifle put out. But my pride in you would not waver. That, too, is true. Ardith, did you meet any of the noted eccentrics when you were in London? The ones who manage to go their own way yet retain a place in the ton?"

"None who are accepted everywhere."

"No. There are high-sticklers who cut anyone who does not strictly conform to their rigid code of what is socially acceptable." He went on thoughtfully. "They are dead bores and not among those I call friends. So that argument is shot down, m'dear. My friends may be startled if you walk out in the middle of the soup course and disappear for the evening, but they will not give you the cut direct as a result."

"There is another problem," said Ardith after digesting that thought. "Summersend. My stable and breeding stock. My plans for its future and the managing of it. I could not give that up."

"Why should you?"

"It is time-consuming, my lord. You have no idea how many hours I spend schooling my horses and overseeing the men."

"I've a very good idea the time you put into managing your stable. Could you bear to cut back a trifle? I ask because I'd wish you to spend more of that precious commodity with *me*, m'love."

"I don't know. Perhaps," she teased, "*you* could work more with your own stock and we could combine the studs."

"An excellent notion. A definite possibility."

Ardith glanced at him. He was serious. "I was roasting you."

"No, you've suggested a compromise. We would both work our stock, but you doing less and I doing more. Is that reasonable? Our land has a mutual boundary. What if we build new stables, yours on your side and mine on my side? We could take down a portion of the wall for freer access."

"I could not afford such a project, my lord."

"I would write it into the marriage contract that I provide all."

"You spoke of *our* lands, my lord. Summersend is mine. If I marry you, it, as well as all else, would be yours."

"I hear a touch of bitterness, Ardith. Have I asked that Summersend be part of your dowry? I believe I've never suggested such a thing."

Ardith frowned. "I don't understand."

"Your father provides your dowry—as is proper. It is more than adequate. Summersend is yours and will remain yours by jointure."

Ardith reined in her mare, turning it to face him. "The law . . ."

"The law provides for the sort of woman you insist I should marry, a woman who could not manage her own property, assuming she has any. You manage very well. Far better than many men I know. Why should I insult you by suggesting you cannot?"

She blinked, looked away, and moved off slowly. "St. John," she said when he'd about given up hope of an answer, "will you give me time to think about this? You are certain I would not have to give up Summersend and my work?"

"I believe I can control my jealousy of all that takes you away from me if you can bear to give up some of it for our time together."

"But how *much*? Oh, I realise it would not be fair of me to expect to carry on as I do. I'd have a duty—"

"Don't," he interrupted sharply, "speak of a duty to me. If you cannot freely give and *wish* to give me the friendship and companionship I need then I will leave and never bother you again! Do not speak of duty."

A pain clutched at Ardith's heart. He meant it. He would go and she would never see him except on those social occasions at which they were both guests. No more companionable rides. No more chess. No more long discussions about their mutual interest in their stables and their land, or arguments about something they'd read and disagreed on. He would treat her as a casual acquaintance, polite and cold as only he could be. "I could not bear that."

"Good. Because I believe it is more than I could bear as well."

They rode back to the manor, each deep in thought, each feeling tense and worried. Ardith glanced at him as he dismounted, stared at him as he spoke to Tomlin. She loved him. He loved her. She *knew* that deep inside although she didn't understand it. Would never understand it. But could she bear to marry him? Could she change—adapt to double harness, having for so long jogged along by herself? He turned and they stared at each other. Deep in his eyes she saw a longing, an almost lost and lonely look which frightened her. It was as if he believed he'd lost her. As if he were thinking ahead to long, lonely years.

He came to her side. "Ardith, I do not mean to push you. You must decide for yourself." He laughed but the sound had a sour note. "Which means, m'love, that I must leave. I will continue arguing, pushing, and prodding if I stay. I will come again tomorrow."

His eyes held a questioning look. She met them, knowing what he was asking. Finally she nodded. "Yes. Tomorrow. I will give you my answer tomorrow." Again they stared at each other. He lifted her down, his eyes never leaving hers and abruptly—with something very close to a good-bye in it—placed a gentle kiss on her forehead. Then he backed away and lifted her hand, bowing over it in a formal manner unlike their usual leave-taking. A shiver raced up her spine at the thought of the way he'd looked at her. It was a hint of how it would be if she said no to him.

St. John mounted, back straight, nearly rigid. She watched him ride slowly towards the gate. Marry him? Could she? Why was it so difficult to do what she wanted so badly to do? He understood her needs and had met them with more generosity than one might have expected. Her needs . . .

But what of his? He said he wanted her companionship, her friendship. She thought briefly of the passion which had flowed over and around her, drawing her into a maelstrom of feeling unlike anything she'd ever imagined and put the thought away. St. John had demonstrated beyond question he could bring her to the point of meeting *those* needs, and although she knew herself unsophisticated and untutored she had no doubt he'd patiently take care of that particular aspect of their marriage.

She watched him, his receding figure symbolic of their future. She longed for him but it was the time and energy needed to be those other things which frightened her: Companion. Friend. As she had been this summer? She'd enjoyed the hours they'd spent together and she didn't try to deny it. Marry him? It was the wrong question! Could she bear *not* to marry him? Panic, pure and simple, welled up in her.

"St. John!"

He pulled up, turned in the saddle, too far away for her to see his expression clearly.

"St. John," she repeated and heard a note of desperation in her voice.

He turned his horse and cantered back. "Ardith?"

"Oh, St. John."

He dismounted, running up the steps to take her hands in his.

Tomlin cleared his throat. "I believe the salon is empty, m'lady."

The hint they were allowing their emotions too free a rein in a very public way brought a hint of a flush to her cheeks, a deepening of colour up St. John's neck. They smiled at each other and hand in hand followed the footman as he led the way and threw open the double doors. Very gently Tomlin closed them and the couple was alone.

A fleeting thought that her footman had somehow guessed that this was the day, the moment, she'd formally accept or deny St. John brought on an instant of silent laughter. But what *had* she decided? The moment of humour faded. Ardith moved away, then turned. Her riding skirt, which she'd forgotten, nearly tripped her up. It seemed as if every time she neared a decision—the yes they both longed to hear her say—another problem would come to mind.

Ardith sighed. She was being unfair. She expected all the changes, all the compromise must be on his side. Had she become so completely selfish and self-centered? Did she expect a promise of idealistic perfection from him? That he demand nothing of her in return for all he was giving her? He'd want a son and heir. She brushed that aside. She, too, wanted children. That was not what she meant at all.

She believed in compromise. And compromise could not be one-sided. Ardith sighed. Why was it so difficult to simply say the single word which would settle it all for ever? She raised her eyes to meet his.

He watched her closely, and she smiled slightly when she saw how firmly his jaw was held, how his eyes were very slightly hooded and his expression carefully controlled. Hidden somewhere behind that expression was pain. Pain she caused by her indecision. Ardith straightened, her hands loosely clasped before her, her body held with dignity, and her features as calm and serene as a madonna. St. John, too, straightened—almost into military rigidity.

"Well, Ardith?"

For one more instant she hesitated. "On conditions . . . yes."

He seemed to deflate, happiness lightening the stern expression he'd adopted and held so firmly. "Those conditions?"

"The things we discussed—the new stables for me of my design, for instance. But not at our mutual border. I think they'd be more convenient if they adjoin your present stables, my lord." He nodded. "And, that I retain possession of Summersend, of course. Fremby will continue to live here, if she wishes. That goes without saying, I think." Again he nodded. "Then, you will not interfere when I'm needed by the sick or the confined." Once again he nodded without hesitation. Ardith tipped her head, her eyes gleaming. "That you allow me go my own way in all things and . . ."

His expression changed and a gurgle of laughter built inside her. He strode towards her, taking her by the shoulders and giving her a gentle shake. "I think not."

The laughter broke loose. "I wondered how far you'd let me go. If it were my length, I'd have withdrawn my answer. No man, especially you, should be a doormat to any woman." She smiled. "Of course it is my belief no woman should be a doormat to a man, as well, which you will agree is rebellion of the worst sort, is it not?"

"You will never let me walk all over you, Ardith. But be warned that I won't lie down and let you walk on me either."

"I'd be ashamed of you if you were to do so, as you well know." She studied his face. "Have you no conditions of your own, St. John? I am not an easy woman. I am not conformable nor will I adjust my ways to fit the expectations of society."

"M'dear, you have excellent manners in company, you are a lovely woman, and, except for worrying about what your response will be to some man who spouts some ill-considered pronouncement, I have no worries about taking you into society. Come to think of it, I'll not worry about that either since I'll most likely back you up with any additional arguments which come to mind. Ardith, can you not understand that I love you for who and what you are? That I love *you*?"

"I have been forced to acknowledge that." The faintest of frowns formed on her brow. "*Why* you should is hopelessly unclear. I can only pray your delusion continues. That you always love me. As I do you, my lord."

It was St. John's turn to look a little concerned. "Ardith, m'love, how have I earned your anger now?"

"Anger? I am not angry with you."

"But you call me 'my lord' only when you are in a temper. It is always a clue I've somehow managed to get into your bad-books."

She shook her head. "Very obviously I do not, my lord. I am feeling very happy and light-hearted and *free*. That last surprises me, you know. I expected to feel as though I were in a trap!"

He ignored her admission. "Dammit, Ardith, don't do it."

"Don't do what?"

"Don't call me 'my lord' that way except when you are angry."

Ardith bit her lip, her eyes twinkling. "Oh no, *my lord*. It wouldn't do to make life easy for you. You'd succumb to ennui within a fortnight! You'll have to figure out another way to recognise my incipient tantrums. And once you do, I'll just have to find some other way of misleading you."

"Ardith . . ."

"Oh, St. John, will you stop talking and kiss me. I've wanted one of your lovely, special, impossible kisses ever since it occurred to me I *had* to marry you."

Still he held her away from him. "Had to marry me?"

"Of course."

She'd never tell him of her cold analysis of their relationship, the logical balancing of points for and against their marriage. Or the fear of losing him which had led to her decision and the deep need to make him happy—as he was *not* when he awaited her answer.

"I suddenly remembered," she said, blithely, "I am unable to waltz with anyone but you, and I discovered at my father's birthday party I *liked* the new waltzing and so, St. John, it is obvious I could not turn you down and find you treating me from that point on as a stranger. Why, you'd never do something so *fast* as waltz with a stranger!"

He studied her face for a long moment. He knew she was hiding something, decided it was unimportant. "All right minx. I'll allow you a few secrets. The fact you've admitted you love me will have to be basis enough for your reasonable and rational decision to marry me."

So, she thought, he knew and understood how difficult it had been for her. Keep secrets from him as she'd thought to do? No. He *always* knew.

Sometime later, unable to bear the suspense another moment, Tomlin very reprehensibly peeked through the barely opened door. He discovered his mistress and her love dancing around the room to the slightly off-key humming of a waltzing tune. After recovering from his surprise he also noted how happily they gazed at each other and, smiling to himself, Tomlin quietly closed the doors. He turned slowly, dignified in every inch, and looked at the servants waiting breathlessly nearby. He nodded.

A muffled cheer filtered through to the happy couple, but since it merely reflected their own feelings neither attempted

to discover if it was real or their imagination. They waltzed on, stopping occasionally for a kiss, a cuddle—perhaps just a bit more than that—and didn't care that the room gradually darkened as they danced and talked.

Decisions were made. They'd buy a special licence and have a quiet wedding before Lord Winters married Mrs. Mallingham. After her father's wedding, they'd travel by easy stages to honeymoon at St. John's Scottish property. And they spoke of the special things lovers tell each other. And danced. And kissed. And hoped they'd be left alone like this for ever.

Tomlin forbore to interfere even though he *knew* it was time to draw the curtains and light the candles. There were times a good servant had to be wise. He had to know when to do what was proper, but more important when to forget. A trifle smug, he searched the cellars for the very best French champagne in Ardith's limited stock. He had it ready when, sometime later, the inspection party returned from Winters Hall and the engagement between his beloved mistress and Lord Rohampton was announced.

Tomlin, impassive, poured the champagne. Lord Winters looked at his wine, looked at his betrothed, and decided he'd be far too busy to hunt a less infuriating husband for Ardith as he'd intended doing during the Little Season that fall. So there was nothing for it but to accept the inevitable. He raised his glass. Expectantly, the others awaited his toast.

"To a grandson," he said.

If you would like to receive details on other Walker Regency romances, please write to: